A TWIST
IN DESTINY

The horrors of Partition and the birth of Pakistan – the two biggest traumas inflicted on the psyche of the Indian subcontinent. Hasn't every Indian – and maybe every Pakistani and Bangladeshi – wondered at some point of time: Was Partition really necessary? Hasn't nearly every person in the subcontinent tried to imagine a world without Partition – no Pakistan, no Indo-Pak wars, no Kargil, and no Kashmir stalemate.

This novel sweeps across the threshold of that question. Unfurling a scenario, where India at the crossroads of Partition, rejects the division of the country, it moves forward in time to the fifty-first year of Independence. The mood is sinister with fanatics demanding Partition and Pakistan, and the ugly face of terrorism defacing the composite culture of a peace-loving India . . . . Where will it end?

The author fast-forwards the recent past in a touchdown with grim reality . . . . Read on . . . .

Sujata S. Sabnis has a Master's degree in psychology and a postgraduate diploma in journalism from the Indian Institute of Mass Communication, Delhi. She has written extensively for *Indian Express,* Pune, as well as *Pune Mid-Day*. Three years ago she published her first novel, a murder mystery titled *Silent Whispers*. She lives in Pune with her husband, Satish, and children, Rohit and Siya.

A TWIST IN DESTINY

A TWIST IN DESTINY

SUJATA S. SABNIS

LOTUS COLLECTION
ROLI BOOKS

Lotus Collection

This edition first published 2002
The Lotus Collection
An imprint of
Roli Books Pvt Ltd
M-75, G.K. II Market
New Delhi 110 048
Phones: 6442271, 6462782, 6460886
Fax: 6467185
E-mail: roli@vsnl.com; Website: rolibooks.com
Also at
Varanasi, Agra, Jaipur and the Netherlands

Cover picture: Rakesh Kumar Gupta
Courtesy: Private collection

ISBN: 81-7436-204-5
Rs 295

Typeset in Galliard by Roli Books Pvt Ltd and
printed at Pauls Press, Okhla, New Delhi-110 020

Contents

Dedication

This book is dedicated
to my beloved parents
Raghunath and Sudha Apte

*'The reason why birds can fly and we can't
is simply that they have perfect faith,
for to have faith is to have wings.'*

J.M. Barrie
The Little White Bird

Thanks Dad and Mom for
teaching me that faith

Part I

The Twist

One

The bungalow was painted an incongruous shade of bright pink. Not a genteel pale variety of the colour, but its virulent version. The roseate theme was underlined by innurmerable carved blooms spread generously all over its visage. As if that was not revolting enough for the aesthetic-minded, *Lala* Shyamlal Kapoor had topped this with an extravagant bit of fantasy. Perched on the parapet was a surrealistic sample of an artist's imagination – a huge cement moulded aeroplane complete with wings. So unique was this stupendous example of art deco that it had soon become a landmark in its own right, which fact afforded its owner a good bit of smug satisfaction.

For *Lala* Shyamlal Kapoor took childlike pleasure in the knowledge that his *jahaj-wali kothi* (aeroplane-like mansion) was famous in this part of Rawalpindi. As that had been the whole object of the exercise, the barbs – and there were plenty of these – were ignored by him.

Just as he ignored his Bela's grumbles as he got ready for the day. It was a happy, satisfied, ruddy face which looked back at him in the mirror as he adjusted his pugree. Not that he anticipated anything different today. In fact that would have unsettled him, for *Lala* did not like change.

It was his claim that every day in the fiftieth year of his life was exactly the same as any other. And being a practical, pragmatic man with the inherent Punjabi talent for living life to the full, that suited him just fine. The fact that he continued to think this way on the eve of Partition, living on the wrong side of the threatened border, could be taken as sheer faith or misplaced optimism. But Shyamlal Kapoor had the unshaken belief that he was much too ordinary to be threatened by such extraordinary upheavals.

That was the advantage of being a common man – the uncommon never touched you. The unusual usually passed you by. And Shyamlal Kapoor knew that he was as ordinary an Indian as they came. He had a little bit of everything, enough to keep him content at this stage of his life but not enough to give him an exalted air. His was not a story of rags to riches, it was more a saga of rags to mediocrity and that was fine with him. He had started his career with a handcart, and it had taken him years of hard work to become the owner of a small shop in the swanky Cantonment. His Hind Trading Company would never make him a Tata or a Birla but ensured a reasonable living for him. Enough to leave a decent inheritance for his son, Vishnuprasad. And more than enough for his present needs.

Not that he had a taste for high living – he was not one to forget his roots and that special flavour of rustic Punjab was still there in his accent and in his booming, gruff, larger-than-life persona. He had a marvellous capacity for paternal love and an even better one for the romantic kind, his love encompassing not just his plump wife, Bela, but also gathering in its lusty folds quite a few torrid liaisons over the years. Not that Bela had not known about them – she had, God bless her, and had given him hell every time too, each of their fights ending in a passionate tussle on the bed. Hot she had been, his Bela. Hot and fat and fiery like all good wives should be. He would have hated having a mewling, whimpering bag of bones. Why, a weak woman would have run away years ago, frightened by him! And with reason, he had to admit. For his temper was spectacular, his repertoire of swear words extensive.

But then that was him, a typical Punjabi, living a typical existence in the Punjabi city of Rawalpindi. And God willing would continue to live it. Why would he be asked to leave a land where he had lived all his life? He found the whole idea unbelievable, like a badly written story. And if he was scared, he tried not to show his fear, hiding his concern with an excessive outburst of normality.

Dressed in a flowing white Pathani dress with his pugree tied to perfection, he shouted for his wife.

'Bela!' he shouted. 'I am going.'

She came out of the kitchen, holding his joy in her arms, his son's son, little Rajender. A big smile split his face as he looked at the chubby, fair, one-year-old boy, and he made droll clucking noises in an effort to please the little one, giving him a noisy kiss on the cheek and tweaking his button nose. 'Say Dadada.' he said lyrically.

'Where are you going?' asked Bela irritatedly. 'I have made *mooli* parathas for breakfast.'

'Oh, oh, I have to meet my friends. Has Vishnu gone to the shop?'

'Half an hour ago. He does all the hard work while you have your gossip sessions.'

'That is what sons are meant for, woman, so stop eating my head.'

'Listen ji, take care.'

'What do you mean, take care? What about?'

'These are bad days, *Lalaji*.'

'Rubbish. Everything will come back to normal, you will see. I met Karimbhai the other day – he too was saying that nothing will come out of all this Partition-bartition nonsense.'

'Karimbhai may be a big *sarkari* babu, but I doubt he is an authority on these things!' snapped Bela.

'Okay, then at least you trust Mahatma Gandhi? Remember what he said when he came here? That the division of the country will be a division of his body. Now does that count for anything or not? You relax, this is just a lot of hot air and then back to business. You and I are going to die right here in Pindi. And now I must go or I will be late.'

A cherubic bundle of vivacity suddenly emerged from the verandah and threw herself at him. In a moment his face became transformed, as with a positively foolish smile, he clutched the small girl, bouncing her in the air and safely catching her in his arms. His three-year-old granddaughter. Nimmi, could run rings around him and she knew.

'Dadu, where you going? I want to eat. The *golewala* has come. Please, please?'

He placed a big smacking kiss on the bright little face, searched in his kurta pocket and took out an anna, 'Here you go. But don't go alone.'

'I won't, Dadu, I will take Samina along,' she said, prancing away delightedly.

Bela turned to her erring husband, determined to give him another dose, 'You are spoiling her rotten. What do you mean by giving her money for *gola*? These things affect the throat – she will fall sick!'

'Fall sick, nothing! A Punjabi child like my Nimmi? What's wrong with you, woman?'

'Yesterday, our daughter-in-law, Chanchal, was also complaining.'

'Why? What's the matter with *Bahu*.'

'Nothing. Only that Nimmi is getting spoiled. That is not good for a girl, you know.'

He dismissed it with a flourish, 'You women do nothing but complain. You are not talking about any girl. You are talking about *Lala* Shyamlal Kapoor's only granddaughter! You will see, I will find such a good match for her. What a celebration it will be, Rawalpindi has never seen such a marriage!'

'*Bas*, enough, once again you have started on your technicolour dreams. That is years away. But aren't you getting late now?'

Guiltily he checked his new Rolex timepiece – *Rab di saun* (oh my God)! he was nearly twenty minutes late! His friends would be on their second *bhatura* by now! Hurriedly he stepped out.

They met at the place they had been meeting like clockwork, twice a week, for years. A pokey little shop near Hathi Chowk, which served the best *chhole-bhature*

in Pindi. Munnelal was there, as was Champak, Goga
Singh and Amritlal. In other times, they would have
discussed women, business, relatives, women, civic issues,
firangs, women, sons, grandsons, women, wives, money,
women. Not now though; now there were other things
they needed to talk about.

It was a discussion eerily familiar; a fragment of the
collective consciousness of Punjab. Generations of their
forefathers had been faced with a similar problem – the
safety of the future, the threat of complete disintegration
– and had discussed it in worried whispers in a similar
way. The only vital – and tragic – difference was that
then the enemy had been without, foreign, clearly hostile.

But now the threat was from within. The adversary
had the face of a friend, a brother, a neighbour. The
dichotomy was complete – the irony overwhelming.

Shyamlal broke off a big piece of a huge *bhatura*,
scooped up some *chhole*, with a piece of pickle and a
green chilli, and put it in his mouth. Then he looked at
Amritlal, his friend of twenty years, who was pensively
talking about a riot which had broken out in Ram Kund
the day before, killing five people in its savagery.

Earlier this horrifying news would have produced
shock waves; now there was only a sullen, resigned,
collective shiver.

Munnelal spoke, 'You know Krishnakant Sharma, who
lives next to me, the one who has a hardware store in Sadar?
He is moving to Ambala. Selling his house and shop.'

'My sister wants me to do the same,' said Goga. 'Says
I should not wait till the last moment. Says I should
shift to Amritsar as soon as possible.'

A sudden vehemence shook Amritlal, who banged his
glass of *lassi* on the wooden table, 'What do you mean,

leave Rawalpindi? What for? I was born here, lived my
whole life here. All my memories are bound with this
city. And now I am supposed to leave it all behind me,
go to another place, call that my home! I won't do it,
I tell you, whatever happens, happens here. I am not
going to be uprooted at this age, that's final.'

Shyamlal snapped, 'Don't be childish, Amrit, mere
sentiment will not work. We have our families to think
about. But what I say is, this is just a tempest which will
pass. Nothing will come of it, you will see. Who wants
Pakistan, I ask you? Who are these politicians to decide
our lives for us in this way? Why hasn't anyone asked us
what we want? We have lived together for centuries. This
is just a political whim of the moment which will die
down. You will see.'

A diversion appeared in the shape of a young boy,
running, frightened, searching. He saw Shyamlal, and
called out his name.

'*Lalaji!*'

Shyamlal turned. It was Sadiq, the boy who worked
in his shop.

'What are you doing here?' he asked sharply.

The boy huffed and gasped panting.

'*Chhote Lala* is in hospital. Come quickly.'

Shyamlal stood up with a jerk, stunned.

'Vishnu? Vishnu has been hurt? How?'

'Some people threw stones at our shop, *Lalaji. Chhote
Lala* was hurt on his head. He is bleeding badly. Come
quick.'

'Where? Where is he? In the shop? No, you said he
was in hospital.'

'Yes, Ismail Sahab of Merchant Hardware Store took
him to the Cantonment hospital.'

Shyamlal was feeling his age as he stumbled through the hospital corridors, his strength seeping away without warning, making him realise how dependent he had become on his son. He entered the ward with shaking limbs, his eyes hungrily inspecting his son's face – a sickly grey – wrapped in white bandages. He saw the ominously seeping red patch, the saline dripping silent life. He plonked down weakly on a stool next to Vishnu's bed, engulfed his son's limp hand in his own huge one, willing his own strength to permeate through.

'Vishnu! *Puttar*, my son.'

A tremor animated that beloved face, a sluggish opening of tired eyelids, recognition trembling in dark pupils.

'*Bauji*,' whispered Vishnu.

'How are you, son?' Shyamlal found he had suddenly lost his booming voice, and was finding it difficult to speak through the big lump stuck in his throat.

'Okay, I suppose. Have you told *Chaiji* and Chanchal.'

'No, not yet. When I go home. Bela will come in the evening with *Bahu*.'

'Yes, you explain it to them gently. Otherwise they will get scared – you know how mother is. Gets upset at the smallest things.'

Softly, bitterly Shyamlal said, 'But this is not the smallest of things. What happened?'

'Some young louts came to the shop, demanded money. When I refused, they cursed me. Said that Hindus should go where they belong. I got angry and threatened to call the police. So they went out, and the next thing I knew, they were stoning our shop. And then this big stone came straight for my head.' He shook his head in disbelief, 'I tell you *Bauji*, if Ismail

Chacha had not intervened, anything could have happened.'

'But why?' cried Shyamlal helplessly, plaintively. 'Why am I frightened in my own city? What kind of sickness is this?'

'*Bauji*, this is nothing to what can happen if the country is divided. We must seriously start thinking about whether we should leave Rawalpindi.'

'Let's wait for some more time, son. The country will not get divided; Gandhi will find a solution. We will emerge from this trouble and things will become normal again. I'm telling you, let's wait.'

'Okay, we wait, and if the situation worsens? Then what?'

'Then it's in God's hands.' Bitterly he added, 'I have always been proud of the fact that I am a self-made man. And now, at this age, to discover that I am a mere puppet in the hands of politicians, that my future depends on the dictates of their conscience and their ambitions. Why doesn't anyone ask us what we want?'

His words were mere rhetoric without effect. On the brink of power manipulations, India's politicians would turn a deaf ear to the wishes of the common man. Never before would the future of so many be in the hands of so few, and those few so obsessed with their own truncated visions. But as of now *Lala* Shyamlal Kapoor did not know what destiny had in store for him. He could only hope.

Two

They came to kill, rampaging, runting beasts swooping down on their prey, delivering death without a particle of pity, without a remnant of remorse. Hideous power, purging hate had turned human beings into slobbering, venomous merciless animals. For the next one hour, death danced inside houses, on the streets, in men's hearts as living, breathing beings were gorged into, cut to pieces, raped, strung up, slaughtered. Bones were broken, eyes gouged, heads chopped, skulls smashed, bodies pierced. Painful screams, unending sounds straight from the depths of insanity. Entreaties – whining, grovelling creatures maddened by fear, pleading, begging for mercy. Fire – scorching, ravaging, its flames scalding skins, melting resistance, turning homes into traps of hell.

That night old men were viciously killed, young girls taken away, small shrieking babies slaughtered in front of their crazed mothers. That night a sixty-year-old father had to collect the broken pieces of his son's body for the last ritual. That night innocence was destroyed when a five-year-old saw his mother raped, when a daughter saw her father burnt alive. That was the night when men stopped believing in God, when the devil reigned on earth, when humanity ceased to be . . . .

Hidayat Ali Beg tiredly kept his pen down, removed his spectacles and rubbed his weary eyes. God, they had been pitiless barbarians – the soldiers of Mahmud Ghazni – so many years ago. What terrible times those were – when men were capable of such unbelievable cruelty to others made in their own mould. He sighed, history repeated itself – so they said, but no one could repeat this kind of history, not in this country. There were no Adolf Hitlers over here – this was Modern India. India of the saintly Mahatma, the pragmatic Nehru, the fastidious Jinnah. India of British rails, British administration, British rules. It could never happen in this spiritual land of religion and compassion, he was sure about that.

He rubbed his eyes again, massaged the back of his neck. It was draining him out, this project of his, making him forget the time, sapping his energy. But at least his book, *The Invasions of Mahmud Ghazni,* was shaping up beautifully. He had already found a publisher ready to take on this capsule of fast-paced history wrapped in a simple, emotional package of writing. But with the entry of a publisher had come the introduction of a deadline, and instead of leisurely hours spent earlier on the book, he was writing at a spaced-out speed. Tiring but

satisfying! He yawned, stretched out, peered at his watch.
God, it was nearly 9 p.m.! No wonder he was hungry.

He locked his manuscript in the desk drawer, and
wearily came out of the quiet study to a scene of utter
chaos. The huge dining room of his Daryaganj mansion
seemed to be in the grip of twin tornadoes, who for
some bewildering reason, were intent on chasing each
other, making a holy mess in the process. It took him
some time to sort them out, to realise that his first-born,
Javed, a seven-year-old rogue, was running fiendishly after
Rehana, his five-year-old daughter who could do no
wrong. And adding his bit to the madness was chuckling
one-year-old baby, Parvez, delighted by the ruckus and
adding his gusty gurgles to it.

The whole scene was too much for him, and after a
stunned moment he did what he invariably did at such
times. He bawled for his wife, 'Noor! Come here, see
what's happening.' She came rushing out of the kitchen,
a slim waif-like creature, looking unlike anyone's mother,
leave alone of three.

It was her name which had first instigated the historian
to see the girl who had inspired matrimony in his *Ammi*'s
mind. But there had been nothing queen-like about this
Noorjehan. She had been a frail, dreamy little thing and
Hidayat had rapidly changed his ideas about what his
ideal wife should be like. But beneath the touching
fragility, Noor was endowed with a startling amount of
strength and an instinctive knowledge about how to keep
her man happy. Within a few days the teenage wife had
taken the measure of her studious, absent-minded
husband and quietly gone through an in-depth training
under the aegis of her mother-in-law on the running of
a household.

Three children later, she was the de facto chief of not just the house but also the hundred-odd ancestral acres in Mehrauli, complete with a sprawling farmhouse, keeping the entire estate running without a crunch. But her biggest talent lay in managing her resident scholar, who had become a professor at Jamia Millia. For Hidayat Ali she would always remain the delicate fawn he had fallen in love with, someone who would break apart if she was not protected by a strong man. She allowed him to continue weaving this charming fantasy, and because she truly loved him, let him enjoy the illusion of this masculine myth. Now she responded to his call and surveyed the scene. Then she said quietly, 'Javed, Rehana, stop it this minute. Come here.'

Hidayat Ali could have said the same words, in much louder decibels, till the cows came home, but without the slightest effect. You could call it maternal hypnosis. You could call it magic. But it worked. Rehana tumbled into *Abba*'s arms. Javed ran towards his *Ammi*.

'I am not sleepy, *Ammi*, I am not. Put this stupid Rehana to sleep, I am a big boy. Why can't I stay back and talk to *Abba*?'

She soothed him softly, 'Tomorrow, I promise. Not today, for *Abba* is much too tired. Come on,' she cajoled. Gently enticing Rehana away from her father, she patted the two in the direction of the staircase. Stooping down expertly to pick up Parvez and his ball, she managed a soft lamb-like smile at Hidayat. 'I will settle them and come. Dinner in fifteen minutes?'

For Hidayat Ali dinner time meant moments of complete contentment. Good food with a serene Noor by his side had always spelled marital bliss for him. Usually she listened intently as he passionately discussed his book and softly interspersed her comments. But today she was paler, distracted. It took him some time to realise that something was wrong, but to give him credit, the minute he did so he was concern personified.

'What is it, Noorie,' he enquired anxiously. 'What is wrong?'

'Nothing much. It is just that my aunt Binto *Foofi* came today.'

'Oh!' he made a grimace. 'What about her?'

'Well, it seems her son Kadar Bhaijaan has come to a decision and *Foofi* is worried about it.'

As his opinion of the intellectual capacity of Binto *Foofi*'s son, Kadar, was not flattering, he asked sarcastically, 'And what has that great brain thought of now?'

'He is shifting to Lahore next month.'

'What!' Hidayat Ali was flabbergasted. 'You mean on a permanent basis? How can he do that? His shops, his bungalow . . .'

'He has put his property on sale. He has already found a buyer for his Chandni Chowk shop. And talks are on for the rest.'

'But why? Why?'

'He says he doesn't feel safe in Delhi any more.'

'That's ridiculous,' snapped the professor. 'So all right, these are testing times. But as far as security is concerned, we are perfectly safe!'

The pensive face did not respond.

Sharply he asked, 'What? What is it?'

'I didn't tell you. But something happened at our Mehrauli farm three days ago.'

'Really? What?'

'There was a fight between three of the farm workers. One nearly died. He is in hospital now.'

He shrugged, 'Well, it's sad, but these people are a violent lot. Drunk all the time.'

'Two Bihari-Hindus attacked Shamsuddin with a knife because he was praising Jinnah and his demand for Pakistan,' she said quietly.

'God!' he sat stunned for a long moment. 'I didn't know that, my God!'

'There is something else,' she added gravely.

'Now what?'

'Javed came home crying today.'

His silence posed the query. He waited for the answer.

'He had a fight with another boy in school. Javed defeated him. You know what the boy said?'

Hidayat Ali's heart sank, almost knowing what was coming.

'What?' he asked sharply.

'He asked Javed what he was doing in this country. "Why don't you go to Pakistan," he said. Javed asked me where he belonged, wasn't India his country? What could I answer?'

There was no answer with him either. Not for the moment.

'For years you have taught in Jamia Millia. You are a reputed professor of history. Answer this simple question – where do we belong? Are we not Indians too?'

The question vibrated in the air like a rumbling volcano, its echoes becoming muted but refusing to die down. As Hidayat Ali Beg, thirty-five, professor of history, father of three children, contemplated the ceiling, the question hummed around him like a mosquito.

What was happening to human relations forged through centuries of coexistence? Were they so weak that one tug could rip them apart? And yet he could not be emotional – he had to be pragmatic. He was after all a historian, and what could be more practical than that? The years he had spent in studying the story of ages had skinned away the false veneer of mankind, and given him a perspective on the barbarian within. If history was a saga of man's evolution, it was also a testament to man's depravity, his inhuman cruelty, his increasing brutality. What Mahmud Ghazni had promised, Adolf Hitler had delivered. Modernity was a mere sham, the layer of humanity extremely thin.

And yet Hidayat Ali Beg had not given up hope. He hoped, for there was nothing beyond. He hoped because he dared not think of the alternative. What alternative did he have anyway? How could he leave tracts of ancestral land near Mehrauli, in his family for centuries, gifted to them by Shahjehan? How could he leave his home in Daryaganj, a graceful, elegant house built by his great-grandfather? How could he leave his beloved Jamia Millia? And yet the cold winds had brought with them some ugly changes, pinpricks which could turn into suppurating wounds. Nothing blatant, nothing he could scuffle with, just a change in attitudes, a suspicion in minds, a slow festering hatred. And with this awareness had come fear. Sneaking in slyly. Refusing to go. Making him face facts. And the facts were that though he was preaching unity and nationalism every day in his university, it was the desperate attempt of a desperate man. India was breaking up with a loud, ugly crunch. And nationalism was dissolving under the fiery lava of communal hatred.

For the first time in his life, Hidayat Ali Beg was frightened. Were they really safe in India? Or was he destined to stay the rest of his life in a country he had never asked for, had never wanted? He who had thought of himself as an Indian in his every conscious waking moment. Would he soon be a foreigner in his own motherland? So many confusing conundrums, so many tragic paradoxes. What was the solution? He who could glide through the devious labyrinths of the past with such expertise was frightened of the present. And the future was wrapped in an impenetrable fog of politics and hatred. Where was hope?

* * *

NEW DELHI, MARCH 31, 1947

The shining black sedan swerved smoothly around the massive arch of India Gate, and scrunched softly up the Raisina Hill, towards the imperial edifice of Lutyen's creation in red and cream sandstone – the seat of British power, the residence of the British Viceroy. Entering the magnificent forecourt, the car slowed down, became hesitant, almost as if the powerful engine was afraid of harming its fragile, precious load. Had the chauffeur instinctively held back its strength, muting its energy in awe of the forlorn-looking man settled in its luxurious interior? For that matter, how could anyone be so fragile yet have so much inner strength? Enmeshed in poverty, yet priceless? But this was not the first time that the figure inside had produced this confusion. For someone so direct in his approach and so sure of his principles, he had managed to perplex a generation of government heads and assorted power brokers across the globe. Confounding them with the very simplicity of the conundrum he represented.

Thin, with his body shrunk from years of self-imposed

starvation and self-denial, yet with an indomitable inner strength that could move political mountains – a man who held no posts, owned no land, boasted of no crowns. Yes, he was unarguably the most important man of the time, of the century, in a subcontinent teeming with faceless millions. He barely tipped the scale at a hundred and ten pounds on his best days, yet carried more 'weight' than any other Indian. After all, how heavy ought a soul to be? For that is what he indubitably was – the soul of India. That is what he carried in his weak, wasted frame – the spirit of a subcontinent. The messiah of the anguished millions, the Mahatma of the masses.

But today, when he was on the verge of getting the prize for which he had struggled for nearly three decades, he looked anything but triumphant. Mohandas Karamchand Gandhi, at the pinnacle of the supreme success of his doctrine of non-violence, was full of anguish. Betrayed by his acolytes who were allowing this violence to eat into the ideas he had cherished, to destroy the dream he had created.

And today he was on his way to meet the reluctant writer of this tragic betrayal – Lord Louis Mountbatten, the new Viceroy of India and its last. He was going to meet the man who was ready to shrug off the white man's burden, but in a way which could leave scars on souls for years to come. The British crown would relinquish its most shining jewel, but was threatening to do it at the price of dividing it into two halves. And that was unacceptable to the little man whose dream of independence was unequivocally entrenched in a subcontinent not just free but also united. He could not come to terms with anything less than that. And he was here to see if there was any way to turn the tide, stop the forces of division, bottle back the communal genies who were threatening to create ugly history by parting a nation into two hurting halves. Could he do it? Would his inner voice inspire him in this moment of his toughest test?

He jerked his head in a sudden bird-like movement, desperately tense, desperately determined. He would not let the unthinkable happen. India would remain united. He would allow it to be divided only over his dead body. It would be a whole, unscathed country which would break away the shackles of an alien domination, not a pieced-out, mangled mockery. That was one last legacy he would try and ensure for the future generations. But he could do it only if God was with him. 'Lead kindly light,' he murmured helplessly, momentarily strengthened by the beautiful inspiring words of an inspired poet. Would there be a light at the end of this tunnel?

Edwina Mountbatten took a cursory look at herself in the mirror to check the thin elfin face staring back gravely. It would do, the simple touch of artifice giving her elegance without overdoing things. Today everything had to be just right, perfect. Which is why her normally cool Dicky was fidgeting with his tie, checking his cuffs, flicking an imaginary thread from his beautifully cut white uniform. A flicker of sympathetic understanding crossed her expressive face – he was so tense, his nerves stretched unbearably, his mouth grim. And not without reason. Today's meeting would be a crucial one, possibly decisive, its effects touching millions of lives, capable of contorting the future in unimaginable ways in dark directions.

Until now everything had been positive: her charm, Dickly's silver-tongued oratory, their obvious sincerity, had soothed many ruffled feathers, softened hard attitudes, created bridges, built up an edifice of diplomacy, covering it with the mantle of acceptance.

But today's guest could prove a tough nut to crack, this man who puzzled and irritated Lord Wellesley. The 'naked fakir' who swamped the unconquerable Winston Churchill with hatred and helplessness. Her gamine grin flashed, made bubbly by irreverent humour as she saw in her mind's eye a grim, highly baffled, cigar chomping, nattily dressed, obese Winston. Confronted by a man half his weight and wearing one-fifth of the clothes he wore. Spouting a theory of non-violence utterly incomprehensible to a 'bulldog' who had just recently defeated a tyrant. Churchill and Gandhi, two men so diametrically opposite. And yet Edwina was sure that history would judge both of them as the greatest men of the century.

Today, one of these great men was coming for something as innocuous as tea with Dicky. And could do something as lethal as put a spoke in the grand plan they had been working on. She looked at her watch and went to Mountbatten, gently touching his elbow.

'He should be coming any moment, Dicky. Let's go.'

He grimaced in the mirror, adjusted his tie, looked at her, 'Edwina, what do you think will happen? Do you think he will agree?'

'God, or rather, Gandhi's God, knows. But you have a tough job ahead of you. If he proves to be as stubborn as he was with Lord Wellesley, we are in trouble.'

'Blast it, I must convince him, I have to. I have to make him understand that Partition is the only way for India. The only solution to an unsolvable problem. Sardar Patel has accepted that fact. So has Jawaharlal Nehru.

Now it's Gandhi who is left. He knows he is fighting alone – his own party members do not support him on this issue. Surely that should help influence his decision?'

'You think so? I think the only thing in the world that can influence his decision is his own mind. A stubborn old man he is, from all accounts. And with more inventive ways of protesting than any other man alive. What will happen if he decides to go on another fast unto death to protest against Partition?'

'God, Edwina, don't even say it! If he does that anything can happen – he has the capacity to make Indians follow him blindly. But this time he has got to see reason, he has simply got to.'

'I suppose your best bet is to convince Jawaharlal completely. If anyone can change Gandhi's mind, it is him. You know that.'

Mountbatten shrugged, 'I suppose so. But let me try first. Are you ready? He should be coming any moment.'

'Dicky, I've been ready for the last ten minutes. Please stop fiddling in front of the mirror.'

They made a superbly regal-looking pair, she knew, as they stood patiently under the porch waiting for their guest. Her Dicky was handsome, really handsome, with those faultless features, that patrician nose. As for her, she never thought of herself as beautiful, but she knew she had that certain something. Something elusive. Intangible. For want of better word, you could call it charm. She smiled to herself ruefully. Would it do any good today? Mahatmas were notoriously insusceptible to such mundane qualities. Frankly she was anxious about today's outcome. Either they would win this battle, conquer a situation which had beaten Wellesley and go back with glory pinned on their crest. Or it could be the beginning of a miserable end. The old man was unpredictable and much depended on his attitude. Surely the threat of an impending civil war would make him cow down somewhat? At least enough to understand that he was in a corner with his back to the wall?

The car came to a smooth stop inside the porch and the liveried doorman rushed forward to open the door. But before he could touch the handle, the door was pushed open and a tiny, frail figure jumped out. A beaming face, eyes alive with a bright light, he spotted the Viceroy and Vicereine half a dozen feet away. He smiled and walked towards them, hands outstretched, uncaring about protocol and power games.

The spontaneous gesture shook the stunned Mountbatten from his state of suspended animation and he rushed forward to meet the old man halfway, Edwina just a step behind him.

'Mr Gandhi, it's a pleasure to meet you! A great pleasure!'

Gandhi nodded his head energetically, a happy smile on his face, 'Yes, for me too. And this is your wife? The charming Lady Mountbatten? I have heard so much about you.'

Edwina smiled sweetly and gently held his hand, 'Mr Gandhi, Bapu, may I call you that?'

An elfin smile lit up Gandhi's face, a typical bird-like jerk of his head as he chuckled, 'Yes, I'm used to it – everyone calls me Bapu. Only don't call me Mahatma, for that I don't like. I've told everyone that, but they don't listen to me.' His eyes twinkled, 'I'm no great soul, you know, just an average one. But they persist in deluding themselves.'

Mountbatten smiled widely, gently took his guest by the elbow and led him inside to his inner sanctum.

Looking lost and small in the oversized stuffed Victorian chair, Gandhi settled himself and looked around with frank interest.

'Very nice. Very nice indeed.'

'Do you really like the decor, Bapu?' asked Edwina. 'From what I have heard you do not care much for luxury and pomp.'

He chuckled genially, 'Yes, but that's because I'm a simple man with simple tastes. I don't fit in with these kind of surroundings you know. I feel awkward, I look awkward. The fact is that austerity has spoiled me over the years. I've become addicted to it.'

He wanted to talk about himself, Mountbatten realised, amused by this frailty in his armour. He wanted to talk about his life in the wilderness, his experiences with truth, his philosophy of freedom. And the Viceroy let him, skilfully prodding him on, genuinely interested in what he was saying. For though Lord Louis Mountbatten had met and chatted with scores of important world figures, Gandhi was the most unusual of them all.

It was after quite some time that Gandhi said, beaming, 'Now that's enough about me. I am not that important. We need to discuss many important matters as you well know.'

Mountbatten said softly, 'Yes, we do. Rather we need to discuss only one thing.'

Gandhi looked up, tiny lines of tension adding to his already lined forehead. 'About this ludicrous demand of

Jinnah's, I suppose. And I am telling you right now, I will never agree to it. Never. No one can divide our country. Not Jinnah, not you.'

'But Mr Gandhi, what is the solution? You know the country is falling apart fast. India is on the brink of civil war. The subcontinent is sitting on a keg of dynamite. One spark and it may explode, making the whole system fall apart. And when that happens there will be communal violence, confusion, chaos.'

Gandhi stopped him midway with a gesture of his hand, almost snapping, 'You don't mind my being frank with you?'

'No, Mr Gandhi, of course not.'

'All right. I will.' He took a deep breath before he spilled out his feelings, a depth of emotion in his words: 'You talk about communal violence. I say this evil genie has been created by you, and by that I mean the British. We lived together in brotherhood for years. For your own selfish interests you sowed the seeds of hatred. You talk about confusion. But what can be more confusing than a nation torn apart on an unnatural basis? You talk about chaos. Well, let India head for chaos. Chaos is better than Partition. Just leave us to our fate.'

Mountbatten said patiently, 'You know we can't do that, Mr Gandhi. We can't just leave the country before the issues are settled.'

Gandhi argued passionately, 'Why not? You have controlled our destiny for too long. Let us handle it now. Whatever the price to be paid, we will pay it. Who are you to decide that India should cease to exist as one country? Let's leave that in the hands of the Gods, of our countrymen, of their conscience.'

Mountbatten interrupted quietly, 'The subcontinent

will go up in flames, Mr Gandhi. Would you want that to happen?'

'Can you give me a guarantee that will not happen if you divide the country? That there will be no human loss? No communal rampage?'

Mountbatten was silent, unable to answer the old man.

Gandhi shook his head in despair and continued raggedly, 'You don't know the immeasurable harm Partition can bring in its wake. You haven't lived in India's villages. You don't know the real soul of the people. I do. And I warn you that if you divide this country you will let loose an evil you can't even imagine. One you will find difficult to bottle, which will leave this subcontinent forever scarred, its psyche forever damaged. Now you tell me – would your conscience allow you to do that?'

After a pause Mountbatten said softly, 'It will if I have no alternative. And as of now, I don't. Mr Gandhi, I can appreciate your feelings, understand them, but I can do nothing about it. This is the only way of saving the situation and I'm not the only one who thinks that way. Not just the Muslim League, but even the Congress leaders have veered around to my viewpoint. Sardar Patel has, Mr Nehru has.'

Gandhi nodded quietly, 'I know, I have had a talk with them. But I will never agree to Partition, I have yet to decide what to do about it, how to guard against it. The voice of my inner soul hasn't guided me yet, I'm waiting for its inspiration. And then I will act. As for Jawaharlal, he does not agree with me on this issue, I know, but it's not too late. Something may happen to change his mind. Some miracle may take place.'

'And if it doesn't? What then?'

'I'll protest against it in my own way. Let the whole Congress Party agree to Partition – they have their own compulsions to do that. I'll never agree. If I don't have the support of the Congress, I will go back to the common people. Politicians are no longer the real representatives of the common man, you see. They have been corrupted by the twin temptations of personal power and personal gain. They are slowly losing their connection with the real soul of India. That is where I will go to find my inspiration, my strength. Now I may fail – I am not infallible – but I will die trying.'

'Mr Gandhi, it's too late for any movement of this kind to be effective. The time for that is already past. Only an immediate, even ruthless decision can save this country from being dragged into a quagmire. I can assure you it will be taken only as a last resort. And my request to you is, help me in this. Don't make matters worse. Think calmly about what I'm proposing. Doesn't one cut off a gangrenous leg to save a life?'

'Yes, but one doesn't cut the heart out,' Gandhi jerked out unhappily. Then softly, beseechingly, he said, 'Partition is not the solution to our problems. You requested me to think rationally about Partition. I'm requesting you to stop thinking about our country. We are no more the white man's burden. So don't think for us. Don't decide for us. Just leave us alone. Go. Leave India to chaos, if necessary, but leave us.'

Three

CALCUTTA, MAY 15, 1947

As the Calcutta Mail chugged into Howrah station, the vast platform exploded in a maelstrom of action. The supreme metro of British India, Calcutta was already bursting at the seams with faces and faeces, many parts of the city festering like an open gutter behind the shining, cultured facade it presented to the world. It was a schizophrenic megalopolis, the duality confusing, incongruous. A major axis of the freedom movement. A hotbed of militants. A pinnacle of culture. A stable for a battalion of slavish babus. So many faces, grotesque or grand, together making the city pulsate with vivacity, slightly sleazy, yet vibrant with greedy life.

The man stared at the bewildering scramble on the dirty, stinking platform as he sat passively in his window seat, watching the jostling human mass trying to disgorge itself out of the train. He was in no hurry, he would wait. A twisted smile contorted his mouth – it was amazing how faithfully Howrah depicted the city it belonged to. Bright with bustle, with throngs, with energy and vitality. And yet, scratch the veneer and you would see suspicion in the eyes, fear in the minds . . . quick glances to gauge a man's faith . . . a subtle wary, shrinking . . . urgent whispers, mistrust fogging perspective . . . a city torn by terror, on the brink of a holocaust.

The man walked out of the station into the magnificent yet mean streets of Calcutta, a shabby tin suitcase in one hand and frayed holdall up on his shoulder. He surveyed his environment, standing below a lamp-post which was ineffectively trying to brighten the dull atmosphere. The night had a moody quality with dark clouds threatening to burst, the raucous streets made more noisy by the utterly still air, the human movements made more urgent.

That same urgency was mirrored in the face of the man as he looked around for a rickshaw. He glanced at the faces around him, keeping an eye out for anyone showing undue interest. He needn't have bothered though – the harried Calcuttans seemed to be in a hurry as usual and that was just what he liked. Shadows were where he belonged; the limelight and attention would have been corrosive to his welfare.

But then it was very rare that the man attracted any prolonged attention from a chance stranger. He was too ordinary, he melted too easily amongst the crowd. A limp white dhoti, tied carelessly. A kurta which was white when new but now verging on grey. Generously oiled hair, combed back stringently. A mouse-like moustache nestling on unsmiling lips. Mouth full of paan, the red spittle threatening to dribble down the corner. Rubber chappals on cracked feet, a torn old black umbrella in one hand. Anyone would have taken him for an ordinary trader. Perhaps a tobacco merchant. Whatever. Who cared? He was just another faceless face amongst many other faceless faces. His identity, his name, his ideology, his very life was of no value.

The ordinary viewer would have been totally wrong, of course, in this analysis. His identity was suspected by the British, his name whispered amongst a few Bengali freedom fighters who kept their ear to the ground. His ideology had created its own following and his life was about to turn the fortunes of India on its head.

Finally, he found a cycle-rickshaw as rundown as the street, but he was not complaining. He gave crisp instructions to the rickshaw*wala*, agreed to the exorbitant fare without haggling, and sat on the cracked shiny red seat, the first drops of rain chasing him on his way.

As the rickshaw swished along the road, he rubbed his forehead tiredly. He had not slept for the last two nights, worrying, planning, thinking. The clitter-clatter of the rain steadily gaining in strength hardly bothered him, nor did the clamour of city noises. His mind was focused on more important happenings. The information he had received was heavy with significance, valuable in result, far reaching in effect. And today he would be talking about it to his group. Let them decide. What was weighing on his mind was whether that decision, that action would be tinged with the colour of betrayal. Well, maybe, but history would judge him more kindly, he knew. Certainly his country would. And what else was more important? For a minute he allowed his mind to drift to the pages of his life which had left an indelible print on his susceptible years.

It was another such night, stormy and scary. Quiet shadowy figures entering his house, the door opened by his Baba. *His* Baba *closeted with them in the living room, windows shut, door locked. He remembered his affront at the way he had been hustled out of the* baithak *by all of them. Overpowered by the force of their collective adult mind, he had left, seething with fury and rebellion. And he had not gone to his mother as he had been told to do. No, he had strained his five-year-old ears through the cracks. Listened as quiet as a mouse to the passionate, hot-headed voices inside. And understood as much as a mouse too! In fact the only word he recognised was the one spoken by his Baba – he was talking about a gun!*

That had excited him, he remembered. A gun now, what would his father need a gun for? Could it be possible that Baba *had at last decided to stop doing something as boring as teaching in school? Go in for something much more thrilling like being a robber?*

The prospect had pleased him immensely, and he could almost see the envy on the faces of his friends when he told them this excellent piece of news. His dad – a robber! Now that would be wonderful fun indeed.

The door had banged open, startling him, his eyes still dazed with his dreams. His father had frowned as he looked down at him.

'What are you doing here, Manu? I told you to go to Ma.'

'I . . . I . . .' he had gulped, then closed his eyes shut,

sure that he was in for a beating. But instead of the expected smack on his bottom, he had felt warm hands on his waist. Up, up in the air, enclosed snugly by strong arms. He had opened his eyes in wonder – for months now his father had not picked him up.

And then he was arrested by the look in Baba's *eyes. A curious hungry look; a strange combination of love and apology, of fear and hope. Not that he had deciphered all these emotions then. That had come later. At that point he had just been glad that his father was not angry.*

'Baba,' *he pinned up enough courage to ask,* 'are you going to become a robber?'

'What! What do you mean?'

'Baba, I heard you talking about a gun. I thought . . .'

His father's arms suddenly clenched around him.

'Manu, don't talk about this to anyone, do you understand?'

'Not even to Ma?'

'To no one. It will be our secret.'

He had nodded solemnly with as serious a face as he could make. The unbelieving thrill that he had become his Baba's *friend had stayed with him forever.*

'And no, I'm not a robber, son, not even a policeman. I am just a fighter.'

'Oh, like . . .' *trying to come to grips,* 'like as in wrestling?'

His father had smiled indulgently, 'No, I fight for freedom.'

'Oh,' *he had been more confused than ever.* 'But Baba, we don't live in a jail!'

'No, but our mother is in chains, Manu.'

He had been horrified then, 'You mean Ma is going to prison?'

'No, but your other mother is.'

He was even more horrified by this, with all the fairy tales chasing his imagination. In deep accents of foreboding he had asked, 'You mean I have a stepmother?'

Baba had laughed then, hugged him fiercely in his arms, taken him back to the baithak. There he had sat down on a huge rocking chair, placed the five-year-old on his lap and explained exactly which 'mother' he meant.

Manu had not understood everything, but his immature mind had grasped one mature thought - India was his motherland. And to serve India was the biggest service one could do. The exact phrases and words his father had used that night had faded in his memory, but their meaning hadn't. Nor the passion. Even now, after so many years, he felt that he could touch that moment, touch its throbbing emotion . . .

'Babuji . . .' the urgent voice of the rickshaw*wala* pierced his reverie, startling him.

He looked around, his eyes confused.

'What is it?' he asked the man irritably. 'This is not Bahubazaar.'

'I won't go beyond this point, Babuji. You will have to walk the rest of the way.'

He snapped, 'What's wrong with you? It's at least ten minutes away. And why can't you take me?' A long silence, no answer. 'Well?' he prompted bitingly.

'This area is not safe at night. Not these days. Not for me. Don't you know what happened here one year back?'

He knew. He remembered. Jinnah's call for Direct Action day. The killings. The toll of dead, the figures of injured. The petty reason which sparked off the tragedy.

'But that was a year back! Its been peaceful for many months now!'

Stubbornly the man shook his head, 'No, Babuji, there was a small incident here – two men injured in a community fight. Not big enough to merit headlines in newspapers. But sufficient to act as a spark in these sensitive days. Who knows when the situation flares up uncontrollably? I can't take that chance.'

'I see. So I am supposed to walk for a mile with luggage in hand at this time of the night.'

In a pleading voice the man said, 'I shouldn't have come at all, Babu, if it was not for the money. Please understand, I can't come any further. I have three children.' Slowly the anger left him as he saw the live fear in the eyes of the rickshaw*wala*, in his shaking hands as he stared at a group of sullen youngsters standing some distance away. Even after one year, the fear had not died, nor trust regained. What was happening to his Calcutta?

Without another word, he got down, paid the fare, shifted the luggage in a more comfortable position, and started off on foot.

It was a long narrow road, pock-marked with holes, clogged with drain water, splattered with mud and lined with a cluster of shanty-like cement houses, the small rooms clobbered together relentlessly, boxing a morass of humanity. Ordinarily the street would have been milling with people at this time of night with customers hovering around paan shops, *mithai* sellers, a few pimps, some whores.

But that was usual – these, however, were unusual times, the orgy of hatred which had ripped apart century-old links last year still alive in people's minds. There were more pockets of shadows on the street today. More hard faces. More fearful eyes. Strangers were suspect. A threat hanging unconsciously on anyone not belonging to the right community.

Manu tramped his way through the potholes and the dirt with practised ease and a fake nonchalance. Nothing vague about his eyes now, sneaking quick looks around. Gauging danger. The shoulders still stooped as befitting the middle-aged man he was supposed to be, but the pace of the walk crisper, younger.

It was when he was striding around the corner that they confronted him. Young faces with old expressions. Mean with menace. Hostile with simmering rage. Fortified with false courage which comes from numbers. Sticks in hand, feet apart, spewing venom.

'Wait, what are you doing here?' snarled the leader, still in his teens, drunk with power.

Manu quietly looked at the motley group, estimating strength.

Then he said evenly, softly, 'I want to go to Bahubazaar. I am simply passing through here. So please let me go on my way, if you don't mind.'

'We mind,' snapped the leader. 'Tell us who you are, only then will we decide whether we should let you go.'

'What do you mean who am I?'

Impatiently, 'Are you a Hindu or Muslim?'

'Does that matter? I am a citizen of Calcutta. An Indian.'

Growled another youngster, 'Ah, a smart-ass. Cut that nonsense and tell us straight, are you a Hindu or Muslim?'

'And I told you, does that matter? Aren't we all Indians?'

The leader stepped nearer to Manu, stared in his eyes with contemptuous fury.

'Keep your damn sermons to yourself! If you don't want to tell we have other ways of finding out.' He signalled crudely to one of his chums, ordering harshly, 'Pull off his dhoti!'

The boy stepped ahead, a hand stretching towards the knot, a satisfied grin on his face. A brief bang as Manu unceremoniously dropped his suitcase. And then with stunning speed the boy's hand was clutched in a vice-like grip, twisted and turned, the pain shooting out in waves, his voice screaming to match its intensity.

'You . . . you . . . '

Quietly Manu said, 'I have let you go easily. Next time I will break your bones.'

The group hovered with indecision for a moment, then the leader surged up with anger, his stick raised to intimidate, to grasp back the power slipping away.

'My God, you bastard. I will show you how bones are broken.'

Another voice came from the shadowy corner, urgent with meaning, shaking with discovery, 'No! wait, wait you fool!'

The leader stopped, confused. Stared suspiciously at the middle-aged man, who stepped forward from the cover of darkness.

'What's wrong with you? What do you mean by stopping me in this way? How dare you call me a fool!'

'Because you are one!' bit out the man. 'Let him go. Immediately.'

Silently the group let him pass and without another word he picked up his suitcase and walked away.

In another five minutes Manu reached his destination, a shabby, rundown building, with patches of dirt streaking the ugly greying walls.

As he entered the silent portal of the grimy, maudlin hall, a figure detached itself from the shadows.

In that murky decor, a shady menacing character would have been more fitting. Instead the face which met Manu's eyes was warm, smiling, glowing with simple pleasure as the young man stepped forward, clutched his hand, chuckled with immense relish.

'Well, well, look who is here, finally!'

Manu smiled, the veneer of gravity falling away as he met his friend.

'Bishu. God, it's good to see you, though you are an idiot if ever there was one!'

'Ha, better an idiot than a two-bit clerk like you, you pen-pushing babu.'

'No, no, don't insult me! I'm supposed to be a jute trader for anyone excessively curious about my profession.'

Bishu laughed, took his elbow in a gesture of affection, 'You are mad. You are also late – we have been waiting for ages. Was the train delayed?'

'What else? Have the others come in?'

'Oh yes, for quite some time now.'

'Then let's go.'

'Would you like to clean up first? We have kept a room ready for you here. You must be tired.' Critically Bishu looked him over.

'Yes, and filthy and grimy and stinking. If I make them wait for ten more minutes, will they go berserk?'

Trenchantly said his friend, 'I don't know about that, but if they see you like this, they definitely will. Off

with you, hobo, get normal and then show your face.
The meeting is in the main hall as usual.'

It was after fifteen minutes that a very different Manu
emerged from his room. Clad simply in shirt and
trousers, clean looking, clean shaven, hair parted in the
middle. The removal of the moustache seemed to have
stripped years away from his face, peeling away the
ordinary, imparting it a certain charm. Or it could have
been just the trick of the chameleon changing with its
surrounds. He turned left, went up the huge, knee-
breaking stone stairs, stepped over the splintered wooden
floor to tap at the thick, chipped door. After a pause it
was opened a crack, a right eye stonily stared at him,
blinked in recognition. The door was then opened wider,
enough to let him pass through before it was shut again
firmly and latched.

He looked silently at the strained faces of the dozen
people gathered inside that small room. Sitting around a
shabby table, the overhead bulb throwing an eerie light
over them. Revealing faces hard with purpose, strong
with commitment. The oldest man of the group, as
wrinkled as a prune but with a fierce light in eyes which
would have been more fitting in a youngster, nodded
briefly towards the entrant.

'Jai Hind,' he saluted in crisp tones unmarred by a
single hint of elderly wavering.

'Jai Hind,' echoed Manu, allowing a brief smile in
greeting and sitting down on a wobbly stool.

'You are late Manu, we waited yesterday too.
Anxiously I might add.'

'I know, Dada. I came as soon as possible.'

'And what's the news from Delhi?'

'Bad. As bad as can be. The situation is tense. The demand for Partition is gaining strength. Emotions are being incited by the power groups. Religion is being dragged in and misused by politicians.'

Snapped Dada, 'We know that Manu. It is the same here in Calcutta. What we want to know from you is – what exactly is happening in the political circles.'

'Well, Mountbatten seems to be winning the game slowly but inexorably. He has been convinced that Partition is the only solution to our problems and now he is selling the idea to other parties. Pretty successfully, I might add.'

'What do you mean?'

He has been holding parleys with leaders of all the major parties. He is good, I tell you, he and his wife together. He has created a rapport, established influence, generated trust. When he says that Partition is an evil necessity, these leaders are listening. Wondering if he is right. And slowly agreeing.'

'Sardar Patel?'

'Yes. Not difficult either. His bitter experience in the state government had him thinking on similar lines.'

'Nehru too? Not him surely?'

'Well, yes, but with more reluctance. Afraid of the threat of civil war. Doesn't want to pay the tragic human price.'

'And what makes him think that Partition won't extract its own price?'

'He thinks it won't. He thinks that it would instantly defuse the communal bomb, put people back on the track of harmony. Get them to coexist peacefully again.'

'He may be a great leader – in fact he is – but he is not much of an expert in human nature, is he? If he thinks that Bengal and Punjab can be partitioned without bringing unimaginable suffering and wholesale massacre, he is deluding himself. What about Bapu? When I met him in Noakhali, he was vociferous that he would never allow it to happen.'

'Dada, Gandhiji is the only one who is resolutely, completely against Partition.'

'Then why isn't anyone listening to him?'

'Well, he seems to be losing his previous hold on the average Congress leader. They are in a hurry to get power in their hands. After too many years in jails, too many sacrifices, they are scenting victory, losing patience.'

A young man sitting near Dada leaned forward the nerves in his temples throbbing with anger. His Cambridge accent, brimmed with nationalistic passion. His clenched fist banged on the table, 'There must be some way of stopping the forces of division. There has to be.'

'Ganesh, in politics it pays to be practical,' snapped Dada. 'It is not very easy to fight against a huge tide, to mobilise public support. There are big guns out there, son, trying what we, Hind Mata Sevak Sangh workers, are trying to do in our small way. When they seem to be giving up, how much will we be able to achieve?'

Ganesh stared at Dada, surprised, 'You say that? You, the creator of the HMSS? This is the time when India needs us and our ideas the most – and you are afraid?'

The old man smiled bitterly, 'I have worked on this canvas for years now. I can gauge realistically how much difference we can make. And it's not enough, it's simply not enough. Our intentions are great, Ganesh, but battles are not won on intentions.'

'So what do you suggest, we simply give up?'

Manu turned his head slightly to look at Dada, his eyes a pinpoint of serious thought, 'May I say something?'

'Yes, Manu, of course.'

'You are right, Dada, that ordinary, traditional methods will not work here. The deadline is approaching fast, the tide has gone too much against us. Only one thing can control it now, only one thing may stop the worst – an explosion.'

Bishu literally jumped out of his seat, 'What? Explosive? You mean a bomb? What will that achieve, Manu?'

'Just hear me out, will you? When I meant explosive, I did not mean a stick of dynamite. An idea, Bishu, I'm talking about an idea. Sometimes an idea can be more deadly than any quantity of weapons, you know. A plan. Something reactionary, dramatic, crazy. A gamble which just may pay off. A wild card which may clinch the game.'

'And from where are you going to get this wild card?'

'Well . . .'

'Yes, Manu, you have some idea don't you? This is why you called an urgent meeting of the HMSS?'

'Yes, Dada. But I don't know whether it will work or not.'

'We can decide that later. Tell us about it.'

'I have got hold of some information. Very sensitive. Very significant.'

'Reliable too?'

'Very. The only difficult thing is to get the evidence to prove it. I know where this evidence is – getting our hands on it will not be an easy task.'

'But you think it can be done?'

'Well, we can certainly try.'

'For the sake of argument, let's presume that we somehow manage to get this evidence. Then what?'

'That information and that evidence, in the right hands, just may do the trick. Not a certainty, but maybe.'

'So what is this information?'

Manu told them.

The silence was complete, the shocked faces aware of the threat, like a coiled snake, ready to strike out at the smallest hint of danger.

There was a long pause while Dada sat deep in thought. Finally he spoke, 'I see.' Another deep breath, 'I see.'

He looked up, 'Manu, how sure are you of your informant?'

'Very sure.'

'The envelope is in Bombay?'

'Yes, in the safe of the doctor's clinic.'

'And under conditions of maximum secrecy?'

'Naturally. Very few people even know of its existence.'

'Then how will you get it?'

Manu took a deep breath, 'This information was told to me by a nurse who works there. She says she will help – but we will have to open the safe to remove the envelope.'

'You mean steal? How can you manage that?'

'I can always try.'

'Just a minute. This girl, can you trust her? Suppose it is some sort of a trap?' asked Ganesh suspiciously.

Manu quietly explained, 'She is a family friend. I have known her for years. She may not be a member of the HMSS, but she believes in our cause.'

Deep silence with eyes puckered in thought. Then a sigh.

'It's a desperate plan, Manu, fraught with danger. And if it fails, the fallout could be bad. There are moral issues involved here, you understand? And actually even if it succeeds, it may still create a terrible scandal for the HMSS. Something which our supporters may not approve of, as you know.'

'I know that. Which is why I propose that only I handle the plan. Whether I succeed or fail, I will not involve the HMSS in any way.'

'And suppose you manage to steal that envelope – you realise that it may change nothing? It may remain a mere footnote in history books.'

'I know that too. I said it was a gamble, a wild card. The question is can we afford not to play it? Not to take that chance?'

'Even if it is desperate.'

'Yes, even then. Can we? Just forget about it? Do nothing?'

'You know my answer to that don't you?'

'Yes. But I need a confirmed answer before going ahead. That's why I called for this meeting.'

Dada pondered for a minute then looked around the table, the mute question in his eyes. No arguments, quick nods, immediate acceptance. He understood, nodded back, then turned towards Manu.

'We go for it.'

Bishu bent forward, 'What help do you want from us, Manu?'

'Money. And a good safe-breaker.'

Bishu grinned, 'That's the best of being a freedom fighter. You never know what you will be asked to do next. I have a few contacts amongst the not-so-decent people of Calcutta, the *abhadra lok*. I will see if I can find you one.'

Interposed Dada, 'So what's your plan? Once you get this file in your hand – if you get it – what are you going to do about it?'

'Take it to the right people.'

'And those are?'

Manu told them.

*   *   *

BOMBAY, MAY 29, 1947

The setting sun sank in the Arabian Sea, unknowing or uncaring that it artistically depicted the status of the British Raj on the Indian subcontinent. Just a short while ago, the sun had been the bright, buxom, bully ruling proudly over the cowering earth. Indispensable, unconquerable. So drunk had it been on its own glories that it had ignored the stealthy power of nature's forces. Slowly this power was unleashed, the earth moved and with its movements, the equation had changed.

Shadows which had been sulking quietly on the sidelines had thrown their mantle of sufferance and moved centre stage to claim back their domain. The reign of the sun was over, the king was dead, long live the king! Soon the new regent would rise on the horizon, less shining, more soothing. Its gentle, caring moonbeams would cool a burning land with their balmy rays. And the glorious new star would move many hearts with emotion, inspire many poets with passion.

But perhaps it was just as well that the setting sun did not care that it was a sad symbol of a dying age. Anywhere else the scene would have had the poets searching dizzily for couplets, waxing lyrical about its poignant philosophy. At least a few mushy lines, some maudlin thoughts would have come its way. But this was Bombay, already on its way to be the commercial capital of free India. Not that the city did not hide creative souls in the midst of its fast expanding borders. After all, it rocked a thriving film industry within its cradle. But when these artists wrote couplets, they expected to get paid rupees and annas for it. In the city where money was fast becoming God, no one had time to throw away a few free poetic lines for any reason. This was the city where old fashioned values and principles had not been discarded . . . not completely. Where patriotism could spark off fervour and passion and heroic sacrifices . . . still. And yet a new breed was slowly coming up, a breed gearing itself to vacate the spaces of power left by the departing British regime. A breed ruled by Mammon by rampant, unapologetic greed.

But at dusk this evening, Bombay had put on its best face, the humming whirr of a growing metropolis adding its charm to the majestic vista of the Arabian deep.

Manu expertly and hurriedly weaved his bicycle amongst the tongas, Victorias and cars near Fort. He was late, the train would be coming in any moment. According to the telegram he had received from Bishu, a safe-breaker had been unearthed and was arriving from Calcutta. And presently Manu was on his way to receive this crucial human merchandise at the Victoria Station.

Abruptly he had to brake, cursing as he hopped and balanced on one foot. Not another *morcha*, for heaven's sake! He fulminated, glaring at the group of white khadi-clad demonstrators, tricolour flags in hand, Gandhi topis on heads, screaming their lungs out. Slogans of national unity, slogans of brotherhood, slogans against Partition.

Finally the snail-like pace of the *morcha* moved away and he kicked off, going faster than ever.

The crowded street was slowing his pace. Home-returning babus, on bicycles, clad in stiff white shirts. Youngsters ambling along the road, in wide-bottomed Raj Kapoor trousers. Ogling pretty young Suraiyya clones dressed in *salwars*, daringly tight *kameezes* and *mulmul dupattas*. Hair tightly plaited, tied up with the bright ribbons that were such a rage. If he was not so late, he would have given them a few looks of his own. Devoted as he was to his cause, he was yet young. And one of them had looked so much like his favourite actress, Nargis.

The grand old Victoria Station was in front of him and from its elegant belly he could hear the sharp whistle of an approaching train. He parked his bicycle on the side, bought a platform ticket and went in. The ticket checker said that the train from Calcutta had arrived ten minutes earlier. Which left him with the job of hunting for this man from the meagre description supplied by Bishu.

He looked around. First in anticipation, then with growing anxiety. Now that the incoming passengers had receded from the platform with their sundry luggage, the stone stretch was relatively clear of human habitation. He ought to be able to see this man and yet there seemed to be no one who remotely resembled a safe-breaker! Manu sighed – where exactly was he? The prospect of searching for one petty criminal in the wide expanse of Victoria Station did not please him one bit.

Muttering a few choice words under his breath, he cursed in frustration.

Someone mindlessly stepped in his way, colliding with him. He steadied this clumsy customer, noting with displeasure the clean lines, the innocent face, the wavy hair of the youth.

'Can't you look where you are going?' he snapped. And then found that instead of a reply he was being stared at with rapt attention.

'What is it?' Manu asked sharply.

In answer the young man took out a photograph from his pocket and stared at the image and then back at him. Slowly a grin dawned on that absurdly good-looking face and he shot out a hand.

'Bishwanath had given me your photograph but I wasn't sure. You look much more fierce in real life.'

A stunned Manu took a moment to digest the fact that this was the man Bishu had sent to break open the safe. He stared at the figure in front of him with utter disbelief – tall, slim, with neat clothes, neat shoes, neat voice.

'You are . . . you are . . . '

'The man you wanted,' said the newcomer genially.

'You have had experience in this job? I mean it is not an easy one.'

'For the last four years I have specialised in this, sir,' he said in chaste Bengali. 'I am the best there is. And the most expensive too.'

'But you are so young!'

'My face lies. I am about your age. And don't ask me how I know what that is. I do my homework very well, you know.'

'All right. Let's get out of here. We have to meet someone.'

They were passing by the Regal Cinema on their way to the beach, with Manu traipsing slowly on the bicycle and his companion easily keeping pace with him on foot.

'Where are we going now?'

'I told you, to meet someone. A girl.'

'Who is she?'

Manu said impatiently, 'She is a nurse. She is the one who is going to give you exact details about the safe, its position, how to reach it. Whatever questions you have you may ask her.'

'All right. When am I supposed to do the job I came here for?'

'Tomorrow night.'

'And what is your role in this, if I may ask?'

'I'll be accompanying you tomorrow night. It will be my job to get you in. Your job is to open the safe and get the envelope.'

'You a break-and-entry man?'

'No,' said Manu shortly. 'A freedom fighter. Something which your kind will never understand.'

'Never had the luxury, friend,' said he with undiminished geniality. 'When you are an orphan trying to survive in a city like Calcutta, you can't afford ideals. Not that I love my country any less, mind you. Only at present I am more busy in tackling my personal freedom from poverty, you understand.'

'For a man from the shady streets, you speak very well indeed,' wryly said Manu.

'Blame that on the orphanage matron. She laboured under a misbelief that I was marked for better things and accordingly gave me a big dose of culture. Not that it helped me to get any kind of job. In fact I had written it off as a big waste till I realised that it bestowed on me a certain sheen, a skin of legitimacy.

Which, incidentally, is valuable in this illegitimate business.'

Manu smiled ruefully and shrugged. It was not his concern if the morals of his accomplice were not exactly sparkling.

He reached the beach, flanked by this nimble shadow who was amiably humming a tune and looking around with interest. Pushing his bicycle through the sand, Manu headed towards the rocks at the end of the grainy span. The sandy stretch was virgin, no sign of any footsteps, or bicycle marks. Where was she, for God's sake? They had to finalise their plan, survey the spot, evolve a schedule. And for that they had to get the details from her today. Time was running away, stealing with it the future of a nation.

For Mountbatten had scheduled the All-Party meeting on June 3. Once Nehru gave his formal assent to Partition, it would be all over. The information contained in that envelope, dynamite that it was, would be defused even before it could emerge. He had to reach Delhi before that with the evidence. The attempt had to be made tomorrow. Or the plan would be aborted at birth.

A kind God seemed to have heard his plea. For she was coming, he could see her now, walking towards him at a running pace, feet plonking carelessly through the sand. Petite, slim, her lovely small features alive with inner strength. Her serenity rooted in simple untainted beliefs. She stopped a foot away and smiled a greeting. Then suspiciously inspected the young man sitting cross-legged on the sand, at peace with the world.

But he got up as soon as he saw the pretty little thing in front of him, in a simple *salwar-kameez* with a white *mulmul dupatta* across a curvaceous chest.

'Hello,' he said dazedly in stunned shaken tones. 'I never knew Bombay was so nice,' he said, smiling widely with unashamed admiration.

She glared at this unexpected bundle of masculine appeal and looked flustered in Manu's direction.

'Manu, who is he?' she asked sharply.

'He is my friend from Calcutta. The one I told you about,' he replied wryly.

'You mean . . . you mean . . . the man . . . who is going to break open the safe!' she said in utter disbelief.

'I know,' sighed Manu. 'It's difficult to believe, but as he himself says, don't go by his looks. It seems he is seasoned in the job.'

Manu sat down on the sand, gestured her to join them.

'Okay. Now tell us everything you know about the place. The exits, the windows, the layout of the rooms.'

'And the safe. Can you describe the safe to me? In detail?' put in the other anxiously.

She stared at him coolly and nodded. Taking a paper and pen from her bag she started drawing lines on it. The diagram was a faithful representation of the clinic.

'Okay, now this is the main gate and this is the reception. The doctor sits here and this is where the safe is . . . .'

Four

It was the largest *jhuggi* settlement in Delhi without drainage, without a toilet, without any basic civic amenities. Its seething, scourging drains a receptive nursery of any and every disease, every infection. A dirty acre of metropolitan land where humanity huddled in misery, where the stench permeated every inch of your waking moment. Where the nauseous became normal, the dirt an unchangeable, even accepted part of life.

And on the eve of impending independence, this was where the father of the new nation had chosen to live. Not for him Birla's massive masonry built on the sides of the Yamuna. He would rather go to the poorest of the poor, be one of those countless Indians whom the vagaries of fate had deprived of even the most basic amenities of human existence. Obstinately ignoring other invitations, he was staying in Delhi's Bhangi Colony.

The dilapidated hut which was the Mahatma's present abode had magically and temporarily upgraded itself to the Congress Party command centre. The top cadre of the party were there, huddled in the hut, their attention focused on an emancipated 77-year-old man. Cross-legged and spinning cloth, his thin fingers handled the wheel smoothly, expertly, patience stamped on a face which was a curious mixture of uneven features and utter sweetness. With round-rimmed spectacles perched on his nose, Gandhi spinning on a *charkha*, the spinning wheel had become the symbol of an age. The icon which would instantly speak to an Indian's psyche for centuries to come. But the present pose had some differences from the standard image. Bapu's smooth bald pate was covered with a damp towel for a change, the only concession he had paid to the killing heat of June in the airless sweepers' colony.

The second difference was more basic, more significant, less noticeable. Today there was no toothless smile which normally puckered his face, no peace shining in crinkled eyes. No tweak of impish humour flashing on that extraordinarily mobile face. But then that was not surprising either. Peace, happiness, humour had no place in today's meeting of crossed tempers and angry purposes.

For it was a conclave of the rebels. Those who had followed him fervently for so many decades were not assembled here to add their voice to his or their step behind his. The distance between the leader and the led had grown. There was a chasm where there had been complete faith. A parting of ways in place of unity of thought. For so long he had been their Bapu, the guide of their conscience who had charted their course. They would continue to call him Bapu, but take decisions on their own. Let compulsions instead of conscience determine their actions. They called him the soul of the nation. Today while deciding on the future of that country, the soul would be ignored.

Jawaharlal Nehru sat nearest to Bapu, eyes strained, face anguished. This old man whom he worshipped, who he loved as a son loves his father. And yet he was about to take a decision that was absolute anathema to that man. But Nehru really believed that this time Bapu was wrong. That, unable to grasp the severity of the crisis, he was simplifying issues, placing too much faith in a just God. How could one depend on belief to solve major political matters? What Nehru was contemplating was searing him with intense agony, intense self-doubt. But what other solution was there?

And Gandhi's suggestion about presenting the whole of India on a platter to Jinnah and his League, had been so objectionable, so unacceptable that it had been thrown away out of hand. Rightly so, Nehru thought, for the Hindu majority would have erupted in a murderous rage.

With no other magical idea evolving, with Jinnah as unmoving as a rock, and emotions being exacerbated by the hour, the crisis was snowballing at a frightening pace. If the price of independence, of strength, of power, of harmony was dividing India, then Nehru was almost ready to pay it. No, not almost, he had already made up his mind to it. Now all that was left was convincing Bapu about it. Because Nehru knew, better than anyone, that if there was one man alive who was capable of putting a spanner in the works, it was the Mahatma.

The old man was unpredictable, with an amazing hypnotic power over the masses. If he decided to start a grass-roots protest against Partition, the results could be completely disconcerting, totally devastating. Any major upsurge by the masses could affect history in unknown ways. The British regime may decide that the white man would have to carry his burden a bit longer. Mountbatten may extend the appointed tryst with destiny by months, even years. Indians couldn't wait that long. He couldn't wait that long. Patience was running thin, and he was tired of running. The prize which he had hungered for, which he had chased for so many years, through so many turbulent times, which had demanded so many sacrifices from him, and which had always remained an enchanting chimera, a gossamer of a dream, a tantalising mirage. Would it slip away from his hand once again?

He would not let that happen – not now when he had come so near it. Let Jinnah have his Pakistan, he would make the remaining part the India of his dreams. And the only obstacle to its fulfilment was Mohandas Karamchand Gandhi.

Sitting a little way away on the *chatai*, the rushmat on the floor, Sardar Vallabhbhai Patel silently surveyed the scene, quietly impatient, quietly irritated. Sardar Patel had not always agreed with Nehru, but in this they both seemed to be on the same wavelength. It was his considered opinion that this farce had to stop. The first act of the independence movement had stretched to half a century. Time for the second act, first scene and if the curtain could only go up if Jinnah was not amongst the cast, so be it. He was fed up of the whole rigmarole, of this weak pandering to Jinnah's ego.

And today he was here to tell Gandhi about it.

'Bapu,' he started urgently, 'please, listen to us.'

'Patel, how can you expect me to listen to something which my inner voice says is all wrong?'

'But why, Bapu?' pleaded Nehru. 'Why is it wrong? Jinnah, as you know, is adamant on this issue. That is the price he demands. If that is the only way to freedom, we have to pay it.'

'Jawaharlal, I have told you, India will be divided only over my dead body. As long as I am alive, I will never agree to the Partition of India.'

Sardar Patel spoke with a snap, 'Bapu, we are on the brink of civil war. This is no time for grand philosophies, we need some realism too.'

'And you think I'm being unrealistic when I advise you against Partition? I'm not an old emotional fool, stuck on an unreasoning idea. I'm afraid because I can see the kind of hell Partition will bring along with it.'

'I don't see it that way, Bapu,' intoned Nehru. 'You know I don't agree with Jinnah in most things but I agree with him when he says that with a little care, Partition will be a surgical operation. Clean, precise, painless, ultimately healing, ultimately beneficial.'

'You think that way, Jawaharlal, because you have not been in India's villages the way I have. You have not kept your finger on India's pulse to the extent I have. Painless, you say? If you think that any division of Punjab and Bengal can be achieved without unleashing unimaginable pain, untold disaster, you are living in a dream.'

'Not if the boundaries are cleanly marked out.'

'Boundaries you talk about? How will you mark out the shared wealth of history, of culture, of tradition, of lifestyle? We have lived together for centuries in peace,

our lives are too closely interlinked. You cut the country
in two and you will be creating two halves which will
hurt for centuries. Surgical operation, you say? It will be
one which will benefit no one, solve no problems, cause
immense human misery. You talk about paying the price
for independence. But this price will be paid not by us
but by the future generations.'

Quietly Nehru said, 'Yes, it will be very painful. I
know that. I realise that. But Bapu, can you suggest any
other solution? Things have gone too far ahead.
Mountbatten has decided that this is the only way out of
the whole mess. We can't turn the tide back now, it is
too late.'

'Why is it too late? All you have to do is refuse to
agree to Partition.'

'But that may achieve nothing. Mountbatten will still
go ahead and grant Jinnah his wish. He may be the last
Viceroy but he still is the highest constitutional authority
in India.'

Gandhi shook his head, 'He wouldn't do that. Not if
the Congress Party unitedly opposes it. He wouldn't dare
to fly against the veto of the largest party.'

'Okay, I grant you that. But what will that achieve,
Bapu? Civil war? And if the British can't control it and
just leave us to our problems, what then? Without their
administration, their organisation, what will be left?
Chaos.'

'Jawaharlal, I tell you, chaos is preferable to Partition.
Chaos will be temporary. We will get back on track.
Civil wars will die down eventually. Peace will be
regained. Don't you have that much faith in India's
inherent moral strength? But once you partition this land,
you will never be able to join it again. Tell the British

to leave us to our fates. To chaos, to anarchy, but leave. And leave without parting us into halves. Tell them that, Jawaharlal, refuse Partition.'

'I am sorry, Bapu, I am very sorry but I cannot do as you wish. Mountbatten has called a formal meeting on June 3 of all the parties involved to discuss Partition. Congress will be represented by Sardar Patel, Acharya Kripalani and I. And we have decided to give our formal agreement to the partition of India and creation of the state of Pakistan.'

Mutely Gandhi looked at him, a wealth of unhappiness in his eyes, 'And nothing I can say, nothing I can plead will change your mind?'

'No, Bapu, nothing. Nothing short of a miracle can now save India from Partition. Nothing short of an act of God.'

Gandhi whispered defeatedly, 'Then that is what I will pray for. A miracle for India.'

* * *

DELHI, JUNE 2, 1947

Manu descended the rickety wooden steps of his cheap Dariba Kalan lodge near Chandni Chowk, scratching the abundant crop of red mosquito bite marks on his arms. There was no one in the shabby reception nook and he didn't expect there to be – it was only 6 o'clock in the morning.

He patted his stomach gingerly, touching the manila folder strapped to his chest and covered well with his closed-neck kurta. It was uncomfortable, itchy, but he couldn't risk keeping it in his room. Not after the pains

he had to take to retrieve it. He shook his head wryly
at the memory of that night when he and his accomplice
had entered the clinic. He regarded the break-in as one
of grim necessity but not his cheery companion who had
sailed through the illegal procedure in sunny spirits. And
though that had irritated Manu immensely, his emotions
had turned to reluctant admiration when he had seen
the other's unquestionable expertise. The safe had been
no match, opening like a Venus fly when confronted
with this degree of skill. Manu chuckled involuntarily at
the memory and then checked his watch – time for him
to leave.

He walked a little way through the tiny *gulli* to reach
the wide expanse of Chandni Chowk, grand in this
morning light and without the crowds. He looked around
and hailed a tonga.

'Yes, Babuji? Where do you want to go?'

'17, York Road.'

'Ah, want to meet Nehruji, huh? A friend of yours, I
suppose? Ha, ha. Come on sit, but I will take eight
annas, okay?' he warned.

Manu nodded his assent, held on to the side railing
of the tonga and perched on its shiny black seat.

The middle-aged tonge*wala*, resplendent in crisp white
kurta pyjama and red *zari* jacket, gave a fleeting look
behind to check if the passenger was comfortably seated.
Satisfied, he proceeded to exhort his horse to make a
move in choicest epithets and expertly steered the tonga
and horse till it was cantering at a nice steady pace.
Then he looked back.

'You are a stranger in the city?' he asked chattily.
'Where have you come from?'

'Calcutta.'

'Calcutta! Subhash Babu is a great man indeed. If only he was in India, he would have done something about this situation.'

'You mean Partition?'

'Yes. Troubling times these. God knows what they will think of next?'

'I know. It is going to be a bad year.'

He sighed, 'You are telling me? My wife is pestering me all the time. So are my brothers. They want me to go away from Dilli. To some part of India which will come under this new country of Pakistan.'

'But you don't like the idea?'

'It doesn't make sense to me. Why do Muslims need a separate country of their own? This is very much their country too. They have lived here, happily, for years. And now these politicians want to break up this land in two! What for? What will they get out of it? I just don't understand.'

'What is your name?'

'Karim Abdul.'

'So Karim *Chacha* are you going to listen to your wife?'

'Not me! My question is simple – what will Pakistan give me that India will not? Here I have been born and here I will die. There is a saying in Delhi, you know, that even if you leave the *gulli-koochas* of Chandni Chowk, you will leave your soul behind. And I can't live without my soul, thank you very much. This is my *vatan* – I am not going anywhere else.'

'What about your relatives, your friends? If Pakistan comes into existence, would they like to settle there?'

'It's like this, different people think in different ways. They talk about feeling unsafe here, they are afraid of persecution. Of losing their identity within Hindu rule. So yes they may be going.'

'But you don't agree with them.'

'I told you, it's nonsense. What makes them think that there will be more safety in Pakistan, less persecution? Human beings will live there, right? Not angels? Still, who knows, Pakistan may not happen at all. I have great faith in Gandhiji. He has said, hasn't he, that Pakistan only over his dead body? He will show some miracle.'

'But Nehru seems to be agreeing to Partition,' pointed out Manu.

'That's because Nehruji is a man in hurry. He wants the reigns of the Raj in his hand. And he wants it as soon as possible. It's the same with most other politicians. This Jinnah. He was once an ardent nationalist, a Congressman, a firm believer in Indian unity. Why do you think he has changed his colour like this?'

'Why?'

'Power, of course, what else. Gandhi became the most powerful leader in Congress and that pushed Jinnah's nose out of joint. So he changed track completely.'

He shrugged, 'But still as I said, I have hope. Gandhiji will do something. India will not get divided. And we will continue living in these *gullis* of Chandni Chowk.'

He stopped the tonga, 'There is your 17, York Road, the bungalow over there.'

Manu climbed down and shelved out eight annas, 'That was an interesting talk Karim *Chacha* – you seem to be a very well-read man.'

Karim Abdul chuckled, hugely delighted, 'No, Babuji. Never went to any *madarsa* – who would send a poor man like me?'

'But then,' Manu was puzzled, 'you talk very well.'

He laughed, 'All Dilli*wale* talk very well. You ask any Dilli*wala* his opinion about anything on this God's good earth and they will talk for hours. This is a city of politics and talk, Babuji. Give my salaam to Nehru.'

Abdul smiled, whipped his horse and went off at a smart pace.

The voice of the common man, Manu thought wryly. But who cared to listen? He turned away to look at the clean lines of the laid-back, sprawling British-style bungalow where the future Prime Minister of Free India lived. Instinctively he patted the folder hidden under his kurta. Tomorrow was the All-Party Conference convened by Mountbatten to ratify Partition. Nehru had to see these papers before that. Today. He must meet Nehru today, even if he had to wait the whole day to do so. And he did wait patiently the whole day without seeing much action around the gates of 17, York Road. The *durwans* were lolling comfortably on their seats. Not surprising, considering that there were hardly any visitors. By late evening the ones who had been there in the morning had gone away, disappointed when Nehru had not come back. Pointed enquiries had been met with a casual shrug. 'Big man. Busy in meeting. Very important ones. God knows when he will return.' And indeed as one hour after another had ticked away without his entry, the crowd had dispersed. But not Manu who would not give up his vigil. He had to meet Nehru today.

Another hour went by. Suddenly he saw a car smoothly swerving in at the gates, the sharp profile of Nehru plainly visible from the rear window. Manu broke into a run towards the gate, towards the car, towards Nehru. With a growl the gates opened and the chauffeur put the car in first gear. 'Wait,' shouted Manu, desperately. 'Wait, please.' The car crawled inside, gaining speed, and had disappeared in the driveway when Manu reached the gate. 'Wait,' he shouted again. Hopelessly. Nehru could not hear, he knew.

Urgently he turned towards the *chowkidar*, 'Please, let me go inside. It's important. Very important. Just five minutes, that's all I will need. Please.'

'Everyone says that their work is important. Leave the man alone. He needs to sleep too you know. You go and sleep now like a good boy, go. Come tomorrow.'

Manu looked again at the mantle of darkness which had fallen on the somnolent bungalow. It had to be tomorrow – he would have to meet Nehru in the morning, before the conference. Or it would be too late. Too late for him, for Karim Abdul and for Abdul's Hindustan.

* * *

NEW DELHI, JUNE 3, 1947

Manu reached 17, York Road very early, his pale wan face showing that he had slept very fitfully last night. Once again, his precious folder' was strapped to his chest. Once again he had fear in his mind, hope in his heart.

'Is Nehruji inside?'

The *chowkidar* stared at him, 'You again? So early? What is the matter, can't you sleep?'

'Just tell me, please, is Nehru inside or not.'

'Well, of course, he is like all decent men are at this hour of the morning,' he jibed, looking meaningly at Manu.

Manu ignored it, went a little distance away and stood his ground. Waiting, watching.

After a long moment, the guard grew restless. He stared at Manu, took a tobacco pouch from his pocket, slapped some on his palm, crushed it with the other, and with another look at the visitor, gulped it.

'Look, you are wasting your time you know. Today Sahab won't meet you, at least not now. He has a very important meeting. With the *angrezi* Lord. Come in the evening. You may be able to see him then. What is your name anyway?'

'Manu. Look, *bhaisaab*, I have to meet him before the meeting, it's essential that I do so. If there is any way that you could help me . . .'

'What you have to say is more important than the meeting?'

'Yes.'

'Have you eaten *bhang* or what? You young men are all the same. Think no end of yourself, you do. Go, Baba, go, don't eat my head.'

Manu ignored this too. But by now he was concerned. Nehru may not be admitting any visitors today. Then how was he to meet him?

The car horn shrilled behind him, making him jump for a moment. Manu stared carefully at the rear seat, trying to identify out the shadowy person sitting behind, head bent in concentration. The *chowkidar* snapped to attention, went to open the gates. Manu stepped a bit nearer, staring hard, trying to place the familiar face. A dark man, a great hooked nose, an air of intense intellect. And then, with a frisson of excitement, he identified the man. It was Menon, V.K. Krishna Menon! Nehru's confidant, friend, adviser.

'Mr Menon wait, please,' he shouted, his voice grating with urgency. Menon looked up from his papers, stared at the young man for a long moment. Perhaps it was the despairing eyes which moved him? But he motioned the driver to stop and rolled down the window.

'Yes, what do you want?'

'Mr Menon, I want to meet Mr Nehru, it's very important.'

'I am sorry young man, but I don't think that will be possible today. Mr Nehru is busy in a meeting.'

'Yes, I know,' Manu almost snapped. 'The All-Party Conference on Partition.'

'Well, if you know that, you must know why he can't meet you. Come tomorrow. Driver, let's go.'

'No, sir, wait! It's because of that meeting that he must see me. Before he attends it, I must show him something. Please, you don't understand, it's important for our country that I meet him.'

Menon stared, 'Is it? Why? Explain yourself.'

'Not like this, in the open. If I can tell you about it in private . . .'

Menon thought for a minute and came to a decision. '*Chowkidar*, search this man.'

Manu stood quietly, with his hands on his side while the guard frisked him.

'What is this?' he tapped Manu's chest suspiciously. 'What is inside here?'

'A file. It has papers I want to show Mr Nehru.'

The guard turned, 'Saab, no weapons, but a file which he says he wants to show Nehrusaab.'

'Check it.'

The *chowkidar* opened the buttons on Manu's shirt. A manila folder was strapped to his chest with the help of a thin belt. One hard jerk and it was pulled out. The *chowkidar* reached out for the papers inside and glanced through them.

Then he turned to Menon, 'Only papers, sir. And one *eksara*.'

'X-ray?' intoned Menon in surprise. Contemplated the anxious young face for a moment and then nodded. 'Okay, young man, you can get in my car. Tell me what you have to say, what you have to show. And if I think it's important enough, I will take you to Nehru, otherwise not. Is that understood?'

Manu nodded and stepped into the car, closing the door firmly behind. Stared at the man on his side renowned for his intellectual powers and tried to grope for the right words. Then instead of talking, he simply handed over the folder to Menon.

'Read it for yourself, sir. This is what I want Nehruji to see before he goes for that meeting.'

Jawaharlal Nehru was not a happy man that morning. He was going to concede to the division of his country. He was going to cut up his country, allow a separate nation-state to be carved out of that which should have been one. And he was doing it in spite of Gandhi's objections and warnings. In the future, would the coming generations give the same verdict as Gandhi had? That Partition was one colossal, unnecessary mistake, a traumatic wound inflicted on the psyche of the nation? And worse, would they think that the assent of the Congress was mainly self-motivated. A mere quest for personal power? Would they one day blame him for creating this two-faced Janus in the subcontinent – cursed with the dilemma of constant physical proximity and equally constant, visceral hatred?

Involuntarily Nehru shook his head. No, that would not be. Partition would not prove to be a trauma, instead it would be a clean operation, cutting through the bleeding, festering wound of communal hatred, releasing the venom, cauterising the abscess. Only then could the process of healing start.

And once normalcy returned, as it soon would after Partition, the people would be able to forget the past. Rediscover human bonds of brotherhood and cooperation. Remember the common bonds of culture, of history which had linked them together for so many centuries. It would be impossible for them to fight, they had so much in common! And there would be no wars – for where would be the reason for hatred or enmity? After some initial difficulties, India and Pakistan would simply accept the reality and adjust to it. Get on with the job of living. Get on with the task of building a nation. Or so Nehru hoped. Gandhi thought otherwise. Which one would be proved right in the remorseless spotlight of the future?

Nehru quietly clinked his coffee cup back in the saucer, leaned back in his chair as he gently rubbed his hand across his bald pate.

He would become the first prime minister of a brand new nation, with power to guide millions of human beings towards economic freedom and social welfare – why was he feeling so helpless? With a sigh, he pushed his cup away and dragged the pile of papers once again towards him – he had read them a dozen times and yet the words mesmerised him like some evil magician. The revised Mountbatten Partition Plan – a blueprint of hope, a blueprint of heartbreak. An ordinary combination of alphabets and words which signalled the amputation of one nation and the birth of another. Innocuous phrases on paper which would ruthlessly cut through of a generation.

Nehru grimaced and looked at his watch. After a few hours this blueprint would become a historical fact. With his blessing. For it was the only medicine, though bitter, for the ills which India suffered from. Well, wasn't it?

A knock on the door, firm, even urgent, distracted him from his reverie.

'Yes, come in.'

'Good morning, Jawahar.'

The quiet, familiar tones caught his attention. He looked up at Krishna Menon with a smile and gestured towards a chair.'

'Rather early, aren't you? Well, come in. I have already ordered a big pot of tea for you. Let me just go through these papers once again, then we will talk.'

'No, Jawahar, this is no time to read those papers. I want you to meet someone, immediately.'

'At this time? Right now? Surely it can wait? Whoever this man is, tell him to come back tomorrow – I will meet him then.'

'No, it will be too late. You have to meet him now. It is very important, Jawahar. No, it's more than that – it is essential.' Nehru stared curiously at the set face of Menon, his expression deliberate, controlled, only the eyes giving away his intense excitement.

Quickly, quietly he came to a decision. Softly he said, 'Okay, who is this man then?'

That hoary old cliché, pin-drop silence, was true, he
thought. But no one in that room had the slightest
inclination or the time to drop pins. Nehru sat poring
over the contents of the manila folder which had
travelled all the way from Bombay. Reading it
compulsively as if he still did not completely believe the
contents. And as if to assure himself he opened the cover
again, took out the X-ray with its white orbs in the
centre, held it against the morning light, and put it back.
He picked up the thick white sheet below it, reading
the crisp, professional words written on it for the third
time. Words which coldly, unemotionally signalled death
for a man, and prescribed a time-span for his life on
earth.

His muscles moving in slow motion, Nehru kept the
file back on the table and looked up at the young man
who was watching him with quiet expectation.

'This is factual information? You have verified it?'

'It was stolen from the doctor's clinic, sir. You have
read the diagnosis with his signature. It is genuine.'

'And why did you want me to have it?'

'You know why. Because I want you to think over
your decision of agreeing to the Partition of India.'

'What makes you think that this information would
change that in any way? Or make me rethink?'

Manu looked at him quietly for a long moment.

'Doesn't it, sir? Shouldn't it?'

Another tense moment of suspense and then Nehru
nodded crisply, 'Yes, it should. I must seriously think
about the implications. About the effect it may have on
the future. And yes, on my decision about the Partition
Plan too.'

He nodded again and turned towards Menon with a

tense face, 'Can you ring Patel and Acharya Kripalani? Request them to come here immediately. Tell them that there is a serious development. That we have to think about its strategic consequences. Reassess the situation. And that we have to do it before the meeting with Mountbatten.'

Without a word, Menon gulped down his second cup of tea, got up and went out of the room, a certain spring in his steps. Nehru turned towards Manu and contemplated him, 'I haven't yet understood who you are but I am grateful for your action.'

'May I request something?'

'Anything.'

'Could you keep my identity a complete secret?'

'Is that what you want?' Nehru was surprised.

Manu nodded, 'In fact, if you can bury the whole story, it would be better. For everyone concerned.'

Quietly Nehru surveyed the strong face, 'Yes, it would be. All right, your name will be kept a secret. But I won't forget. You may have done a big favour to me, young man. And to the nation.'

'Sir,' said Manu quietly, 'whether my action was a signal service to a troubled nation or a wasted effort will be determined in the next few hours, after today's conference. It all depends on you – and on your decision. Do you still think that Partition is the only solution?'

Patel the Iron Man of India was immersed in deep thought, legs crossed, fingers on his chin. He was known to be hard as nails, his inner strength awesome, his force of mind capable of shaking up the most stoic adversary. The legend held that once he reached a decision, his follow-up action was like a bolt of thunder, the irresistible hammer of unstoppable force but it took him a long time to come to that decision. Not for him an impulsive thought or an unreasoned act. He carefully deliberated on the pros and minutely inspected the cons. His legal brain coldly separated emotions from fact, analysed details, contemplated their implications. This process of decision-making could be tortuous but it was thorough and complete. And was followed by rapid implementation, executed at lightening speed.

Right now, Sardar Vallabhbhai Patel was at the stage of absorbed reflection. And today's deliberation would be colder and harder than ever. Because the case was complicated. Convoluted. The outcome fluid and dependent on any number of unknown factors. The decision affecting millions of human beings. A huge nation. An entire subcontinent.

Finally, he uncrossed his legs, sat up straight. Looked at Acharya Kripalani. Then at Nehru. Then he said tersely clipping his words, the first he had spoken in a long time.

'If this information is true, it may change everything.'

Nehru said wryly, 'I know, that is why I called both of you here.'

Acharya Kripalani thoughtfully put the papers down and stared at his colleagues in the greatest freedom struggle of the world. Softly he said, 'Let me get this right. I had always known that Jinnah suffered from tuberculosis – I think both of you did too – but I never knew that the situation was so serious. According to this X-ray of Jinnah's chest and Dr J.A.L. Patel's diagnosis, the tuberculosis has affected his lungs badly. And that he has no more than one year to live from today's date. Could this diagnosis be right? Is there any chance of a mistake here?'

Nehru shrugged, 'There is a chance in anything one does. Dr Patel is not God after all. But he is a renowned physician specialising in such cases. One of the best in India.'

Sardar Patel bent forward, biting words, rolling each one around in his mind before grunting them out.

'So essentially, what may happen is that after one year Jinnah may not be with us?'

'That is what the medical diagnosis says.'

'And he is the one insisting on the partition of India. Not prepared to compromise, to listen to reason, to meet us halfway.'

'Yes.'

With a jerk Nehru got up from his chair, its comforts too confining for his restless spirit, his agonised mind.

'I have never got along with Jinnah but it is shocking when you hear this kind of news about someone you have closely known for decades.'

Patel, the perennial pragmatic said coldly, 'Jinnah can take care of himself, we have to think about India.'

Nehru turned away from the window and nodded, 'I know. And the fact is that, though a sad event, this could be the miracle Gandhi was talking about. The act of God which will save us from Partition. With Jinnah gone, there is no other leader of national stature in the Muslim League. At least no one strong enough to grab the imagination of the Muslims of India.'

'And no one fanatic enough to fan communal fires,' snapped Patel.

Nehru grimaced.

Kripalani interpolated, 'And so? What next?'

Patel said crisply, 'We have to think about our decision again. Carefully. In the light of this information. We have to rethink our decision on Partition.'

'But last night we forwarded to Mountbatten a formal letter of assent to the Partition Plan!'

'We can always revoke it. We have not yet authorised it.'

Anxiously Kripalani asked, 'Have you thought about the consequences of not agreeing to Partition? Remember what happened in Calcutta when Jinnah gave his call for direct action? Five thousand people died!'

'In a civil war it will be worse. We have to think about that too.'

'But according to Bapu, Partition too will come at its own price,' Nehru said reflectively, softly. 'Now that we know that within a year Jinnah will cease to be a factor, the whole political equation changes.'

Nodded Patel, 'And the way I see it that equation doesn't add up to Partition.'

'But it's a risk, a gamble! It may prove to be terribly wrong.'

'How do you know that Partition would not be a bigger blunder?' asked Nehru, tensely. 'How do you know that our political heirs would not castigate it as our biggest mistake?'

Softly he touched the blushing red rose on his lapel, 'I just read a few lines by an Urdu poet:

Lamhon ne khata ki thi
Sadiyon ne saza payi.
The mistake was made in moments,
centuries paid the price

Nehru shook his head pensively, and sat down in his chair behind the huge desk. 'Gentlemen,' he said emotionally, 'it's time to ensure that the moments of June 3, 1947, should not prove to be a terrible legacy for our subcontinent. A burden which may become unbearable in years to come. In the light of this startling piece of information, what should be our future course of action?'

* * *

NEW DELHI, JUNE 3, 10 A.M.

The very air of Mountbatten's study was silent, heavy with history in the making. And around the table in the centre of the room were sitting the makers of that history. Designers of India's destiny. Arbitrators of India's fate.

The focus of the round table was Lord Louis Mountbatten, the man who had managed to create a political solution for the conundrum that India had become for its *firang* rulers. With judicious and effective use of wile and guile he had effected something which would have been deemed impossible a few months earlier. By cajoling and convincing the warring politicians, he had artfully negotiated a plan which was to rewrite the history of the subcontinent. Reshape its boundaries. Realign political equations in the region.

By any standards it was an awesome single-handed, single-minded triumph. A dazzling culmination of an illustrious career, the Mountbatten Plan, a two-edged sword which would partition India and create Pakistan. And today his agenda for freedom would get the official sanction. A formal anointment by leaders on the brink of achieving pinnacles of power. At a price to be paid by millions with no voice in that decision.

Looking elegant in a well-cut suit, Mountbatten glanced to his left where flanking him were Mohammad

Ali Jinnah, Liaquat Ali Khan and Rab Nishtar – supremos of the Muslim League, self-appointed guardians of Muslim sentiments, expectant fathers of a new nation. Next to them was Baldev Singh, representing the valiant, exuberant community of the Sikhs. Then there was the Congress, the party, which for the last three decades had relentlessly fought for the independence of a subcontinent. And now, on the brink of gaining their prize, had capitulated to its carving. Nehru had informally signalled his consent yesterday. A letter written at midnight had made that assent formal. Today would simply be a public ritual, a peaceful protocol.

'Gentlemen,' said Mountbatten, opening the historic meeting on a formal note. 'We have come here to register acceptance of the plan promulgated by me as a solution to India's problems, as a prerequisite to peaceful transfer of power to Indians, and an essential step before India can be proclaimed independent.

'You know the blueprint of this plan, its broad features. I know that all of you have certain reservations about it, certain doubts which you have confided to me. But I think that you realise that it is the only workable solution for the present political impasse. To put this plan in action, I will now ask for your formal assent to it for the sake of record.'

Mountbatten looked around at the range of emotions which flit on the faces flanking him. He took a deep breath and called out crisply.

'Mr Baldev Singh? You agree to the Mountbatten Plan on behalf of the Sikhs of the country?'

Singh nodded bleakly, unhappily, 'Yes, I do.'

Mountbatten turned towards Jinnah.

'I know that the Muslim League also consents to the Plan. In a long and friendly conversation last evening, Mr Jinnah had assured me that the plan was acceptable. Yes, Mr Jinnah?'

He stared at Jinnah, willing him to say yes, petrified that the habit of years would make him compulsively say no.

But Jinnah would give him no shocks today. After a long moment of suspense, he unsmilingly gave a small nod of agreement. And with that frugal gesture, the Muslim League's assent was in Mountbatten's kitty.

He then turned towards Nehru, for the first time that day managing a whisper of a smile. He was on surer ground here, agreement a mere formality.

'Mr Nehru, do you agree to the Plan on behalf of the Congress Party?'

There was a long silence, humming with meaning. Too long, too unexpected. Confused, the Viceroy stared at Nehru, surprise marring those perfect features.

'Mr Nehru? You agree to the Plan, don't you?'

Nehru looked fleetingly at a stoic Patel and at an expressionless Kripalani. Then with a determined expression on his patrician face, he stared back at Mountbatten, shoulders stiffened with resolve.

'No, Mr Mountbatten,' he said firmly, staunchly. 'The Congress Party will not be a part of any plan which divides this country. We categorically refuse to agree to the partition of India.'

The shock was total, its effect stunning with the unexpectedness. Paralysing with its surprise. It took a moment before Mountbatten could get his breath back. His wits together. His forehead knit in puzzled creases, he said in an unbelieving tone, 'What? What do you mean, Jawahar?'

'I mean what I just said. I do not give my formal assent to the Mountbatten Plan.'

The Viceroy looked in the eyes of the man he had come to consider as a dear friend, saw the resolution shining in Nehru's eyes. And for the first time he was shaken by doubt that Nehru really meant what he said.

'But I don't understand! Yesterday you gave me a letter to that effect . . .'

'We have changed our minds. That letter stands revoked from this moment.'

'But why? What has happened? What is the cause of this turn around?'

'We just decided that Partition would not benefit anyone, neither Hindus nor Muslims. And definitely not the country.'

Jinnah snapped, 'Who are they to decide on what is good or bad for Muslims? Let the Muslim League decide that.'

'Mr Jinnah, Muslims are a part of this country. They are first and foremost Indians. You are inciting them to forget their own motherland. I can change their minds. I can remind them that for good or bad, this is their birthplace. That the legacy given to us by our forefathers should not be squandered away in a fire of communal passions.'

Jinnah bit out furiously, 'You think they will listen to you? Muslims in India know that they have no future in this country. That division is necessary for their benefit.'

Quietly Nehru countered, 'They will listen to me for I think that in their innermost hearts they too don't want Pakistan. I will show them that no one will win by this division. That we both will lose. And the scars may never heal. I will make them understand that together we can achieve greatness, an apex position in the global polity, economic independence, military glory. United India has the capacity to become a superpower of the world. An Asian giant like no other. With the strength of our natural resources and sheer vastness of size, we can dominate world events. But if we divide we lose out on everything.'

Jinnah was about to retaliate when Mountbatten interrupted, 'Just a minute, Mr Jinnah, I'd like to say something first.'

He stared hard at Sardar Patel and Acharya Kripalani in turn, 'Do you agree to what Mr Nehru has just said?'

The Iron Man stonily stared back, 'Yes, Mr Mountbatten, we completely agree. We have taken this decision jointly and unanimously.'

'Mr Kripalani?'

'Yes, I am absolutely with Nehru on this.'

Mountbatten nodded his acceptance of the verdict, turned towards Nehru and contemplated him. Then he asked softly, with just a hint of a threat, 'Do you realise that as a Viceroy I can still go ahead and implement this Plan with the authority inherent in me?'

'I realise that.'

'And?'

Patel interrupted tersely, 'You won't do it. Without the agreement of the majority party, you dare not force the Plan on India.'

'Granted. And you are right. I will not be able to implement it without your agreement. Apart from anything else, the British Parliament will not give their sanction. But do you realise something else?'

'What?'

'The British Parliament may, in frustration, scuttle the

plan of granting independence to India. Postpone the date indefinitely.'

'We know that.'

'But you still think that your decision is the right one?'

'We have waited for so many years for freedom. We will wait a few more. But when it comes, it will be a real freedom. Untainted by the tragedy of Partition. A unified strong India ready to take its legitimate place amongst the great nations of the world. That would be a dawn worth waiting for, don't you think?'

'No, Mr Patel, I don't think so. For you are forgetting something very crucial. In your fantasy of the unknown future you are forgetting the cold reality of the bleak present. And the reality is that India right now is on the brink of a civil war. A communal conflagration of colossal proportions. Only this Plan can save India from that disaster. Stop millions from massacre. Bring everlasting peace to the region. Are you ready to sacrifice these on the altar of some Utopian dream, which sounds great and noble and is impossible to attain?'

Nehru interrupted, 'Your argument is a valid one but there is one basic fallacy marring it.'

'Which is?'

'Your presumption that Partition will be a peaceful act of amicable separation which will douse the fire raging in the country. But how do you know what Partition would be like in reality? How do you know that it would not turn out to be a demon which would demand its own sacrifices? Uproot families? Destroy lives? Create havoc? Even, perhaps, result in terrible bloodshed, wholesale massacres?'

Jinnah interrupted with cold ferocity, 'Gandhi has

managed to brainwash you, hasn't he? Once again he gets his way, but this time, it is going to prove costly, I warn you.'

Mountbatten gestured to him helplessly and turned to Nehru, 'So do I take it that this decision is final?'

'Yes.'

'You would like to think about it perhaps . . . '

'No.'

'So be it. The Mountbatten Plan stands terminated as of now. As does the plan to partition India. Whatever happens after this is your responsibility. You have taken a great gamble Nehru, I hope you are ready to cope with its consequences.'

'You don't worry about that, Your Excellency. It's our country, we will take care of it in our way. And if India is destined for a civil war, we will face that too. Better a temporary civil war than a permanent partition of India. We will allow no one to break up our motherland. It will be one whole unbroken India which will keep its tryst with destiny.'

Part II

Crossroads

Five

Such moments come very rarely in the life of nations. It is the moment of judgment, the moment of decision. An instant, carrying with it the baggage of centuries past, the responsibilities of the centuries ahead. A moment born of a conflict between two warring factions in the ocean of time, in the womb of murky night, in the deep sludge of poison. Would there be nectar at the end of it, or was it an illusion, to be shattered with the coming of a false dawn?

A nation caught in the throes of such moments is ruled by one king, ambiguity, which no nation should be ruled by. And yet in that ambiguity, that uncertainty, may lie the genesis of future glory. But then again, it could turn out tragically different. The shimmering light glimpsed through that ambiguous haze may prove to be nothing but a mirage, a betrayal, a negation of promised greatness. A nation standing at such a crucial crossroad in its journey through time is more like a melting pot of emotions. With disjointed forces pressing power buttons. And in the ensuing mindless melée it is difficult not to be swayed by the momentum. To step through the visceral jungle of pouncing events.

This is the difference that divides the sun from freakish stars, statesmen from mere rabble-rousers. This magic ability to lead from the front, to keep sanity intact in the midst of rampant madness. To provide the healing touch of humanity. To keep the nation on an even keel with the sagacity of a Solomon. In the end much will depend on these Solomons. They will be called on to end the ambiguity. To decide on the direction and let sanity flow.

In 1947, a subcontinent was standing at a crossroad, its destiny controlled by politicians pulling it in conflicting directions. Manipulations and manoeuvres, strategies and counter strategies, the motives ranging from sublime to selfish.

It was indeed a staggering dilemma faced by these midwives assisting in the birth of a new nation. A decision imperative, its result unknown. One starting point, two different roads. Where did India's destiny lie? In that second of immense significance, India could have turned either way. The choice was open. The alternatives confusing. Difficult to predict which way lay the proverbial gold.

The politicians in 1947 would naturally not know, but on one side lay the horrors of Partition, the three resource-sapping, tragic wars, the constant enmity, the killing borders, the dreadful division and emergence of Bangladesh. And something even more terrible. Slowly the poison would grow as would the distance. It would breed hatred, fan suspicions, create rivalry. Brothers at birth, enemies forever after.

On June 3, if India had decided to accede to the demand for Pakistan, to take the easy path to independence, history would have had a different face, as would the subcontinent. As for the citizens of the region, it would change their lives in uncontrollable ways, rewrite kismets, reshape destinies.

Hidayat Ali Beg, for example, would lose both hope and heart at the first brush of a communal backlash. He would forfeit his ancestral land, his ancient house, his beloved Jamia Millia. He would pay huge amounts of money to a trucker to transport him, his family, his belongings and ultimately go across the border almost empty-handed. But bankruptcy would be a minor misfortune in his tragic saga. The truck would be stopped near the Wagah border, ambushed, robbed. His Noor would be carried away by the maddened animals, clutching in her arms one-year-old baby, Parvez. Hidayat Ali would meet his wife again only after six months, a battered, beaten ghost in the refugee camp. An insane frightened wraith compulsively reliving the trauma of multiple rape. He would never meet Parvez again, the baby's fate unknown till Noor's screams in the grip of a nightmare would reveal the horrifying story of his death. Hidayat Ali would live out the rest of his years in near penury in a two-room dwelling on the old streets of Karachi. The years would be spent in nurturing his shattered family, his traumatised wife. He would never publish his book on Mahmud Ghazni. He would never again dare to hope or hope to dream. He would never again believe in humanity.

Lala Shyamlal Kapoor would cling to his hope and home until both were literally burned away. His precious *jahaj-wali kothi* in flames, he would exchange all the gold in the family for a berth on the last train from Pakistan. It would be a journey straight to hell. The train would be stopped with the Indian border just half an hour away. The wholesale pitiless massacre would leave a stash of bloody unrecognisable bodies, beyond identification. But Shyamlal would know that Bela was one of the grotesque contorted corpses. And his only son, Vishnu. And Vishnu's wife, Chanchal. And his beloved granddaughter Nimmi. He would always wonder what quirk of fate had made him take the one-year-old Rajender to the bathroom just before the attack. He would always wonder how he could have stayed inside that small hole, listening to screams, knowing that his family was being killed just a few feet away. He would always wonder why he had not died that night. The marvel of the survival instinct, that is the heritage of every Punjabi, would come to his rescue. He would clutch his grandson, stay in that small stinking cubicle for four days, he and the baby surviving on nothing but water. When the train finally reached Amritsar, he would get down, head for Delhi. Occupy a vacant small room in Paharganj – the previous Muslim owner having been slaughtered.

With no resources, no backup, and a baby to support, he would go back to the point from where he had started. He would again become a *raddiwala*, roaming the unfamiliar streets of Delhi with his handcart. He would get used to being called Shyamlal without the affix of *Lala*. It would take him all of twenty years of backbreaking work to buy a minuscule shop in

Panchkuin Road. He would name it Hind Trading Centre and cry like a baby while reading the board. The deja vu and the difference would break him up finally and within six months he would die of a heart attack. But twenty-one-year-old Rajender would understand. *Lala* Shyamlal Kapoor had tasted death twenty years ago on that doomed train from Pakistan, with his Bela, his Vishnu, his Nimmi. His body would receive its last rites two decades later in the Nigambodh Ghat on the banks of the Yamuna.

Manu would become a victim of the madness that would strike Calcutta in the wake of Partition. He would die a horrible death in the midst of Gariahat trying to save a screaming family from their burning hut. The maddened arsonists would grab him and throw the writhing, struggling man into the hungry flames. His charred body would not arouse any pity, the sight would be much too common.

Karim Abdul's story would be just as common. The shocking would turn ordinary in the holocaust which would grip the bowels of Delhi in those scorching months of 1947. Abdul, the politically savvy tonga*wala* from Chandni Chowk, would refuse to go to Pakistan, clinging stubbornly to the fact that this was his country too. He would pay for his mistake on the streets he had lived all his life. One evening the *gullis* of Chandni Chowk would turn into killer stretches, and Karim Abdul would be beheaded by maniacs, after witnessing the killing of his wife and two sons. His three-year-old daughter would find her way to an orphanage, about ten minutes distance from Chandni Chowk. She would never remember her father, she would never know what those streets had cost her.

These and countless other numbing miniature tragedies were ticking in the dark pit awaiting India's tottering over the edge. But at the last moment, the nation would change track, regain equilibrium. On the point of keeling over the brink, it would step back. Turn away. Change course. And with this reversal, the stories of Karim Abdul and Manu and *Lala* Shyamlal and Hidayat Ali Beg would change. At that confusing crossroad, India would choose to go a different way and that moment would reshape its future.

The refusal of the Congress Party to accept the conception of Pakistan would turn the geopolitical situation on its head. Its ripple effect would push the country's freedom calendar three years further. India would get independence, but not on August 15, 1947. Instead it would taste the first moment of freedom on August 15, 1950.

But what a colossus would be this India! Swaying over a whole subcontinent like a soaring eagle ruling the horizons. The newly independent nation would encompass within its boundaries a bewildering bounty of variations. Stretching giddily from the turbulent heights of the Khyber pass to the stunning vistas of Kanyakumari, from the rice fields of Bengal to the orchards of Quetta. With a galaxy of metros like Delhi, Lahore, Bombay, Karachi, Calcutta, Rawalpindi, Madras, Dacca within its expansive folds.

The diversity of its four hundred million people would be mind-boggling. But the silken thread of unity binding them would create a behemoth of a nation straddling proudly the whole of Asia. With its treasury of natural resources, sheer size and manpower, it would have a staggering potential for greatness. A cohesive green revolution would transform vast areas into a granary and industrial innovation with some inspired leadership would work its own mantra. Increasingly India's influence would be felt in global affairs.

On May 11, 1998 this eminence would be rakishly underlined with a brilliantly orchestrated outburst of the atom. The world would be stunned by the news that a series of nuclear blasts had been carried out simultaneously in India's twin atomic sites – Chaglai Hills and Pokharan. The self-appointed guardians of World Peace would moralise, threaten sanctions, spout condemnations. But ultimately they would realise that it is difficult to make a pariah out of the biggest middle-class market on earth. Ultimately economic mathematics and profit motives would direct a rethink of global strategies. The Asian giant would be accepted as the sixth member in the charmed circle of nuclear haves. And by circa 2000, in the fiftieth year of its independence, India would be an acknowledged superpower in the world.

Part III

Destiny

Six

There was a peculiar smell pervading the jostling, bubbling Mcleod Road. And no, it was not the stink of sweat oozing out from hundreds of armpits that hot afternoon. Instead the busy commercial street of Karachi was reeking with that special odour that all busy commercial streets are burdened with, the stench of avarice, of greed, which rises from the collective coveting of minds.

But just for the present, the monetary motive had taken a backseat – this being the lunch hour – and the gastric God ruled everyone, from the suave executives to the 'chippy' clerks.

Not over him though. He walked across the pavement, making his way unhurriedly through the pressing bodies. Head bent, with just on occasional glance to scan the field. Effortlessly merging with the crowd but his antenna sharpened to sense danger. But no one was seemingly interested in so ordinary a specimen of humanity, from his oily, backcombed hair, to his slightly frayed light blue shirt, shiny polyester trousers and scuffed shoes. The only touch of the unusual about him was his shoulder bag in expensive soft leather with strong brass tacks.

A little ahead of him loomed the mammoth FINCOM Bank Plaza building and he slowed down his pace even further. He stopped casually near a paan*wala*, about thirty feet away from the gates of the building. Looked around indifferently, searching. Then he saw the face. Eyes locked for a second, identity confirmed. His contact raised a listless hand, wearily rubbing his forehead. A pre-decided gesture, the significance known – the field was set, the territory safe, proceed. He turned his head away, heft the bag, and walked ahead.

It was difficult for anyone to miss the thirty-storey building of FINCOM Bank Plaza, towering both in structure and status. One floor of the imposing concrete and glass edifice given over to the sprawling FINCOM Bank, the rest of the floors crowded with offices of international banks, multinationals and mega companies. A colossus in cement playing house to a concentration of financial muscle.

It was this muscle he was going to twist today – get them running, press them into panic. There was a grim smile on his face as he entered the imposing gate of the Plaza. They loved their skins, these money barons – one pinch and they would go cawing all over the place, creating more ruckus than a dozen crows locked in a pot.

A quick check of the premises. Satisfactory. A look for the familiar face, and infinitesimal eye contact. Immediate signal – schedule activated, time period accelerating. Move.

He went to the rear of the building, towards the doorway of the basement. The parking attendant was standing at the entrance. More ornamental than efficient, smoking a *bidi* and gossiping, giving him only a cursory glance. But then the look turned sharper, a gesture asking him to stop. Keep cool, stay casual. His business was legitimate! Remember that. Act that.

'Yes, what is it?' a hint of arrogant impatience. 'This is a car park.' The implication being that he did not look as if he could possibly own a car.

He clicked irritatingly, 'I know that. So?'

'Well, no one is allowed to go inside except the owners and the drivers. And I don't think you are the chauffeur of any car that I know of. Never seen you before.'

A bored voice explaining facts of life to a mentally deficient person, 'I am not. I am a clerk and I have to accompany my boss to a meeting. He has asked me to come down and wait for him in the car.'

'And who may that be?' Still suspicious.

'Bikram Goenka. Mahalakshmi Finance Company. Tenth floor.'

A new respectful acceptance on the attendant's face, 'The new silver Mercedes! Oh! Well, go in, then turn left. Fourth in the row. Beautiful car, beautiful! How many lakhs did he pay for it, do you know?'

He politely declined knowledge, went rapidly down the cement ramp, turned left as advised. Saw the silver sleek lines of the car he was supposed to wait near but instead of stopping, stepped up speed. The time-span was accelerating. Precipitate action. Catch up with schedule. Hurry! To the end of the basement, in the shadows, near the wall, the predetermined action centre. A Fiat was parked there, part of the plan, providing the necessary bulwark, a temporary cover from curious eyes.

He reached the car, looked around. No one in sight. Another covert look, last check before the plunge. Satisfactory. He hastened to the back of the car, in the narrow space created between the boot and the corner of the wall. Grimy, paan-stained and urine-drenched as it was, that dirty, dusty pocket of earth would be acting as a womb, nurturing rage, delivering death. For many stretched out moments he stooped there, his face hidden in shadow, his hands busy. It was done. The pieces of destruction were in place, cohesive, ticking. He stood up in one sharp move, picked up the bag, now almost empty, and made his way towards the entrance. He had to get out of here, time was everything. Ten minutes, that's all he had, that's all they had. He galloped up the ramp, huffing slightly, hoping that he would not encounter the attendant again. He did. The man saw him, got up from his chair, approached nearer.

'What happened?'

'My boss has not come down yet. I thought I would go up and see what the problem is.'

'Well, take the lift! Don't you know where that is?'

Damn! Improvise! Hurry!

'I know. I tried it, but it seems to be stuck. Maybe that's why the boss has been delayed. I better go.'

'Wait! The lift is not working? No one told me that. I must check on this, come show me what the problem is.'

Time was his enemy, ticking mercilessly.

'I have to go. I am really late. You check it – something wrong with the buttons, I think.'

He rushed away, not waiting for an answer, not caring that the man was looking at him with faint suspicion. Soon it would not matter. That man would not be in a position to confide his suspicions to anyone. Not ever. As for him, he had to remove himself from the field, from the orbit of effect immediately. The explosion could not be allowed to touch him, he had to live. He had to carve out a dream, give substance to a vision. He tried not to think of those who would be blown up within a matter of minutes. Their destiny was inevitable death. His the achievement of a vibrant passion. Calmly, coolly he walked out of the shadows in to the brilliance of the harsh sun. And kept walking towards the beckoning boundary of safety.

* * *

NEW DELHI, JUNE 25, 2001

The silence in that huge wide-ceilinged room at North Block was deafening, turning the quiet efficiency of an air-conditioner into a jarring hum. It was a big room, generously designed by Lutyen for a different era, designed for power. The era changed hands, the power lingered on. The moments trapped inside the four walls like silent storehouses of decisions, rulings, policies. The second biggest power centre of Delhi, next only to the Prime Minister's office. The central node of governance in Federal India. Controlling authority over the states. The domestic arm of a benignly strong centre.

A Home Ministry is always a powerful portfolio as well as the toughest. In a federal scheme of polity it becomes even more so, acting like a spider, sitting in the midst of a finely knit web. Or like a tigress who lets her cubs play independently. The big cat disdains to constantly interfere or unnecessarily intrude on her playful progeny. She just sits benignly. Watches carefully, and acts with rapid speed if there is an intruder, a threat, a predator.

Farzana Hussain, however, did not resemble a spider in the slightest, nor yet a tigress. Some of her spiteful detractors did call her horsy, but prudently forbore to mention the fine thoroughbred featuring in their imagery. Strikingly tall, strikingly slim, strikingly elegant, she was, in one word – striking. She was also the most powerful woman in the subcontinent, the Home Minister of a country fast emerging as a superpower, a star charted for further political glories. In the last two years she had set up an excellent track record, notching successes, hammering through tough, necessary policies and ruthless implementation. Naturally she had shattered more than a few egos in the process, crumbled reputations, angered powerful factions.

The risks she had taken should have led to her downfall long before had it not been for one fact. She may have gathered enemies by the dozen, but she had also earned a grateful nation's trust. Her very toughness a blessing in an era of vacillating politicians. Her acknowledged impartiality unusual in politics dominated by narrow-minded factionalism.

Farzana Hussain was also acerbic and forthright, with a bellicose temper which she expressed with murderous verbal ability. But for the last ten minutes she had not spoken a single word, her cold logical mind analysing the facts, reaching conclusions, her sharp, well-polished nails drumming a background score to her thoughts.

The staccato drumming stopped abruptly as she looked up from the file she was reading at the man sitting across her. Parvez Ali Beg, at 54, straddled the Central Bureau of Investigation with a reputation as hard hitting, as tough and as brilliant as hers. But right now, neither of them were thinking about their careers – they had other things on their collective minds.

Fine lines of worry marred her otherwise smooth brow as with puckered eyes she stared at the Director of the CBI. 'One week since the FINCOM bomb blast, and this is all the information we have?'

Beg simply shrugged, the action eloquent.

'Twenty dead, a hundred injured. Amongst them a head of a multinational, three chiefs of foreign banks. A vice-president of a conglomerate. These countries are baying for our blood, complaining about security measures, threatening dire consequences. Already I have had two diplomats approaching me with angry enquiries. If we don't come out with results, it could escalate into a multilateral issue.'

'I know that.'

'So tell me, no concrete suspects, no evidence, no firm pointers to the perpetrators, nothing at all?'

'Nothing that is workable, Farzana. Nothing that can be conclusive or accepted in a court of law.'

The fact that Farzana Hussain did not take umbrage at this familiar use of her name, did not mean that she allowed such liberties commonly. But she had known Parvez Ali Beg for twenty-five years now, the association traced back to the fact that one Farzana Quereshi, a brilliant student at Jamia Millia, was also the favourite student of Professor Hidayat Ali Beg. Farzana had frequented the professor's house, got along famously with his wife Noor, argued vociferously with his youngest son Parvez, and ended up having a crush on the young police officer. That it had not been allowed to develop any further was an excellent example of just how practical Farzana could be. Though she found him interesting she clearly understood that he was much too strong to suit her. She preferred a man she could mould to her needs, not one who would try to mould her. The fleeting romance had died a fast death, but friendship had remained.

When two decades later Farzana Hussain became the Home Minister of India, she had handpicked Parvez Ali Beg as the boss of the Central Bureau of Investigation. And Beg had proved over the last two years that her judgment had been impeccable, her trust well deserved.

Farzana sighed in frustration, 'Okay, then tell me about the inconclusive, the unworkable. Knowing you, you have to have those. I'll settle for them for the present. What about this car park attendant, Karim Ataullah? How did he get saved by the way?'

'An act of God rewarding diligence in duty. Ataullah smelt something rotten in the man's story, the one who entered the basement twenty minutes before the explosion. The story he had given while leaving made our man think hard and he decided to call the offices of Mahalakshmi Finance from the gatekeeper's office. That's when the blast took place.'

'Well, has he been able to identify this man?'

'Easier said than done. We have been trying just that for the last six days. Ataullah has gone through all the pertinent records, Interpol identifications, crime files. No match. Negative confirmation.'

'And yet?'

'And yet, what?'

'Your inconclusives. I am waiting to hear about your unworkables.'

Beg smiled, conceding the point. 'Modus operandi, Farzana, my theory is based on just that. A continuum of events, a connection which no one suspects, the motive buried, the goal camouflaged.'

'Look, can you spooks talk ordinary English which us poor common folk may understand? What the hell are you talking about?'

With a grin he elaborated, 'Simple, this bomb blast could be just a link in a complex chain of other events which are under investigation. Disparate in content, but with a shared core.'

Farzana sighed, 'You are losing me again, you know. What kind of events.'

'Remember the kidnapping of Amar Sengupta in Dacca?'

She nodded, puzzled, 'Last year. Senior Finance Minister of the state of Bengal. Released after seven days. Kidnappers unknown to date.'

'Right. Then the bomb explosion at Sita Kund near Rawalpindi four months ago. One dead, three injured. Natural corollary being panic, fear, suspicion. Result? A visible strain on communal ties. I can identify at least ten such incidents in the past eighteen months. None of them as serious as the FINCOM blast, but they have been effective in destabilising the surrounding area, touching divisive nerves.'

'Okay, so what's the connection? Why can't these be

unrelated actions of maverick groups? Criminal elements operating with a profit motive?'

'Well, maybe. But it gives me furious food for thought. Especially when you consider the canvas of their operation.'

He opened his folder and removed the map of India, certain spots highlighted in fluorescent, handed it to her.

'I have marked the cities where these unexplained activities have taken place. Can you see any cohesive pattern, any draft of a design?'

Confused she stared at the map, marking places in a murmur, 'Lahore, Rawalpindi, Karachi, Amritsar, Hyderabad, Kashmir, Dacca, Chittagong, Calcutta. Well, most of them have a dominant Muslim population.'

'And?'

'And what else?' She shook her head, stared again at the map and the penny dropped, her eyes widening, then narrowing in slits, 'Are you saying what I think you are saying? 1947?'

He nodded, 'Got it. These are roughly the areas demanded by Jinnah in the 1940s to create the separate state of Pakistan.'

'My God, you think someone wants to stir up that spectre once again?'

'I have got a nasty smell about this, Farzana. Call it professional instinct, but I see an ugly pattern.'

'Based on what? There has to be something more tangible than this.'

'Okay, there is.'

For a long moment he was quiet, reflective. Then he bent forward, 'Ever heard about an organisation called Quom-e-Majlis?'

She thought, shook her head, 'Well, vaguely. One of those fringe groups, I think. What about it?'

'A bunch of right-wingers. Plenty of talk, very little action. Fundamentalist hotheads who feel that the Hindu majority is rough riding their very existence.'

'But nothing more active than hot air?'

'Until now, no. But it's surprising the way the Majlis seems to be popping up in some form or another in these recent episodes.'

'For example?'

'Take the case of Amar Sengupta. His trusted clerk went missing ten days after the episode. We checked and found a paper in his house which points to the fact that he was an active member of the Majlis. Or that theft in the Amritsar arms' depot. The superintendent's movements had been unusual to say the least so we dug a bit.'

'So, what did you find? That he was a member too?'

'Oh no, nothing so obvious. Instead he was having an affair with a man who was.'

'Oh, oh! Blackmail?'

'That's what we suspect, but we can't prove it. He simply denied everything and we had no concrete evidence of his culpability.'

'But you had evidence of this affair?'

'Sure we did, but what the hell? Homosexuality between two consenting adults is not a crime, you know.'

'I see. Well, what about FINCOM? How does this Majlis figure in here?'

'It's an incongruous connection. The cream Fiat which was parked right next to where the bomb exploded was a stolen vehicle. A police complaint was registered by the owner two days before the incident. On a hunch I checked up on the man – his brother is a member of the Majlis.'

'Well, pull the man in! Throw the book at him!'

'On what basis? He is the injured party. And India is a democracy.'

'Accepted. But you can still probe a little further. Turn on the pressure.'

'Oh, we are doing that, but he seems too unaffected by it. Knows his rights to his fingertips.'

'But surely it should not be difficult to get some dirt on this organisation?'

'Not easy either as they are extremely tight-knit, secrecy maximum.'

'But impractical, don't you think? Defeating their very purpose? They would have to come out in the open to get any kind of mass base. Anonymity will get them nothing.'

'But anonymity could be just the first step of a long-term plan. The first step being mass discontent. Growing discord. Social unrest.'

'And the second move?'

'Generate disorder, create hysteria. Then step out of the shadows. Use the prevailing chaos to get what they want.'

'And you think they want Pakistan?'

'I suspect that, yes. As I said, I have no definite proof to back up my hunch.'

'And you think they are increasing their activities? Becoming stronger?'

'It is difficult to be certain as everything is assumed. But that is the worrying factor, the fact that it is quietly contagious. Seems to be spreading itself like an octopus. The tentacles touching all the sensitive spots of India.

And growing in influence. Loyalties bought by dogma.
Or forced into submission by threats.'

'How much of a support have they garnered, do you
think?'

'Well, if you had asked me this question one year ago, I
would have said, insignificant. Now, I'm not so sure.'

'What's made the difference, do you know?'

'There are rumours that a new leader has taken over.
A lethal combination of brilliance and obsession. But
presently he has chosen to be in the shadow so it is not
easy to trace him.'

She nodded thoughtfully, then came to a decision.
'Let's try, shall we? Get the evidence Parvez,' she said
briskly. 'I will back you to the maximum. But we need
some proof of this, for I tell you, the whole thing sounds
like the plot of a bizarre Ludlumesque novel to me. Give
me something concrete and I can think about further
action. Otherwise, I can't do a damn.'

'Right, ma'am,' he smiled wryly. 'I'll see what I can do.'

'And in the meanwhile what do I tell the media and
that gaggle of diplomats gunning for me?'

'The ubiquitous foreign hand, Farzana. Use that. The
surefire support of all sinking politicians you know.'

She snapped, 'The day I have to take cover behind
that moth-eaten bromide, I'll quit this job and knit
sweaters instead.'

'I need a pullover badly Madam Home Minister.'

'Oh, shut up, Parvez. Why don't you use your wit
for something more constructive instead?' She frowned
thoughtfully for a moment.

'And what do I tell the cabinet now?'

* * *

NEW DELHI, JUNE 26, 2001

The cabinet meeting of the Central Government of India
was proceeding with bewildering quiet. Normally the
atmosphere at such a meeting was exciting to say the
least, with no two heads agreeing on anything and ready
to express in depth their reason for disagreement. This,
of course, was an inevitable fallout of the federal system
of governance prevalent in the country, with every
minister's inclusion in the cabinet dependent to a large
extent on his power base. Which is why nearly all of
them were near satraps of their individual domains and
least inclined to be shy lilies in this supreme power arena.
Each of them had their own calculations, motivations
and support structure. Each of them sharply watching
their flank, blatantly looking at number one.

And yet, despite their power manoeuvres and greed,
there was a vein of unity running through their collective
psyche. The concept and the reality that was India was
much stronger than any of their selfish manipulations.
And a certain love of this land and faith in this dream
was what bound them together, provided that necessary
bridge which could on occasion span their differences.

But today the cabinet meeting was so quiet that it
was disquieting. This silence was partly due to the fact
that they were together watching a series of images
unspooled by a projector. The other part was that each
of them was gripped by a certain shock, thrown out of
gear by that feeling of undefinable dread. The images
were horrific indeed, imbued with ugly significance. One
after another the screen showed scenes of carnage, broken
men, shattered lives, damaged buildings. The cabinet sat
there riveted, revolted. None of them were new, splashed

as they had been on the front pages of newspapers in the last one year. But their collation together was troubling, the inference showing a disturbing pattern.

With a squeak the projector put an end to the visual rampage, the screen went blank and lights were switched on. A buzz went around the conference table, but petered out as the man at the head of the table cleared his throat – his usual way of collaring attention.

When Shiv Charan Shukul had become the Prime Minister two years earlier, it had been on sufferance, as a compromise candidate. Caught between two roaring lions clawing for the crown, for once the rabbit had benefitted from the crossfire, emerging as the dazed winner. Not that anyone had given any odds as to how long it would take him to wobble down like Humpty-Dumpty. For someone who had been a career administrative officer all his life with no power base of his own, being anointed as the official leader of wily power barons was like throwing him to the wolves. But the rabbit had fast learned the ropes, shown hidden grit, set out a risky agenda. And with surprising force and unexpected finesse, totted up gains on the nation's totem pole of achievements. His skill in the subtle art of striking a balance was amazing. And his experience as an able administrator had enabled him to clean up the governmental Augean stables with a ruthlessness unmatched by any other prime minister. It was his image as a simple man with moral integrity and good intentions that helped him score victories over his detractors.

But today there were no detractors in that cabinet meeting, only men as worried as him.

'So gentlemen,' said Shiv Charan Shukul, 'what do you think?'

Jagdish Chowdhury, Finance Minister, turned a tight face towards him, 'I thought this meeting was to discuss the repercussions of the FINCOM bomb blast. But these were a series of violent acts perpetrated over the last year, spanning different times, different cities. Why have you clipped them together like this. You think there is a connection?'

Shukul pursed his mouth briskly and shrugged, 'I don't know, Chowdhury, but Mrs Hussain thinks so. She has given me a set of facts and figures about them which have been placed before you gentlemen. As for their significance, Farzana, would you like to explain?'

Farzana put down the pen she was fiddling with and nodded, 'The FINCOM blast doesn't seem to be an isolated event or a violent aberration. From some of the facts we have managed to put together, there is a clear indication that it could be a part of a cohesive plan. And with hindsight, these other episodes may form links of this chain. Again not conclusive, but probable.'

'What kind of a plan?' Farhad Hashmi, the soft-spoken man, immensely fond of reciting Urdu couplets to make a point, just as fond of his job as the Minister of Industry.

'Basically the destabilisation of India. As for the exact motive, it would not be proper to comment unless I get further information. CBI has some leads and I think I will be able to get something soon.'

'Excuse me, Mrs Hussain, I don't understand this at all.'

The silky voice made her look up sharply. Her rival, her constant baiter, slimy, snakelike Mushtaq Peerzada – Minister of Agriculture, hungrily coveting her portfolio.

Farzana said calmly, coldly, 'Exactly what don't you understand, Mr Peerzada?'

'Well, I would have thought that we should have been discussing FINCOM – definitely not watching garbled video fiction of this kind.'

Wryly she countered, 'Sometimes it's necessary to discuss garbled fiction, especially if it is likely to have a fallout in the future.'

'What are you talking about, Mrs Hussain?'

Shukul interpolated softly, 'The World Energy Conference to be held in the third week of August, Peerzada, that is what she is talking about.'

Farzana continued, 'As you know, fifteen premiers and ten presidents apart from significant representatives will be coming to India to attend the conference. The world's eyes will be focussed on India. We cannot afford any glitch, even the smallest of snags. Any security breach can lead to serious repercussions.'

A quiet man sitting at the far end of the table went vocal for the first time. The Foreign Minister of India, S. Aravindan, was an erudite scholar-cum-career diplomat and was universally considered the best Foreign Minister India had in a long time. The chief architect in securing the hosting of the prestigious conference for New Delhi, he was like a paranoid mother with a fragile infant.

'Just a minute, Farzana. Do you mean to say that you suspect a security threat at the meeting? Do you have some information about this? This is serious. We can't afford to compromise security here, you know.'

'I know, Aravindan, which is why this meeting. If there is the slightest possibility that there is a pattern of collusion in these vicious episodes, we have to be careful. The conference will be much too tempting for the conspirators – providing them with a ready-made target. They have to be thinking about it.'

'And what are we doing to counteract the threat?' snapped Peerzada.

'I've asked the CBI to undertake an in-depth enquiry, penetrate.'

'Penetrate? You mean you suspect a particular group or organisation?' softly Aravindan asked.

'Beg does. And I back his instincts. He is going to try and get more details before the conference, but in the meanwhile, I just thought I would brief the cabinet regarding this threat. We need to tighten up security measures in any case.'

'You can say that again, Farzana. Find out about this group. Arrest them temporarily if necessary. But we can't afford anything insane. India can't afford the fallout from this kind of insanity.'

Seven

The shadows in the room were deepening, darkness creeping in silently towards the sole inhabitant of the room. In the translucent, purple haze it was barely possible to make out the lonely figure, wrapped in deep thought. The salt and pepper head was still, concentrating, the mind in an emotional whirlpool. But no hint of this turmoil was reflected on the tight face, tight with an effort to control feelings. Feelings were dangerous – they weakened, they put roadblocks of morals, of ethics, in the way of logic. And nothing was going to stop the plan germinating in the dark recesses of that scheming mind, nothing, no one.

After meditating for many convoluted moments, after exploring all the possibilities, after many harrowing hours of indecision, the course of action had finally been decided. It did not matter that this action was immoral, unethical, inhuman. These words had become meaningless.

The figure leaned back, thinking of every factor coolly, calmly, sanely. The target had already been decided. The aim of the whole exercise a single one – to accelerate the movement, create violent ripples at the grass-roots level, to instigate a backlash, grab the sympathy of the world for their cause. The beauty of the action was that it was capable of achieving all of that effortlessly. The flaw was that failure could boomerang with equal destructive effect. The mind proceeded logically, ruthlessly, checking and rechecking. Was there any wrinkle of defect, any stain or blemish in the fabric of the plan? The effort made the face frown with deep thought. No, there was none – the plan was perfect – its perfection lying in its simplicity, in its attention to detail. The eyes closed, satisfied. Now for the phone calls to summon the core group for a meeting. Today's meeting would be a crucial one, where details would be thrashed out, the modalities decided.

The hand reached out to pick up the cordless phone and buttons were punched. A brief hello, a few crisp instructions and a squawking response later, the phone was kept down, a satisfied smile settling on the face.

The dream was inching nearer. What was not accomplished in 1947 would come true now. The birth of Pakistan was predestined. Inevitable. And no one could stop the inevitable from happening.

* * *

RAWALPINDI, JULY 16, 2001

The sun's morning rays bounced off the shining white stone of the house, making its translucent beauty come alive. It was another of those ordinary Pindi days, bright with heat, vibrant with promise and the cacophony of humanity. Just like any other corner of the country you would have thought, except that in Rawalpindi everything was maximised. Vigorously alive, passionately emotional, your average Pindite was incapable of seeing greys or sticking to averages. Emotions were magnified, passion was intense, responses extreme. There was a lavish love for life, for its shimmering colours, and naturally the palette had to be as grand as possible.

This love for grandness was reflected in the big brash bungalow, where once stood peacock-like the *jahaj-wali kothi* of Lala Shyamlal Kapoor, now deceased for the last two decades. The transformation of his *kothi* was simply a parallel to the spectacular reincarnation of his big but spartan Cantonment shop, Hind Trading Centre, into the elegant emporium Fantasia. This gratifying growth of the family business was largely due to the enterprise of Shyamlal's son, Vishnuprasad, and later, his grandson, Rajender. Presently the happily bickering old pair of Vishnuprasad and Chanchal were not in residence at the bungalow, preferring to stay in their Murree farmhouse during the summer. But to add to the house's depleted strength, Rajender's elder sister, Nimmi, with her two granddaughters, had decided to descend on them. Life was going on as life usually does, boring in parts, exciting in points. No one knew that it was going to turn unpalatably exciting for one member of the house. Especially when that one person was hardly heroine material, not being a simpering sex kitten.

With her genetic gift of delicate features, sparkling black eyes, unruly mane of dark curly hair, and blessed with plenty of bubble, Reshma Kapoor was a live wire made human. Which is why Vishnuprasad grumbled incessantly about his granddaughter on a daily basis, yet thought that the house was dead without her. She bought sheer life and charge to an otherwise normal, rich Punjabi family in Rawalpindi.

Dressed in a crisp cotton *salwar-kameez* with the *dupatta* wrapped carelessly around her neck, Reshma Kapoor came cascading down the stairs, hair flying, heels scraping the marble. She was running late for her appointment and she had better hurry up. On the breakfast table her father, her brother, Rajeev, and Nimmi *Bua* were busy doing what they loved – verbose, vociferous argument. This time the target was the latest local politics. Rajeev with his usual passion said, 'Papaji, what has the corporator done for us in the last two years, you tell me? Hasn't even managed to repair the roads as he had promised. The potholes on Peshawar road are not even funny any more. How can you support him?'

His father, as usual calm, 'Listen, Imtiaz Ali may be ineffective in some ways, but you must grant that he is honest. That is more than you can say about Vijay Mathur.'

Nimmi *Bua* butted in, 'Frankly all these corporators should be given a holiday, Look at what they have done to Rawalpindi! In our days Pindi was . . . .'

'Oh *Buaji*,' pleaded Rajeev, 'don't start that old record of yours, please.'

'And you guys stop arguing, will you?' chipped in Reshma. 'Such shenanigans so early in the morning!'

'Talking about shenanigans,' retorted her father, 'how was your night at the pub last night? I heard you had gone there?'

'Yes, Rajender, and she took Mona and Sona along,' said Nimmi *Bua* giving her a fulminating look.

Rajeev grinned, '*Buaji*, knowing your granddaughters, it was probably the other way around.'

'What rubbish! They are just sixteen! Now see Rajender, I don't mind giving freedom to a girl, but you have given too much of it to Reshma. She is twenty-two, isn't she, what is she doing running around as a poorly paid journalist? You should get her married!'

Fortunately for Reshma, at this critical juncture her mother emerged on the scene, carrying a tray of stuffed potato parathas in her hands.

'Not everyone can write well,' snapped Minu Kapoor. 'It takes talent which my daughter has. As for marriage, so many wonderful proposals have come, but where is the hurry? Such a name she is making for herself in Pindi. Everyday her name comes in the paper.'

Reshma looked at her watch and groaned, 'Got to go, Ma, I have an interview.'

The natural feeding instincts in her mother upsurged, 'No, no, you haven't had any breakfast! Have one paratha, you must.'

'Ma, they are so damn fattening! This apple is enough, really. And I'm running late! Got an interview lined up.'

'Who are you interviewing, Reshma?'

Midway across the living room she turned back to answer her father.

'It's interesting, Papaji, I'm going to meet Salamat Kidwai.'

'The historian who has written books on India's freedom struggle?'

'That's it. All part of the series *Indian Morning* is putting together on India's independence.'

That started off Nimmi *Bua*, of course.

'Reshma, that's something I can tell you about. Rajender was just a baby, but I was five years old. The things which happened in Rawalpindi at that time, the things I saw . . . .'

Reshma escaped.

Two hours later she smoothly turned her white Maruti Zen across the Adamjee road to enter the gates of Shagufta, a tall cream-coloured building. The offices of *Indian Morning* – the newspaper with a definite chip on the shoulder when it came to officialdom – were on the fourth floor, the lift was probably out of order, and she was disastrously late. By now her boss, that termagant in human form, the notoriously brilliant editor, would be throwing tantrums and paperweights, which would have the sub-editors hiding with fright. She chuckled as she fondly thought of the sixty-year-old Rahmat Khan, the irascible, cantankerous, opinionated rebel who ruled the newspaper, saw red at injustice, and could drum up more enthusiasm for an interesting scoop than the full contingent of young reporters. A stickler for journalistic rules, he was paranoid about punctuality, and she was one hour late. As the star reporter – a piece of information he had confided to her in one of his rare expansive moments – her heinous crime in not keeping her appointment would have him climbing the walls.

She whipped inside the spartan, functional office with its open cage-like offices and grimaced enquiringly at Suru, the pretty but goofy receptionist. Suru grimaced back, rolling her eyes and signalling calamity, to get her meaning across. Reshma mimicked a prayer to God, took a dramatic deep breath and marched into Khan's room.

'Hello, sir,' she chirruped. 'I'm here.'

Khan, who had been ferociously staring at the computer screen in front of him, and angrily banging at the keyboard, glared, took care to save what he had written and swivelled his chair around to face her. Mottled red with fury, he barked at her.

'Now you deign to come, madam, now! What is this, a holiday camp? A national convention on bullock carts? Do you know that your visitor waited for half an hour before he left in a huff?'

'Sorry, sorry, I'll phone him up and apologise, but just listen to this.'

'Listen to what? Some rubbishy excuse?'

'No. Today I had gone to interview Salamat Kidwai.'

'The historian who specialises in the Indian freedom movement? What about him? He couldn't possibly have given you a scoop, unless you think a story which breaks after more than fifty years a scoop. But considering the sleeping beauties around here, I guess that would be just about par for the course.'

'No, it's no scoop. Just something curious, makes you think.'

'Well, well, glad to know something does.'

'Very funny, Mr Khan, maybe I should come back later on.'

Suddenly his temper melted and he almost grinned.

'When you call me Mr Khan, I know you are really mad and really serious. Okay tell me.'

'We were discussing 1947 and why India did not get freedom in that year and had to wait for three more years for Independence.'

'And so?'

'You know that in 1947 India was on the brink of Partition and the formation of Pakistan was very much on the cards. If Nehru had acceded to this demand, India would have been free in '47 and we would have been citizens of a country called Pakistan.'

'Or maybe you would have been creating hell in Delhi while I would be blessedly free from such so-called reporters who can't keep appointments.'

'You would have missed me terribly you know,' she said.

He frowned disbelievingly, then grinned, made the sign of peace and struck an intense listening attitude. 'You were saying?'

'But that did not happen, the Congress Party turned down the Partition Plan and in the ensuing flare-up, the British found they were obliged to continue with the Raj till peace was restored.'

Khan nodded and said, 'And it was not till 1950, after the deaths of Gandhi and Jinnah, that a formula was found which would satisfy both Hindus and Muslims. Which is why India found freedom not before August 15, 1950. Now I know that and so does a fifth standard student. Where's the story in this?'

'The story is that from all reports, Nehru had completely made up his mind to concede to Partition and the birth of Pakistan. He had even given a verbal assurance to Lord Mountbatten to that effect. This was the scenario till the evening of June 2. On June 3, the day Mountbatten called for a formal All-Party meet on the Partition Plan, Nehru refused outright! So what made him change his mind so suddenly at the last moment?'

'Well, it has never been adequately explained and Nehru has never answered it. But the general opinion was that Gandhi was responsible for it. That he played some last minute magic, convinced Nehru that Partition would be disastrous for everyone. And thank God he did.'

'Sometimes I wonder. Maybe if India had opted for Partition, don't you think that there would have been less riots and communal flare-ups? More peace, less disruption?'

'Don't you believe it,' Khan said wryly. 'If the communal factor had ceased to exist as an issue, our worthy countrymen would have invented something else and carried on the good fight. Basically you see, we enjoy complications of this sort. Life becomes more interesting with some brawl handy. And yet if you have noticed, the situation blazes momentarily, courtesy the hotheads of both communities, for some time the rabble goes crazy, creates a bloody ruckus and then the sane fellows take over and the whole thing dies down. I tell you, Reshma, an average Indian is vastly tolerant, and to a large extent the coexistence between the two communities is exemplary. When Jinnah demanded the creation of Pakistan in 1947, you think your average Muslim wanted it? I have my doubts.'

'Anyway, I didn't witness any of that upheaval so it is difficult for me to imagine India as two countries. It seems so unbelievable! But the point is that according to Kidwai, Gandhi may not be the reason for this last-minute turnabout. On the evening of June 2, Gandhi was a bitterly disappointed man. There was a literal falling out between Gandhi and Nehru on this issue.'

'Really? Then who worked this magic according to your precious historian?'

'He doesn't know but he is intrigued. Kidwai's hypothesis is that something very drastic happened between the evening of June 2 and the Mountbatten conference on June 3.

'Really?'

'Well, what could have brought about such a dramatic change in Nehru?'

'Nothing. He must have simply thought things through from Gandhi's perspective and given in. Nehru had immense respect bordering on idolatry for the old man, you know. And tremendous faith in Gandhi's knowledge of the Indian pulse.'

'I don't know. Doesn't sound convincing to me.'

'That's because you have grown up on a staple of Ludlum thrillers. When you are my age, my child, you will realise that the obvious is the norm. Now, instead of troubling your head over mysteries which never existed, how about solving the mystery of the missing article?'

'Which missing article?'

'The one I was supposed to get yesterday. An overview of the political developments of the years 1947–50, a capsule of the front page news?'

'Oh damn! Sorry, sir, I will browse through the Internet and get the stuff right now.'

'Does that mean that I can expect the article today?'

'Aye aye, sir!'

She was fascinated as she read the front page splashed across her computer screen. Modern technology making history come alive. She could almost smell the flavour of those times, experience the tingle, the fervour of those days. She was jealous of the freedom fighters who had lived through that era, envying them their passion, their lust, their moral motive. How wonderful to be able to feel so fervently, to live so daringly, to vibrate with the purest passion of all – the dedicated, reckless encompassing love for your country. Their lives meaningful, with glowing hope for the future. What heady power it must have been, this certainty that you were the creators of history, makers of your destinies.

The headlines faithfully gave glimpses of a canvas lost in the passage of time. The arrival of Lord Louis Mountbatten in the country, the accompanying grainy photograph catching the handsome features but not the turmoil within. Gandhi's anguish, Jinnah's obstinacy, Nehru's conflict. A country helpless and hurting with the sting of communal venom. The dark clouds of division inching ahead, spinning hatred. Momentous events caught within the power of black print.

And then the sudden reversal of fates. The unexpected twist at the crossroads.

'Nehru says NO to Partition' blazed the headlines of June 4, 1947. 'Mountbatten stunned.'

June 5 headline, 'Jinnah threatens civil war.'

On June 10, 'Mountbatten calls for extra troops from Britain to handle escalating communal tension.'

In the next three months India had turned into an inferno.

'Calcutta on fire. 175 killed, 400 injured in unprecedented communal violence.'

Soon Punjab had caught the virus.

'Lahore burns. Bomb exploded by extremists. Citizens fleeing. Situation worsens. Army called in.'

And so it went on – Calcutta, Chittagong, Dacca, Rawalpindi, Lahore, Amritsar, Lucknow, Delhi, Hyderabad, Kashmir. They had become battlefields. A blazing vortex which melted the slightest vestige of pity, of humanity. Animals roamed the streets, death shrieking, madness reigning supreme. Insanity everywhere.

And then it happened, slowly, quietly.

The sane elements emerged. Gained strength, fought back. Peace marches were organised in cities, leaders exhorted the public to oppose violence. The Army swung into action, fanatics by the hundreds were put behind bars.

The leaders of the country did not fail the nation in its darkest hour. An inspired Gandhi went on a fast unto death and managed to control the inferno that was Calcutta. Many Muslim leaders and Abdul Gaffar Khan, the Frontier Gandhi, spoke out for peace, for tolerance. Sardar Patel and Nehru took charge of Punjab and Uttar Pradesh.

Slowly the madness faded, temperatures cooled. The land of Buddha, sick of the violence, sought shelter in peace. Talk of partition weakened. Search for peace formulas began. Began, but failed, and failed again.

Calamity time. The father of the nation was shot dead. The world mourned. But amidst the tears there was satisfaction of a different kind. For Bapu had died an intensely happy man in the knowledge that India would remain united.

One more tragedy waiting in the wings. Mohammad Ali Jinnah died of tuberculosis. The country was shocked.

And then it happened. Imperceptibly at first and then gaining momentum. The lost brotherhood was found again as was the capacity for tolerance. Like two brothers hanging together to face the rough seas.

Compromises were made, demands diluted. Agreement struck on the political structure of the country. Federal would be the rule of the times. United in major matters. Separated in the nitty-gritty. The British were formally informed of this accord. With a sigh of tired relief they agreed to hand over power. The date for freedom decided on mutually was the fifteenth day of August in the year 1950.

'Reshma! Hey Reshma!'

With a jerk she realised that someone was shouting in her ears. She turned fuddled eyes away from the computer screen towards the source of the screech. Suru, the receptionist.

'Yes, Suru?'

'I have been shouting for the last two minutes. You were lost!'

She smiled ruefully, 'Yes, in a page of the past. What is it?'

'Your mother called. Asked me to remind you that you have to go to Rukana's wedding, the *nikah* and that you should go home on time.'

'Yeah, yeah, I know. Thanks.'

She turned back towards the screen and stretched out her stiff shoulders. Yes, what an era, throbbing with romance, with youth, with life. Why had life become so prosaic, so predictable now?

She looked at her watch. Should she exit or maybe just check a few sites on the net. Take a browse through the National Archives. There was a page dedicated to Nehru documents. That could be interesting. She clicked on it and unrolled a list of contents. Nehru's letters, minutes of Nehru's meetings, Nehru's speeches, Nehru's appointment book. His appointment book! It may include the appointments of June 3! She clicked.

Ten minutes later a bundle of energy burst into the editor's office, buzzing with pent up excitement. Rahmat

Khan looked up from the papers he was reading, his eyebrows flared at her shining face. Expansively he summoned her to sit down and leaned back in his chair.

'Now what, Miss Bright? Another of your ideas?'

'Sir, I was researching through old newspaper editions on the net.'

'And you found something there?'

'No, but then I just browsed through the National Archives on a hunch and checked out the site of Nehru's papers. Guess what, one of the listing is Nehru's appointment book.'

Curiosity dawned in his eyes, he bent forward silently, body language urging her to continue, 'The 1947 record is there?'

'Huh, huh. Now June 3 is a curious page. The first entry is in blue ink and it is a scheduled visit by V.K. Krishna Menon. The second entry is the Mountbatten conference, again in blue. Got that?'

'Okay, so?'

She took a deep breath, 'But, in brackets next to the Menon entry, someone has scrawled in black ink the name of another visitor named Manu. Just the name, no details given, purpose unknown.'

'What's the point?'

'The point is that Nehru had kept his morning completely free of appointments, in lieu of the conference. So why this sudden change? Can you imagine Nehru entertaining any ordinary requests for appointments on such an important day and that too so early in the morning? The interesting part is that this man was talking to Nehru for nearly half an hour.'

Khan shrugged, 'So? Could have been a representative of some influential group against Partition.

And Nehru must have taken some time in explaining the rationale behind the decision. What's so mysterious about that?'

'Well, explain this. Between this unscheduled visit and the Mountbatten conference appointment, another entry has been scrawled. In black. In other words, another unscheduled appointment.'

'Who was it this time then?'

'None other than Sardar Patel and Acharya Kripalani. And the timing is interesting too. They came in around twenty minutes after Manu left. With a little stretch of imagination, I can see Nehru listening to this guy, then in a sudden flurry phoning his associates and asking them to come for an urgent meeting. The three of them were then closeted for more than an hour. Now does that give you something to think about or not?'

'I don't know.'

'Well, Kidwai is certainly interested. I called and told him.'

'And what does he think about it?'

'He feels that this Manu could have been the catalyst in the surprising volte-face of the Congress.'

'That's nonsense. How could one ordinary man change a party's policy on a crucial issue like Partition?'

'Well, what if he brought certain information which was highly critical?'

Sceptically Khan pointed out, 'Decisions of this magnitude are not changed just on the basis of some last minute information, no matter how important. In an event which covers a large canvas no one piece of information can reverse the picture sufficiently.'

'I don't know, but I'm curious. It would be interesting to find out more about this man, wouldn't it?'

'Well, if there is any chance that this man's visit changed history, then yes, interesting would be an understatement.'

'God, how I wish I could get a track on him.'

'Well, doesn't the register carry anything about him?'

'I told you it didn't. No address, no affiliation with any organisation, just the name.'

Khan grimaced, 'And anyway if there was such a man, he could be dead by now.'

Reshma made a face, 'Maybe. But if he is alive what a fantastic story that would make!'

Rahmat Khan scrutinised the passionate young face in front of him. And smiled, 'You really seem to be hooked on this.'

'It's exciting, don't you think? Stuff which thrillers are made of. A mysterious man comes in and rewrites the destiny of a nation. Wow!'

'But you have to be in Delhi if you want to dig deeper into this story.'

She sighed and nodded morosely, 'I know. And *Indian Morning* cannot afford to fund reporters on wild goose chases of this sort.'

A beatific smile spread over his wrinkled, angular, bearded face as he fished around in his drawer, removed an official-looking letter and brandished it triumphantly in front of her face. 'Have trust in Godfather Khan, my child, and all your wishes will come true.'

She looked suspiciously at him and then at the letter, 'What do you mean, what is this?'

'This is an invitation from the Central Government to send a representative to Delhi to attend the World Conference on Energy to be held on August 15, 2001.'

She was fascinated, 'And?'

'You, my dear Reshma, are hereby appointed as the paper's representative for the event.'

'No!' she squeaked. 'That's ridiculous! I'm not that experienced at all!'

'You think you need experience to cover this sort of thing? Come on, it is high time you got your perspective right. I'll tell you what you will have to do. Like a nice child you will attend the keynote function and then skip out for the day, coming back only in the evening for the press conference where you will be handed over a compact little press note. Like a lamb you will change a few words here and there as a matter of form and fax it to us. Do this every day religiously and you will have earned your trip. You think any journalist worth his salt works at these conferences? It's one of the perks of the profession!'

'But you were going for the conference! You told me that last week.'

'Well, I can tell you, but don't confide in the damn office grapevine. They will know soon enough. You see, my doctor has scheduled my bypass surgery in the first week of August.'

'Oh hell. That's terrible!'

'Don't be idiotic, Reshma. Bypass has become common these days. And this will give you a chance to dig out dirt on your story, won't it? You can go a few days early if you like. I'll sanction the necessary leave. But, of course, maybe you would like to ask your parents about it.'

She butted in, shrill with excitement, 'They won't say no, I can convince them. Mr Khan, this is great! You are a wonderful man.'

'That I am, of course, I've always known it. Its always amazed me that I seemed to be the only one to know it!'

She grinned in delight, 'I will go in the first week of August, that will give me around ten days to snoop around. And Mr Khan, with a little bit of luck, you will soon know why you are still living in India and did not acquire the status of a foreign national.'

She called up Salamat Kidwai again, this time about her impending Delhi visit, her voice eager with excitement, 'So what do you think, Mr Kidwai, I just may be able to get a trace on Manu, huh?'

There was a smile in the old voice which came over the line. 'Well, at least I know that you will try. And Reshma, there is something else.'

'Yes?'

'This Manu, I wonder if he is the same man who was a member of the Hind Mata Sevak Sangh.'

'What's that?'

'It was a small secretive organisation based in Calcutta. One of their leaders, known as Manu, had quite a cult following, if I remember.'

'I will follow up the lead, Mr Kidwai.'

'Do one thing – when you are in Delhi, get in touch with a Professor Satyen Sengupta of St Stephens College. Teaches history. Good man. He may be able to give you more information on the Hind Mata Sevak Sangh, maybe even on Manu.'

'I will, sir, and I will keep you posted on the story. Wish me luck.'

'*Amma*,' she shouted from the porch, punching the doorbell and banging at the door for good measure. 'Open sesame, Ali Baba, come on, hurry up.'

A shuffling of feet and Rukshana Bi opened the door.

Having worked in their house for forty years, she had become less a servant and more of a tyrant, and immensely enjoyed her status. Fiercely protective and caring, she was also a disputer, opinionated and hot-tempered, with a penchant for choice rustic expressions. She was capable of putting the young girl of the house in her place and did so regularly with great aplomb.

'What kind of a girl are you? Jungli, absolutely wild.'

'Where is Ma?'

'She is in the kitchen making samosas.'

'No wonder, there is this heavenly smell a mile off. Has Papaji come back?'

'Yes, just now.'

She hugged Rukshana in high spirits and went dashing into the kitchen.

'Hi! baby,' she cried, encircling her mother's neck in an expansive way.

Her mother slapped her hand sharply, '*Besharam,* you shameless child, calling me baby, indeed. All these foreign serials are spoiling you children. Is this the way you talk? Next you will call me by my name!'

'Yeah, Minu babe! And who is the one who is glued to the big bad telly every day to watch those serials? But all crimes are pardoned for anyone who makes such supreme minced meat samosas. Oh good. And *kalajams* too! Someone coming? You can't be making all this for my benefit.'

'As if!' her mother sniffed. 'But yes, Zeenat rang up. She is coming around. Sounded like something important.'

'Oh!' Reshma was quiet for a moment. Zeenat, was her mother's friend given the courtesy title of *Maasi,* mother's sister, by the children. A God-fearing lady. But for her, Zeenat Bakhtiar was significant as something else, something tender, something aching. She was the mother of Anees.

A gasp in her mind, a jerk in her throat. The memory of Anees was still capable of doing that to her. A year ago it would have been worse, of course. A year ago, that slight gasp would have been a scream, the jerk would have been a gash, and her hands would have gone cold. She was much better now, getting there, and there were moments when she thought that he was not wiggling inside her skin, that she had finally managed to rip him out, out of her heart, out of her life. But then memories were vicious, ruthless carnivores, creeping in when least expected, voraciously eating into one's essence. Get off me, she whispered. Let me go. Let me be.

A lump wobbling inside her, she casually turned away, peering into the *kalajam* vessel, biting into a samosa.

'Reshma!' her mother called sharply.

She kept her back towards her, answering with indifference, 'What?'

'Reshma, look at me!'

She turned around, deliberately deadpan.

'Reshma, you have not started seeing Anees again, have you?'

'I haven't seen him for a year, Ma. You know I haven't.'

'But for a moment – your face – it just wouldn't have worked Reshma, you must realise that.'

'I do. I did. Now can we talk about something else?'

Minu surveyed her daughter's hurt face and nodded, 'So tell me, what were you excited about when you first came?'

Reshma gave her a strained smile, her mind whizzing with life once again, 'Rahmat Khan has asked me to cover a conference in Delhi, Ma. I will be staying there for nearly fifteen days.'

'*Bilkul nahi,* absolutely not, you are not going so far off. Delhi? Just forget it.'

'No, Mum, I'm going, going, going. Come on Ma, this is important to me . . . .'

'Oh well, in that case, you must stay with Zahera Beg, my childhood friend.'

'The one who is the wife of the CBI Director, Parvez Ali Beg?'

'Yes. She will take good care of you. I will call her up.'

Huddled over her bedroom computer, viciously she punched the keys, deleting them the next minute in frustration. The words refused to take shape. Thoughts played hookey with phrases, ideas hoodwinking sentences. She had to write her story and fax it within half an hour and she was not even halfway through.

It was a simple subject, a fascinating one too. She was the one who was off-key, out of tune, unfocused. She was supposed to concentrate on the Partition which never took place. But instead of Nehru and Jinnah, her imagination was obsessed by the contorted picture of pain that had been Anees's face. One year ago.

'Reshma!' called her mother.

'Coming Ma, just finishing my article.'

'Zeenat *Maasi* is waiting for you. Okay, ten minutes is all that you have, understood?'

In a way, her mother imposed deadlines which helped her to keep the professional ones. The latter half of the article now came pouring out, the words coming together, the flow amazingly simple. Within fifteen minutes she had finished it, checked it and faxed it too. She sighed, stretched, went to the bathroom, splashed the strain away from her face. A neat dash of maroon lipstick, a comb through her mess of tangled hair, a straightening of her *dupatta* and she was ready to encounter Zeenat *Maasi*. And the rush of painful memories.

Anees's smile, the dimple which could suddenly flash in that brown, lean cheek, the love which dappled from his eyes like a blessing, touching her with its heat, melting her bones, making her shiver. After the break-up she had been like an addict without her fix. Without the searing passion which only Anees could convey through a look, a grin, a touch. This meeting with his mother was like getting back into the sickening spiral of withdrawal symptoms. As she slowly came down the stairs, she succumbed mentally to its pain.

'I don't understand, *Bhaijaan*,' Zeenat Bakhtiar was saying to her father as she entered, her face more worried than ever. 'What do I do? You have always given me such good advice.' Zeenat Bakhtiar was a thin harassed-looking woman, very unlike her son, with her fair skin and indistinct features. Only her brown eyes were like those of Anees, warm and soft, gentle like a fawn. Another rapier, another wound, bringing back the past. 'Sexy eyes,' she used to warble, leering mischievously at him and ducking when he threw something at her.

With a shake she forced herself to listen to the constant flow of polished Urdu.

'What is wrong?' asked her father patiently.

'You know, *Bhaijaan,* that Anees is posted at Amritsar cantonment.'

'Yes, yes, two years ago, I think. Is there any problem?'

'It's not a problem exactly, but I don't understand.'

'What's happened, tell me.'

'Well, one week ago my cousin was going to Amritsar and went to meet him too. But Anees wasn't there! He has gone on a one-month holiday!'

'So?'

'But I don't know anything about it, *Bhaijaan*! He hasn't said a word to me about any holiday. I don't know where he has gone, nothing.'

Minu snorted in sudden understanding, hiding a grin.

Rajender, judiciously avoiding Minu's eyes said quietly. 'He must have gone to his friends.'

'That's what he told them in the cantonment. Said he is going to meet Raunaq Singh, his friend in Karachi.'

'Right. So then what's the problem?'

'I phoned Raunaq yesterday. He hasn't heard from him in months!'

'Really? That's curious, yes.'

'Why did he lie? Why hasn't he told me about this holiday? And where is he now?'

The rest of the day was a nightmarish mishmash of incongruous images. Rukana's wedding in the lavish Grand Hotel with its garish glitter. Rukana dressed in a green, gold-spangled *sharara* with hennaed hands, Rukana's shyly sweet *kabool* or acceptance. Rukana's celebration of hopeful love and eternal faith. And Reshma sat through it all in a corner with the weight of her guilt, her betrayal, her cowardice. And with the memory of Anees's pain, his hurt, his bitterness. Why weren't things easy? And why had she lost the nerve, the courage needed to break free from those bonds which ruptured?

Her eyes clouded in self-contempt. Words. That's all she was capable of, complicated words, complex phrases, profound sentences which sounded lofty and had no depth. Just like her. She had accepted that. And she would continue with the charade. She would go to Delhi, she would lose herself in something which sounded deeply esoteric. Grab at a fleeting sense of self-identity by trying to solve momentous mysteries of the past. The mask would be firmly in place. The charade would go on merrily as usual. Reshma Kapoor was all vivacity, all sparkle. The murky shadows within her would remain hidden.

Eight

The black serpentine metal column wove its way through the plains of Punjab, piercing the air with a long shrill whistle. Starting from Rawalpindi late at night, it had a long way to go to reach Delhi, especially as the journey entailed a longish halt at Amritsar. Jolting, shaking, swaying precariously like a drunk, the train moved on, with all the grace of an elegant inebriate. Its rhythmic languorous caress of the cold iron rails beneath produced a beat which rocked one to sleep.

Reshma woke with a jerk as the train came to a stop and a sudden bright neon light shone on the bogie. Turning on her side, she sleepily peered down from her top berth and saw Rukshana Bi peeking out of the window. Fondly she looked at her ample dimensions dressed in acres of cotton. Rukshana Bi had been a part of her mother's package deal for allowing her to go to Delhi. And though Reshma had grumbled as a matter of course, it felt good to be in the comforting, known presence. Especially when she would not cramp her style one bit – she was going to stay with her sister in Chandni Chowk. So it was not much of a compromise to bring her along.

'*Amma*, why has the train stopped? Have we reached Amritsar?'

'No, no, it's only a small station called Wagah. What funny names some of these nondescript stations have. Go to sleep. Or do you want to have a cup of tea? I'm having one.'

'No, but why have we stopped then?'

Rukshana Bi pressed her nose harder against the rail, screwing up her eyes in an effort to see better.

'Can't make out, there is quite a crowd near a bogie. Oh, the police are coming! Allah *khair*, what is wrong?'

She spotted a passing *chaiwala*, yodelled at him to stop.

'Give me a cup. And listen, what's happened?'

The boy poured out steaming hot tea from his kettle into an earthen cup, handed it to her and shrugged, 'There is some terrorist on the train. The police have come to catch him. That will be three rupees.'

'Three rupees,' screamed Rukshana Bi. 'Three rupees for this measly cup? Here, take one rupee. My God, times were when this used to come for 25 paise.'

Rudely the boy interrupted her, 'And how many centuries ago was that, grandmother? Come on, give me two rupees more, this is business.'

Grumbling Rukshana Bi handed over the coin, sipped from the cup with a satisfying slurp and once again angled her neck out.

'I wonder who this terrorist could be.'

In a novel the terrorist would have to have been Reshma's Anees, drama demanding such a turn of events. But then it is only in a novel that you can expect the expected. Real life is not that easily manageable nor moulded. The terrorist who had been caught was a small-timer, a hot-tempered youth, and had nothing to do with the Quom-e-Majlis or future events. Ironically, the train had amongst its passengers one who qualified on both counts, but was snoring noisily in a separate bogie, unaware of the stopover at Wagah.

Alam Khan always slept deep, and not because his conscience was sparkling clean. A professional hit man's conscience can never really achieve that optimal shine. The fact that this did not seem to bother him was because he simply did not let it. He was a complete professional in the field, and his attitude while carrying out any assignment was a mildly apologetic one – no hard feelings but business is business.

Two weeks ago, he had been approached by a man who had put forward a business proposition to be undertaken in Delhi. The bare essentials had been relayed, the terms decided on. Because the job was both dangerous and well-paid, it was essential that he got to first base with his employers. And even more important – got immediate payment. Which is why he was on the train towards that initial conference. And as usual sleeping like a blissful baby.

AUGUST 6, 2001

A sleeping Alam Khan, however, was different from a sentient one, and the four faces carefully scrutinising him would have been hard put to find any similarity between him and an infant. Deadpan, he sat before them at a huge semicircular desk in a plush conference room in a shabby office of a shabbier bungalow in old Delhi. The interview was on, to hire an assassin.

Stoic, bristling with cold efficiency, he crisply answered questions about his past jobs. This was a crucial meeting where details of his assignment would be given to him and naturally he did not blame them for closely assessing his talent. It was a no-names no-introductions drill which was fine with him. As long as they were ready to pay.

And after a long detailed probe, they finally seemed to come to a decision.

Said the face with the beard, 'Satisfactory. You are quite versatile in your profession, Mr Khan. Very inventive too.'

Alam Khan was modesty itself, 'I try to be. This profession needs more creativity and more thinking on one's feet than any other, let me tell you.'

'I am sure. So shall we talk about the payment?'

You bet your last torn rupee we will, friend, muttered Alam Khan silently. He would not move a step till this important issue was settled to his satisfaction. Professional to his fingertips. That was him.

The beard continued, 'You have been paid a certain sum in Lahore, one lakh rupees?'

Another nod.

'The full payment decided on is Rs 15 lakhs, is that right?' He gave a happy assent. This was very close to his heart indeed. 'Of the remaining fourteen, half will be given to you today.'

'In clean, unmarked bills of hundreds,' he interpolated.

'Agreed. And the remaining seven after the job is done satisfactorily.'

'That sounds okay to me.'

The beard removed a briefcase from a drawer in his desk and pushed it across, 'Count it.'

'No need. If there is any less, I just don't do the job, you see.'

'Okay, now that this is over with, can we discuss the details? You have been given some of them. You may need more.'

'Much more,' said he firmly. 'I have been simply told a date, a venue, the approximate time when my target will pass from there.'

'What else do you need?'

'Are there any alternative dates which I can use? Backup schedules?'

'No, it has to be done that day.'

'You still have not told me the name of my target.'

He was told, he listened stunned, his eyes becoming round with unprofessional surprise. This was a really big job then. Really big. But the money was equally big, so that was okay with him. He took a deep breath, kept silent for a moment, planning, mapping, Then took a grip on the briefcase.

'I'd better go to this venue to chalk out my plan.'

Rapped out the beard, 'We will provide you with maps, with transportation and with the weapon of your choice. A white Ambassador is standing outside at your disposal. The rest you will find in the briefcase. But after this you will be on your own, no matter what the circumstances. Is that understood very clearly?'

'Of course. Part of this profession.'

He got up, then thought for a moment and turned towards them.

'May I ask you something? There are hit men in Delhi too. Why have you chosen me for the job?'

Smoothly the beard said, 'For reasons of security we decided it would be better to have someone from outside Delhi. And then we had heard excellent reports about you from a reliable source.'

Unconsciously he preened. It was nice to have your skills appreciated in a place far away from your backyard. His vanity made him accept the explanation, blinding him to its illogicality. That was a highly unprofessional mistake on the part of a professional man. And a fatal one to boot.

Five minutes after Alam Khan left, there was a further exodus from the room. The four men waved a salaam in the direction of a huge mirror occupying half a wall, got up from the table and quietly left. In the ensuing tranquility the focus shifted to the mirror and then the room beyond. To the two people sitting near the one-way glass, hitherto engrossed in silently assessing the assassin. The older of the two took another sip of coffee from a delicate China cup, carefully kept it down and then spoke.

'Well? What do you think?'

The younger looked up, shrugged, 'I didn't understand. What was all that in aid of? Why Alam Khan? Why was all that rubbish told to him?'

The other softly asked, 'Heard the word decoy? You know what a red herring means?'

'Of course.'

'Well, that is exactly what Alam Khan is going to be, a wonderful red herring which will throw everyone off our tracks.'

'But why? Why is this necessary?'

'You don't understand. And you underestimate. A fallacy, my young friend, when your adversary is someone as brilliant and as resourceful as the admirable Director of the CBI himself.'

'Parvez Ali Beg.'

'That's right. And Farzana Hussain's right-hand man.'

'I still don't understand.'

'You see, Beg suspects us. He suspects that the Majlis is planning something big in the near future. And obviously the coming World Energy Conference is perfect in this regard. So he is going to try and seal up security loops. And, moreover, he is going to try to infiltrate the organisation.'

'And?'

The older man smiled thinly, 'We'll pre-empt him. We'll present the plan to him on a platter. After two days, we will deliver our professional hit man to the CBI, all wrapped up in a gift parcel.'

'The CBI may not believe you. They may suspect a foul.'

'They will believe. The source from where they will get this information is extremely reliable. So they think. They will believe.'

'And then?'

'Well, do you see this bird of ours keeping quiet at the first risk of a threat? He will cheep like a robin with laryngitis at a confessional. I think that should send them off in a completely different direction, protecting quarries we never planned to harm anyway. A simple ruse, but effective don't you think?'

'An expensive one,' said the other dryly. 'We have just bought eight lakhs worth of smokescreen. If it works, that is.'

'It will. You will see. And that would make it easier for you.'

The younger man took a deep breath, 'So you are still sure that I am the right person to do the job?'

'More than ever.'

'You know that I have shot and killed before. But it has always been in a battle. Never like this.'

The older man was quiet for a moment and when he spoke his voice was guttural, 'Don't get moral on me. You can't afford that luxury. We can't afford it. And why just now? You were superb during the bomb blast at the FINCOM building. Why these sudden doubts?'

The man shrugged, 'Bombs can be pretty impersonal you know. I did not see the people who died. It is easier to ignore the human factor when you don't witness the face of death. Easy to remain focussed on your ideals. But when you have to shoot someone in cold blood, see them die . . .'

There was a harsh interruption, 'You are our best marksman. Well-trained in arms. Highly resourceful. That is what your evaluation sheet said. We need all of this, the Majlis needs it. If you are really committed to our ideals, then show it. You want to get squeamish, well, you are free to go.'

The young man said softly, like a whiplash, 'No, I am in. But the person I have to kill – it is not easy . . . .'

'The killing of that person will be our short cut to what we have set out to achieve. I have told you

the logic behind it, the pattern. You know what kind
of ripples it will create, its ramifications.'

The young man stiffened his shoulder, 'You are right,
it is an evil necessity. I am sorry for this last-minute
doubt. It won't happen again.'

A brief smile broke the cold countenance in front of
him, 'I know it won't. You are perfect for the job, you
know that. We need someone motivated, not a
professional whore like Alam Khan.'

The young man smiled briefly, 'Let me go out and
start earning this praise then. I must survey the general
area, map out logistics, decide on a time schedule, I'll
report to you tomorrow.'

The man got up, shook hands, and gently said, 'I will
wait for that. Call me when you want to come in. I
wish you luck my friend. God be with you, Anees.'

The Sierra gained rapid speed along the Ring Road,
passing by the Lal Qila (Red Fort) on his right in a blur.
On his left the engorged Yamuna rambled on, its waters
dappled dirty-gold in the dancing rays of the setting sun.
The evening heat shimmered on the hood of the Sierra,
a light warm wind caressing the driver. Both were
incidental and ignored, with Anees Bakhtiar concentrating
on the traffic of his thoughts. His mind on Karachi. On
the day he had accepted twenty sores on his soul. The
twenty nameless human beings who had died in the
FINCOM bomb blast. Because he had been busy playing
God.

Sometimes at night when he couldn't sleep with their
ugly shrieks shrivelling him up, he wondered at the
futility of the action. By morning he generally got over
it, but those moments were his own personal hell. And

now one more black notch. One more death. This time
death with a face on it. How many killings would it take
for him to become completely impervious?

He ignored Gandhi's memorial, Raj Ghat, wiping it
out of his vision as if it didn't exist. The last thing he
wanted was to think about that savant of non-violence
when he was on his way to chart out a violent course.
He had enough of ideals and idealists. This was reality
time.

An impatient horn broke into his tangled thoughts
dragging him away from his troubled past, into the
present. Irritated, he looked into his side mirror, to check
on the player of the discordant notes. A Maruti Esteem.
A girl at the wheel. Something painful grabbed at his
heart, something hurt. She looked so much like Reshma,
so God damn much! The hair, the cheekbone, the
insouciant flick of the head as she overtook him.
Imperceptibly he slowed down, letting the girl go ahead,
as far away from him as possible. He did not want any
reminders of Reshma anywhere near him. His nose flared
in frustrated anger. For hours he had not thought about
her. About her warmth, her love, her betrayal, her terrible
crime.

Violently he stepped on the accelerator. Why did
she still have this power to twist up his innards?
Why did he allow images of the past to take away his
peace?

Shared moments in Rawalpindi. A laughing Reshma.
In that huge emporium on Massey Gate. Choosing his
shirt for him with a proprietary air. The intimacy of the
action alive in their eyes. Vibrant in her lingering
touch as she straightened out a shirt crease on his
shoulder.

Reshma in a deep blue *salwar-kameez*. Bought with his first salary. The secret bringing a provocative smile to her lips when they met at the wedding of a family friend. Her eyes seductively glowing, like those of a woman with her lover's hands on her body. More memories. Late evening, in the restaurant at Flashman Hotel. Celebrating the anniversary of their love. Her long delicate, fair hand looking incongruous in his brown one. Her face serene, beautiful, content.

The small flat in Satellite Town. Borrowed from his friend for a day. She, lying on the bed, unknowingly sensuous. Innocently inviting his touch. Shaken by it. Clutching at him, shuddering next to him.

He swore, an ugly litany of impassioned tortured sounds. No more. He would not think any more. Not about her.

He had loved her once, simply, passionately, completely. His hatred now was just as complete.

Unknown to him, the object of his rampant heartache had already entered Delhi and was ensconsed snugly in the plush residence of the Director of the CBI, Parvez Ali Beg. And being fawned over by his wife, Zahera Beg, who had gone to the station to pick up Reshma, and was now plying her with sherbet and samosas. Overweight is not normally associated with elegance. But then Zahera Beg took a fiendish pleasure in overturning all norms on their head. She did exactly the same in Jawaharlal Nehru University while espousing to her adoring students her highly individualistic (her colleagues rudely called it eccentric) perception of global economy. And because society expected a professor of economics to come packaged in tall, thin, cerebral wraps, Zahera considered it her pious duty to strike a different note. If anyone thought of a pocket-sized, tubby, garrulous, house-proud Frau and a brilliant firebrand thinker as a non sequitur, this woman was more than capable of proving them wrong. Today, in a loose white *salwar* kurta and lustrous Hyderabadi rice pearl jewellery, she was looking both fat and confoundedly elegant. Like a magnificent mother hen, she clucked around Reshma, pressing saffron sherbet and spiced cashewnuts on her, eating much of it herself, possibly as a form of encouragement.

'You have grown up to be very pretty, my dear, but I must tell you not as pretty as your mother was at your age.'

Reshma smiled, 'I know that. I have seen mom's old photographs of her young days in Lahore. You featured quite prominently in most of them, I may add.'

Zahera smiled seraphically, 'That was because I hovered around her constantly. Her most devoted fan, that was me. And though I was a few years younger than her and must have irritated her no end, she suffered me with patience. How is she?'

'Oh, Ma is fine. She has sent you her love.'

'And her daughter. It will be nice to have Minu's daughter staying with me. You will be very comfortable here, you will see.'

Freshly showered, Reshma was combing her damp unruly hair in front of the huge carved dressing table, when Rukshana Bi came from behind. Tut-tutting under her breath, she kept the towel on the bed, pulled away the comb from Reshma's hand and started combing her hair briskly.

'I have unpacked your suitcase and I'll be leaving for my sister's house. You take care of yourself. Don't do anything stupid.'

'I won't, *Amma*. And Zahera *Maasi* is here, of course.'

Rukshana Bi nodded, 'She hasn't changed much over the years except that she has become fatter, much fatter.'

'You must have seen her then. She stayed near my grandfather's house in Lahore, didn't she?'

'Yes, and was more in our house than her own. I must say one thing for her, she loves your mother. Always did.'

The exact sentiment was repeated by Zahera later in the picture-perfect lawn as she sat delicately sipping a Peach Schnapps. It was nearly eight, Parvez would be home soon, mutton chops were frying nicely in the kitchen, life was sweet, and her friend's daughter had revived lovely past memories. She sighed in deep contentment. Reshma looked affectionately at the hedonistically corpulent form draped in a voluminous pink silk caftan, making her look like a forty-nine year old baby elephant with a dramatic taste in clothes. Softly she replied, 'She loves you too. And she cherishes the memories of her childhood.'

'Yes, those were happy days, and Lahore was a wonderful city to grow up in. This was in the early 1950s and I still remember this great, constant interaction between Hindu and Muslim families. There was an intensity about it, a sort of celebration, as if in gratitude to Allah for not letting Partition happen. Yes, very heady times, those. Very happy ones.'

'Are you saying that you are not happy now? If the

answer is yes, then I will take it as a personal affront, let me tell you.'

Zahera turned quickly at the man who had crept quietly behind her and was now smiling with great fondness at the dark head below. She smiled back, 'Ah hah, here comes the Czar of the CBI! Parvez, this is Reshma – Minu's daughter. She came today.'

Reshma got up and went towards the tall man with a patrician profile, a swathe of near-silver hair, stocky muscled body and cool eyes clashing with a smiling mouth. Then the chill went out of the brown eyes as he came forward and gave her a warm handshake and a warmer smile.

'Hello Reshma, how are you? Now I am itching to say that I saw you when you were this old and my, how big you have become! That is one of the most fatuous things everyone says compulsively, but CBI directors are not allowed to say fatuous things. At least not more than eight times a day and I have already run up my quota.'

She twinkled, responding to his brand of quirky straight-faced humour, 'Tell me about those other eight.'

'No, no, this Zahera drives me crazy but not that crazy, not yet. Instead just assure me that Rajender and Minu are okay so that we can get down to the most interesting part of the evening.'

'And which is?'

'Why, we talk about you! I am not exactly brainy like our Zahera here but you don't catch me missing an opportunity of talking to a pretty girl. Now tell me if the Rawalpindi boys are blind or something? How is a lovely, young woman like you still unmarried . . . .'

*   *   *

AUGUST 7, 2001

It was a lovely cloudy morning in Delhi when Reshma came down. At the bottom of the stairs she encountered a servant who informed her that her host and hostess were sitting outside on the lawn. 'You go, please. I'll get your breakfast there.'

She tripped outside, her hair swinging as she hummed the latest Indipop number hitting the charts, and went towards that corner of the dappled lawn from where the sounds of a passionate debate were issuing. During her short stay Reshma had gathered that according to her host and hostess, love was arguing about everything under the sun. She grinned – what new bone had they found today to chew over? It didn't take her long to find out with Zahera promptly enrolling her in as a mediator.'

'You tell me, Reshma, when the global trend is towards formation of bigger blocs, isn't it short-sighted to root for break-up on the basis of medievalist, discarded theories?'

Parvez sighed theatrically, 'Look Zahera, it's not me you have to convince as I'm already a convert! But it so happens that the Quom-e-Majlis doesn't agree with you.'

Ruefully Reshma said, 'I don't have a clue as to what you two are discussing. Perhaps one of you can enlighten me.'

Parvez smiled at Reshma, 'The thing is that I told her about an extremist group whose single-point programme seems to be the two-nation theory of Pakistan.'

Zahera shook her head in disgust, 'Fools, blind fools. That has been the biggest stumbling block in

India's evolution – that we don't know what is good
for us. Look at the way the world is going! In this
shrinking universe, big is better. Even Europe, insular for
centuries, decided to opt for a union for the sake of
survival. But try telling that to these misguided groups
who are fighting for a cause which is intrinsically self-
destroying.'

Reshma was fascinated by the older women's fervour,
her intensity, 'Zahera *Maasi*, all those years ago, if
Pakistan really had been carved out of India, you think
it would have been that disastrous?'

'Not exactly disastrous Reshma, but debilitating.
Disaster is too strong a term to use for any
country's development. And an ancient country like
ours is immensely adaptive in nature. If India had
been partitioned into two, well the two parts would
have carried on, but without achieving optimal
strengths.'

'But during the countdown to 1947 when we came
nearest to Partition, the dogma was that two nations
with clearer identities would become stronger.'

Wryly Parvez said, 'A country does not need an
insular, unidimensional character in order to achieve
greatness. Otherwise that premier melting pot, the
United States of America, would have been in a shambles
by now.'

Zahera looked at her watch with a start, 'Talking of
a shambles, my schedule will be just that if I don't
hurry. What are your plans for the day, Reshma?'

'Nothing much. I called Professor Satyen Sengupta
but it seems he is out of the city for a couple of days.
So I will just hang around. Maybe go to meet *Amma* at
her sister's house in Chandni Chowk.'

'When? Now?'
'Nope. In the evening.'

                        *   *   *

Chandni Chowk. Once the throbbing heart of cultural
Delhi, political Delhi, poetic Delhi, royal Delhi. Now
degenerated to a swampy, sleazy stretch of small-time
traders and wholesale shops. The arterial road, flanked
majestically by the Lal Qila on one end cuts straight
through the heart of Chandni Chowk, and once upon a
time, in the not so distant past, was like a grand sparkling
river, accepting sedately in its folds the myriad mischievous
gulli-koochas made famous by Ghalib.

But with the pressing and depressing increase in
headcount, demanding space, demanding facilities,
demanding sustenance, a desperate Chandni Chowk has
become schizophrenic. Instead of growing old gracefully
it has become a bent, beaten caricature, a garish tart
ready to turn any trick for survival, sinking by the second
into a chaotic quicksand of messy bylanes, stinking drains,
sweaty throngs, tawdry shops. And yet Chandni Chowk
still has the power to surprise you. Unexpectedly, at some
sudden corner, it throws away its whore-like existence
and just for a moment – with an effort of imagination
– you achingly glimpse what a younger, prettier Chandni
Chowk was like.

Perhaps the only places of enchantment that the
Chowk retains are its famous eateries, still faithful to
their traditions, weaving taste bud magic, seducing its
devotees.

Even Reshma Kapoor, a stranger, could feel this power,
this lure as she passed through the Parathe-*wali gulli*.

Amma had told her that this was the landmark, her sister's house being on the adjacent street. What she had not told her was that passing through the street was to succumb to sheer ravishment of the senses as the sight and aroma of the golden-brown parathas, fried in huge *kadhais* tantalised and tortured one.

She was tempted to stop, capitulate, sample. Finally, the only reason she refrained was the preponderance of males inside all the small eateries. Could she endure those searing glances directed towards any female who dared venture alone in this hot-house of masculinity? The prospect was too daunting and she reluctantly moved on.

'Does Fatima Shabbir stay in this building?' she asked a supremely indifferent hawker, pointing to a shabby, squalid, peeling structure, rejoicing under the utterly deceptive name of Aasmaan Mahal.

Carelessly the hawker looked at her, his eyes deepening in interest as he took in her stretch jeans-clad figure. Silently he nodded, his eyes following her as she firmly ascended the stairs. For a moment the enveloping shadows came as a relief from the man's obtrusive eyes, but then the dark dirty walls caved in on her, the dimness increasing the sense of claustrophobia. And it did not help that the wide steps were a foot high in the ancient style, built in an era when there were no elevators and people knew how to use their muscles. She was puffing after a few steps, and at the mezzanine level, she knew she had to stop awhile. She took a deep breath, trying to steady her racing heartbeats.

Stomping from above, someone was coming down. She moved into the corner, swallowed by darkness, standing a little away from the wall, not wanting to rest her body against the generous splashes of paan stains, but leaving enough space for the man to pass her. It was his smell which first caught her throat. Familiarity can sometimes catch you unawares, make your heart ache. Anees's favourite aftershave, the scent clinging to her, around her, for hours afterwards . . . . Ruefully, casually, she looked up at the man who had induced this aromatic nostalgia in her. And then sharply looked again. This time with sudden intent, shocked disbelief. The man – tall, slim – was slowly coming down the stairs. White Nike shoes, black corduroy jeans, a thin leather belt, pale-coloured shirt. His face was in shadow, but something in the walk, in the hands, in the very aura – she was crazy to think the unthinkable. What could Anees be doing here? But the thin light of a valiant bulb falling on his face slit through her doubts. She wasn't insane, her senses weren't befuddled. It was very much Anees!

Hungrily, disbelievingly, stunned, she stood there as he passed her by, his head turned in the other direction. She could have touched him, clutched his arm, whispered his name. Stopped him from walking away. She did nothing. She couldn't. The paralysis of weakness. The shadows of sins. Her sins. The bond was there but the scars were there too. Still raw, hurting. Painful enough for her, worst for him. She let him go. Once again. And once again it hurt to do that, the sudden void like a sharp ache. White-faced, she stood shaking, shocked. The footsteps receded, the stomping became a distant echo. He was going away. As if on their own volition, her feet moved, stepped near the railing, her body bent down, her eyes peered hungrily. Giving in to the temptation of a last look. He had reached the bottom of the stairs, another few seconds and the void would be complete.

Mesmerised she watched, as he was about to step away from the angle of her vision.

What was it that made him look up at that very moment? God of chance? Hand of fate? The sixth sense which reacts to stares? His eyes met hers for a treacherous second. Shock wiped away every expression from his eyes, his pupils dilated, confused, dazed. He turned, took one involuntary step in her direction, then stopped. After a prolonged moment of gouging her face with his eyes, his body whipped around. His shoulders straightened, he walked away, every hard sinew of his stiff back blazing hatred. She stood there shell-shocked, unable to think, to move. It was a noise on the steps which bought her back to her senses. Had he come back? No it was a woman. She stepped away from the rail, took a deep tortured breath, hitched up her purse, and went up the stairs. Shaken and stirred, that's me, she thought wryly, just call me Bond, Jane Bond.

She knocked on the door of Sheikh Mohammad Shabbir and waited. It was opened by a surly teenager, whose eyes blossomed with interest when he saw the visitor. He heard her out, turned and hollered, '*Mausijaan*, some girl has come to see you.' From the corner of her eyes, Reshma saw a mini tornado erupting from a side door and within a blink she was enveloped in yards of cotton *dupatta* and oodles of familiar warmth.

'My *nyani*, my *nyani*, my little only' crooned Rukshana Bi, hugging her, kissing her forehead, patting her cheek.

Reshma gurgled, 'Anyone would think that you haven't seen me in years instead of a day.'

Bi chuckled, took her by the arm, drew her in a corner towards a snugly welcoming *baithak* complete with a quantity of plump cushions. Then, urgently she turned towards Reshma, 'How come you are here? Tell me the truth, *bitiya*.'

'About what?'

Bi realised that her vapid nephew was still to their midst and dismissed him peremptorily with a ruthless gesture which brooked no argument, 'Go and get her sherbet, go.'

Then she looked straight at her, 'Now we can talk. Now tell me.'

'What are you talking about, *Amma*?'

'About Anees,' she said harshly. 'Are you here with him?'

'Anees? No, *Amma*, I am not. What makes you think that?'

'I saw him coming into this building last night. And again today, a little while ago. When you came in I thought – you are sure you are not with him? You know how upset your Ma would be if she hears about this.'

'Would I lie to you? I came to meet you. But yes, I did see him coming down the stairs.'

'Did he see you too?'

'I am not sure.'

'Hmm. Well okay. Stay clear, you understand me?'

'Haven't I, *Amma*?' she bit out.

Bi stayed quiet, just stroking her arm, lost in thought.

After a moment Reshma asked in a studiedly casual tone, 'I wonder what work he could have here in Delhi, in this building. He has come here twice you say. Whom does he come to meet, do you know?'

'Well, it has to be the man who lives upstairs because he occupies the whole floor. No one else stays there.'

'He must be a friend of Anees.'

'No, no, can't be. He's too old, in his fifties, and has the shiftiest eyes I have ever seen, with a reputation to match.'

She asked sharply, 'What do you mean? What kind of reputation?' Rukshana Bi leaned closer, relating with much relish, 'I've heard things. But my nephew ought to know more. We will ask him, shall we?'

Without waiting for a response, she shouted, 'Jameel what happened to the sherbet? Have you gone to pluck lemons or what? Come out!'

A highly offended, dignified Jameel walked in, a Thums Up on a tray. Coldly he stared at Bi, 'I thought she would prefer to have a soft drink, *Mausijaan*. I had gone down to get it, if you please.'

'Good, good. Here *bitiya*, have this. And you, Jameel – sit right down and tell me all you know about the man upstairs. The one you were telling me about last night.'

'You mean Abumiya? What about him?'

'Well, he is not exactly an icon of virtue from what you said. Now why did you say that?'

The topic was right up his alley and his voice lowered to an appropriately ominous whisper as he said, 'I have seen plenty of sinister people going up there. Sometimes at odd hours of the night too. And you know what the talk about him is?'

'I don't, which is why I am asking you,' *Amma* said testily.

'He manufactures guns!' he said in deeply reverent tones.

Reshma asked sharply, 'Are you sure?'

'Well, no, but that's what everyone says.'

'Okay Jameel,' said *Amma* kindly, 'you'd better go and study now. Your *Abba* will be coming any moment. Go.'

Amma turned back towards Reshma, saw the worried look on her face, touched her cheek gently.

'*Nyani*, what is it?'

She was quiet for a moment, then said anxiously, '*Amma*, if this Abumiya is a gun-dealer then . . . .'

'Then what?'

'Why should Anees come to meet him?'

'Well, he is a *fauji*, isn't he? He may be needing a gun as a part of his profession.'

'You think the Indian Army does not provide its officers with weapons? No, its funny. According to his *Ammi*, he is not in Amritsar, no one in his station knows where he is. For unexplained reasons, he is in Delhi and that too visiting an illegal gun-dealer? I don't understand, *Amma*, and I don't like it. Just what is Anees up to?'

As she walked towards an auto-rickshaw, accompanied by a constantly scolding Rukshana Bi, she was alive with anticipation, uneasy with foreboding. Retracting instinctively at every shadow, eagerly searching the shaded nooks in the garish nightlife of Chandni Chowk. Something in her ached for another sight of Anees, but instinct held her back. In the end her passage was unmarked with any sudden surprises. He had not waited. No sudden swooping, no unexpected encounter, no angry eyes torching her. The prospect should have relieved her. It didn't. Instead it brewed up another backlash of memories, a Niagara of pain, a stockpile of guilt. Immersed in her black thoughts, she never noticed an Ambassador following her at a discreet distance. As she got off at the Lodhi Road bungalow, the car slowed down at the end of the road. She paid, went inside, and it was only after she was swallowed up by the huge gate and imposing walls of the house that the car revved up and drove past the gate. An infinitesimal pause while the driver read the golden embossed nameplate, and then the car was put in fourth gear, speeded up, and was soon a speck in the shadows of the night.

Nine

It was one of those unusually pretty mornings in Delhi, when the weather God had quit being irritatingly extremist for a while. It had rained the whole night and the sun was still dizzy from the assault, licking its wounds within the grinning, gurgling clouds, its heated brow tenderly tickled by a soothing cool wind. Delhiites, pleasantly surprised at being neither cooked in a tandoor nor dumped in a freezer for once, were out in large numbers to enjoy the tingling breeze.

On such mornings Delhi takes on an added beauty, especially the splendid area of Willingdon Crescent, whose sinfully lush lawns and sprawling bungalows in acres of land camouflage the fact that it is one of the most powerful areas in India. Its denizens may look like ordinary rich residents but they hold the real power over the vast subcontinent. Changing outcomes, clinching deals, peddling influences. The federal structure of India in this year 2001 has usurped many choice avenues of meddlesome power for the Delhi politician. And given some other similar souls in the regions their share of the power pie. However, the Delhi variety still manage to flex its political muscles with a great deal of effect. Busy in their manipulations, in their mind-games, in their political kho-kho, once in a while this species does take time out and do their bit for their country. If India has prospered in these years of freedom, it is because of these 'bits,' and the inner strength of the country which even this colossal spectrum of collective corruption has not managed to destroy.

But just as there is a joker in every pack, there is a wolf in a pack of hyenas. In Delhi, their is gold amongst the dross, but you have to be a regular Sherlock in order to spot it. Unless, of course, it is someone like Farzana Hussain – a leader of known ability and a matching core competence.

But competence did not seem to be her shining quality that morning as the Home Minister of India hurriedly threw papers out of her cupboard, frantically searching for a missing document, its discovery both essential and time-bound. And just in case she happened to forget the urgency, the chief whip was standing right next to her, anxiously surveying the search, peppering the hunt with frantic reminders.

'Mummy, hurry, my bus will be coming any moment now. Where have you kept my report card? Mummy, please, find it or that Tommy will give me hell. Mom, please hurry.'

'Look, I'm searching aren't I?' snapped Farzana. 'It has to be here somewhere. And if I can't find it I will write a note for Miss Thomas, okay? Now let me see, could it be in this drawer. YES!' She let out a relieved shriek at finally getting her hands on that precious brown booklet, hurriedly signed it and saw her twelve-year-old stuffing it in the bag.

'Asma, you'd better eat your tiffin today,' warned Farzana, 'or you can forget any pocket money this month.'

'Aw, Mom, come on. There comes my bus, bye, see you in the evening. Are you coming home early today or not? I suppose you have another of those sickening meetings lined up?'

She smiled, following her daughter to the door, 'No, I will come as soon as possible. Bye, take care, be good .'

When she turned back from the door she still had that faint tender smile on her face, softening the angles, warming the strong mouth. She was met by a servant, one of the many who managed her home for her while she 'house-kept' the country.

'Madam, shall I get you your tea?'

'Yes, please, and has sahab woken up yet?'

'Yes, madam, he phoned for his tea.'

'Oh good. I'll be in the lawn.'

She picked up her cordless phone, strolled over the emerald dewy velvet and settling in the cane armchair, stretched lazily. This was probably the only hour of her day which belonged solely to her and her loved ones. Which reminded her, It was time for her daily call.

She called on her cordless phone a Mehrauli farmhouse number. A deep voice greeted her, the baritone flecked with age. The friend, philosopher and resident companion of her grandfather. 'Manmohanji, where is Nanu?'

'He is seeing patients. Shall I call him?'

She smiled ruefully, he was going to get upset with her, 'Yes, please do.'

In the background she heard impatient growls and grinned widely. Her grandfather had grown increasingly cantankerous with age and was in a temper this morning.

'Yes?' he snapped, dispensing with polite telephone conversation and getting ready to erupt.

'Good morning, Nanu, how are you?'

'Farzana, I am exactly as I was yesterday morning – just fine. You really don't have to bother so much about me, you know.'

She chuckled, 'I know you are angry with me but you will simply have to put up with this daily call whether you like it or not, okay?'

'You are just like your mother,' he grumbled. 'Now that you know that I am not on my last legs, can I go? I have patients waiting for me.'

She sighed, 'And for your free homeopathic medicines. Okay, Nanu, but remember your promise?'

'What promise?' he snapped crankily.

Patiently she responded, 'That you won't exert yourself, and will phone me if you need anything at all? You have my mobile number.'

The irritation in the old voice lessened, softened by affection.

'You are a good girl, Fazi, but you worry too much about this old man. Concentrate on the country, it's a good job that you are doing. As for me, I can well take care of myself, you know that.'

'I know nothing of the sort,' she countered spiritedly. 'Seventy-five-year-olds don't choose to live in ramshackle farms, miles away from the city and from their only granddaughter.'

'Fazi, old doesn't mean that my faculties have degenerated. And if you think that I want to live with that spineless wonder that you call your husband, forget it. Too much money, not much of anything else, is our Prince Shaukat.'

'Oh Nanu, now don't you start off on him. I have to go, got a meeting.'

'Ha, running away?'

She snapped, 'Have you stopped reading the papers, Nanu? India is playing host to an international conference and world leaders are going to be here, including the British Prime Minister. I have to tighten up security and you know what that entails.'

'I know, I know, just teasing you, Fazi. Now you don't trouble yourself over me, go ahead and do your job. And oh, give my love to him.'

'To Shaukat you mean?'

'To that chinless beauty? Not a chance. I meant the British Prime Minister.'

She was smiling ruefully as she clicked off the cordless, the old man's wicked cackle still echoing in her ears. He was like a stuck record when it came to Shaukat, she sighed. Deriding him as a weak, mediocre man whose only act of brilliance had been to blossom in the womb of the legal wife of the Nawab of Rajapura. And his only talent, an uncanny ability to live through every imaginable illness which had beleaguered his childhood.

When she had pointed out that that itself showed tenacity, Nanu had countered that a leech had plenty of it too. He had never understood nor forgiven his bright granddaughter, a brilliant Jamia Millia scholar, for agreeing to a *nikah* with a man whose only asset was money.

But Nanu didn't realise, she grimaced, that marrying Shaukat had been the best move of her life. It had provided her with ample security, a ready-made constituency in Rajapura, immediate access to the centres of power. And something even more important – freedom. Not many Indian men would have put up with a wife who was the shining young star in the Indian political firmament, completely overshadowing him in the process? True, initially he had tried to object mildly to her increasing foray into power centres, but when she had persisted, he had given up gracefully. He always did.

'Good morning, Farzana, a penny for your thoughts?'

She smiled, Shaukat had done part of his schooling in Eton. But according to him, the only benefit he had derived from this experiment was a marked increase in his passion for cricket and a penchant for using cant English phrases. The former he could indulge in only as a spectator, the latter had become an unconscious habit over the years. She looked up and smiled, 'I was just thinking how good you are for me.'

'Why should that worry you? Your brow was distinctly worried when I came in.'

She sighed, 'Plenty of things on my mind these days.'

'Oh yes, that Energy Conference.'

She nodded thoughtfully, silently, already veering away from her home, towards her work.

He bent forward, cupping her knee gently, the warmth of his hand seeping through, like a snug cocoon of mild heat.

'You will be all right, Farzana. You are a very strong woman. You will manage.'

Impulsively she leaned and kissed him on his cheek, their first intimate touch in days. It had not been like this always, she thought wryly, or Asma would not have been born. In fact sex had been the only time when they had connected, physically, mentally. Nothing earth-shaking or volcanic, but comforting like an old glove on a winter night. But slowly she had found that politics gave her a bigger kick than sex, a particularly tough victory bringing on orgasmic fervour. And seeing her growing disinterest in the nightly callisthenics, he had quietly retreated, as graceful as ever. Sometimes she wondered, if he had a woman stacked up in some bungalow somewhere? God knows he had every right to do that and actually it did not matter to her. Oh well . . .

The phone shrilled. She picked it up.

'Farzana,' abrupt, crisp. 'Parvez Ali Beg. We need to talk. An interesting development.'

'Regarding the issue we were focussing on?'

'Yes.'

'And urgent?'

'Very.'

'Okay, meet me in my office at 10 a.m.'

'See you then.' The phone went dead and she took a deep breath, adrenalin bursting through her. Finally a lead? A breakthrough?

A deep green paisley-patterned *salwar-kameez*, the neatly coiffured head elegantly draped in a muslin *dupatta*. As Farzana clicked her way to her sanctum sanctorum via a series of cubicles and officers, she looked every inch a lethal woman. Another facet of the enigma that had her opponents perplexed. You could criticise Farzana Hussain for many things, but could never accuse her of trying her feminine wiles on fragile male egos. She could win any argument with cold logic. Any detractors to be silenced, she would use her brilliant mind-power and ruthless manipulation. But incongruously, for a woman who refused to misuse her femininity, she took a great deal of pride in being its epitome. The woman who could order fearless, impartial, effective measures, at a tragic massacre, or squelch a communal riot with measures bordering on the despotic, had a love for designer outfits, expensive jewellery, latest make-up trends.

'Mohun,' she briefly acknowledged her secretary's greeting as he came in her office, 'is Mr Beg here?'

'Yes, madam, he said that you had given him an appointment for this slot.'

'That's right.'

'But, madam, there was already a meeting scheduled at this hour. With the delegation from the Ganga Bachao Samiti.'

'Reschedule it. This is more important at the moment. Send him in please.'

Reluctantly the secretary went out, and after a moment Parvez Ali Beg strode in.

She waved him towards the opposite chair, 'So, Parvez, tell me now, what is it that was so important.'

'Yesterday, we made an arrest, a very crucial one I believe.'

'On what basis.'

'On the basis of a phone call from a highly confidential source.'

'And whom did you arrest?'

'Alam Khan. A man who lives in Lahore. Came to Delhi three days back.'

'So what's so important about that?'

'The fact that he is a professional killer. Pricey man. Commands a steep price in the market for his talents.'

'Are you sure about this?'

'Yes, we have some records on him at the CBI. Very sketchy but enough to confirm identification. We have requested the Lahore police to fax further details which they will be doing very shortly.'

'But I don't understand . . . .'

'. . . in what way is his arrest earth-shaking?' he finished for her.

She nodded interestedly.

'Well, Farzana, we put this man through a wringer and he talked to a certain extent. It seems that his visit to Delhi was a business one. A killing which involves a very big name.'

'Who hired him, did he tell?'

'One guess, Farzana.'

She took a sharp breath, 'Not the Quom-e-Majlis?'

'Correct. That's what he says.'

'And you believe him?'

'My dear, Farzana, truth is no longer a matter of moral choices. It has become more chemical in nature.'

'You mean you injected a truth serum.'

Parvez held up his hand, 'You don't want to know the ugly details. As for its veracity, I can assure you of that. Chemically speaking, of course.'

'Okay. So who was his target? And what was the time-span designated for the attempt?'

'It was as we guessed, Farzana. The two-day Energy

Conference. A fixed time, no options. The Majlis wants fireworks in front of the whole world and its press.'

'And now tell me – who was his assigned target?'

After a length Parvez spoke, softly, lucidly, 'Govind Gunaji.'

The silence in the room was as heavy as a sinful conscience and just as worried. Govind Gunaji, the charismatic leader of India's premier Hindu right-wing party, the ubiquitous Arya Andolan Sabha. Gunaji was a man of many parts, of many facets, operating at any given time at different levels. Only a chosen few were able to glimpse the depths within.

For the rest he was like a juggler playing with perspective, a magician's stunning act of lights and shadows, hiding and displaying at will. Govind Gunaji was a chameleon, a chimera. A rabble-rouser. An idealist. A thunder and rumble variety of nationalist. A leader whose world was religion, and who had made religion his world. He was also a man who commanded a great degree of Hindu loyalty, especially of dissatisfied, turbulent elements.

At length, Farzana took a deep breath, 'I should have guessed. Gunaji's assassination would be devastating indeed, changing political equations, provoking a severe Hindu backlash when it is revealed that the assassin was the hired man of a separatist Muslim organisation.'

'Right. The backlash would intimidate the Muslims, who, terrified, would fall back in the arms of the Majlis as their refuge. The support for the idea of Pakistan would grow, the backing for the Majlis increase dramatically with a resultant snowballing of its clout. The dream of Pakistan would become that much more attainable. Yes, a simple, linear strategy, a very workable one too.'

Quietly Farzana asked, 'So what can we do Parvez?'

'Increase security for Gunaji.'

'Yes, but apart from that?'

'What do you suggest, Farzana?'

'I have an idea. Tell me, if we throw Alam Khan in jail, what happens to the assassination plan?'

'It does not get aborted. They appoint another man, at short notice, but it can be done. And they become more careful about the execution of their plan, as they suspect we know it.'

'Exactly, Parvez, which is why I suggest an alternative. Why don't we buy off this man? He was getting paid for a hit, we pay him for a miss. Human error, act of God, it happens. The Majlis does not suspect that we have compromised their man, so no contingency measures, no alternate avenues. What do you say?'

'Logical Farzana, only there is one hitch.'

'Which is?'

'We can't buy him off.'

She was sceptical, 'Are you saying that he will not agree? A man who kills for money?'

'No, nothing so noble.'

'Then what's the problem?'

'Remember what you said a minute ago about human error, an act of God? The man is dead, Farzana.'

'What? For heaven's sake, how?'

'An overdose of Amytal.'

'What the hell was the doctor doing? How could he be so damned careless with such an important witness?'

'I thought the same, but the doctor claimed that he had injected the normal dose. There was no margin of error in this. To establish the exact cause of death, I ordered a post-mortem last night.'

'And the result?'

'Vindicated the doctor. The man had sclerosis in its extreme stage. Severe cardiac complications. The stress of the interrogation, added to the chemicals, worked on him adversely. He died of a massive heart attack.'

'Damn.'

'Yes, but it is curious, isn't it?'

'I don't get you? In what way?'

'Never mind. So now what? We assume that the Majlis will give the contract to someone else.'

'I will go and talk to Govind Gunaji. In this whole sorry mess, that's the one big plus – we have got the lead that we wanted. We know the target, we know the basic operation.'

He started to say something, hesitated, thought again, and clamped up.

After a long-drawn pause he said expressionlessly, 'I suppose so. I am sure you are right.'

But already he had a sense of deep foreboding. The pattern, there was something wrong in the pattern. Nothing overt, or tangible. Just an invisible thread of incongruity. But what was it? Over the years he had learned that it paid to listen to one's basic instincts. As for deciphering the message, he would do that later. Mental peace was a must for this form of mental maths. The action undertaken was over. Its analysis would have to wait.

As the caller kept the phone down, a smile of pure satisfaction spread over his face. The action had commenced, first step initiated. Alam Khan had been captured as planned. Its logical progression – a physiochemical torture. Culminating in death. Just as premeditated. The smile became wider. Phase one over. Phase two starts. It would be rather droll to see the Home Minister of India with her trusted sidekick, Beg, run after that jackass Gunaji. And such a futile act anyway, leaving the real quarry completely out of the suspicion zone. Completely unprotected and vulnerable. Operation red herring was concluded. Time to go for the real fish.

Zahera Beg sailed into the smoke-shrouded study, sniffing in disgust at the cloying odour of tobacco. She stood near her husband's copious armchair, arms akimbo, waiting for his attention.

She didn't get it, not really. He was deep in thought.

'Parvez Ali Beg, what is the matter with you?'

Vaguely he looked at her, 'What Zahera? What did you say?'

She fumed, 'If you look through me once again as if I don't exist, you will get burnt fish for dinner!' Then she relented, pulled a carved chair from behind the huge teak table and placed it next to her husband's.

Quietly she angled her head to look closely at his clean-cut face, 'Parvez, what are you thinking about? Tell me. Is it this Majlis situation? Some more violence?'

He shrugged, 'No, in fact, it is just the opposite. Today we had a major breakthrough. We have zeroed in on their inherent plan. Got a definite pointer to their strategy.'

'So then why are you looking so worried?' she asked reasonably.

'Because I am worried. There is something I am missing here. A pattern that is wrong in some way. And yet I can't figure out what it is that's needling me.'

'Well, don't get tense about it. The subconscious is a great thinking tool, give it time, and it will hunt out this factor.'

Parvez sighed resignedly, 'All right. What are you giving me to eat today – apart from burnt fish that is?'

She chuckled, 'Actually today there is a sort of a feast – all the things which Reshma likes. *Kakori* kebabs, Kashmiri *rogan josh, dahi-pakodi, rabadi.*'

'I hope she stays for some more time. Good for my stomach.'

'Ha, as if I don't cook for you! But you know, Parvez, it is wonderful to have her in the house. I feel as if Samina is with me, and Sohail.'

He looked at the sudden longing in the otherwise vibrant face. Took her hand warmly in his, 'Our children are happy in America, you know that. They have good jobs, good marriages. They come once a year to meet us. What else do you want, Zahera?'

'I know, I know. But to have Reshma here makes the house come alive.'

He smiled, 'Yes, it does. By the way where is she?'

'In her room.'

Reshma, seated at the dressing table in her room, stared at her face in the mirror as she tried to take her mind off those transient violent moments of her meeting with Anees.

She frowned. The origin of her worry lay in a shabby lane in Chandni Chowk. In a building euphemistically called Aasmaan Mahal. And in the man who traded instruments of death. Why was Anees visiting him? What kind of business could he possibly have with a man like that? She wished she could find out. And maybe she

could! She could ask Uncle Parvez about this man –
Abumiya, wasn't it? She nodded thoughtfully,, she would
do it tonight.

It was after dinner that she ventured to broach the
subject.

'I went to meet *Amma* in Chandni Chowk two days
ago.'

'*Amma* means Rukshana Bi, her servant, who's staying
with her sister,' interpolated Zahera.

'Okay. Any problem?'

'No, just a curious thing. On the floor above lives a
man who is said to be running an illegal munitions
outfit.'

'Really?'

'Could be a rumour, but *Amma* is worried. I was
wondering, could you find out about this man, do you
think?'

'But why should Rukshana Bi worry, Reshma,'
quizzed Zahera. 'The man is not going to come gunning
for her! You tell her to sleep in peace and to let that
poor man sleep in peace too.'

Reshma's smile was strained, 'No really, I would like
to know. Please, Uncle, can you?'

Parvez surveyed that tense young face with narrowed
eyes and then slowly nodded, 'What's his name?'

'Abumiya.'

'Address?'

'Aasmaan Mahal, third floor, near the Parathe-*wali
gulli.*'

'I'll check it out.'

Ten

Anees looked at his watch. Five minutes to three a.m., the witching hour, when all good people are in bed, whether their own or someone else's. But there was no sleep for him, not tonight. No sleep for the wicked. He frowned, a quixotic Shakespeare-like phrase. It was most unlike him to think in such poetic terms. And then he remembered – it had been Reshma, of course. Reshma, the avid reader, with a passion for quotes and a penchant for using them in the most unusual places. He could almost hear her, her naked shoulders tantalisingly inches above him, her face languorously close to his, saying huskily with a gurgle, 'No sleep for the wicked. Which means you, my love.'

Stay away from me, he thought harshly. The last thing he needed was that woman fogging up his mind. Not when he needed precision of thought, clarity of planning.

Impatiently he got up from the rickety chair, and strode towards the minuscule window, his only access to a view of sorts and dubious fresh air in this cubby hole of a room.

He looked out at the sea of roofs around him. The area, which was a confusing morass of concrete hutments and overflowing humanity was barely liveable. But safe, promising a degree of anonymity. Here he could melt into the confusing shadows, like a chameleon, his activities unremarkable amidst constant motion. This was Kingsway Camp, the underbelly of northern Delhi, a mean little strip between the laid-back lush area of Delhi University and the mundane morality of Model Town.

Anees peered down wryly at the narrow little street ending in the broad Ring Road. Someone with a nasty sense of mordant humour must have labelled that potholed path as Kingsway.

A sudden outburst of nostalgia shook him. God, he missed Rawalpindi at times. Missed the nitty-gritty and nuances of the city's life that made up its special character. The trouble was that when he thought of Rawalpindi, he thought of Reshma. She had seeped in so deeply into his every memory of the city that it was impossible to separate the two.

But right now, she too was in Delhi. He could meet her tomorrow if he wished! He had come so near to doing that in Chandni Chowk! It had been only the upsurge of anger which had prevented him from turning back and confronting her. And later, when he had followed her and realised with a shock that she was staying with Parvez Ali Beg, he had extra reason to be grateful for that decision.

For his mission was everything. Nothing could be allowed to abort it. It was a brilliant plan, an inspired one, its success completely dependent on his talent, his ability. And he would not let them down, this unique group which was fighting to seize back the inheritance which was theirs by right. Should have been theirs years ago. It was the battle of the righteous against the hegemony of the majority. Wasn't it?

He swore briefly, earthily, as he combed restless fingers through his thick hair. Why should this tiny tinge of doubt creep in to taint his fervour? Why did it reek of the unpatriotic? Why should it savour of the anti-national?

He clamped his mouth tight – that was just emotion interfering with logic. What he was about to do needed to be done. The operation which was sabotaged fifty-four years ago had to reach its logical end.

For India was like a pair of Siamese twins, two souls encrusted in one body. Two nations, forcibly living together as one. Hampering growth, festering sickness. A clean cut was the only solution – two healthy whole entities instead of one grotesque, unnatural one.

The so-called Hindu-Muslim unity was a sham, a facade, words spoken by politicians for their own vested interests. Where was it in reality? It existed only in the imagination of poets, in the hopes of a pitiable few.

For if it had been real he would not have lost Reshma. And something else equally precious. Anger seared him at the thought of what he had lost.

He turned back, shaking his head to clear his mind of the fog of sleep and thoughts of Reshma. For the present.

Which meant that he could go back to work.

He put some water to boil and made himself a cup

of strong coffee. Carrying the steaming cup towards the table, he sat down and drew the papers towards him. He had to make some essential calculations regarding distance, angle and range. Plot out his course carefully on a detailed map of Delhi. He finished his calculations, satisfied with his conclusions. Then he unfolded the map, spread it out, surveyed it meticulously. He thought for a moment, nodded his head, reaching a tenable decision. He picked up a sharp pencil, then unhesitatingly drew a line through two points on the map.

On the ordained day, one point would be occupied by his victim, the other by him. The line was a graphic representation of the distance and direction the bullet would traverse to reach and kill its target.

* * *

AUGUST 10, 2001

Thick rimmed spectacles on his nose, concentration stiffening his face muscles, Parvez Ali Beg closely resembled a professor reading some obscure minutiae of arcane data. In such moments his genetic inheritance from his father was startlingly clear. The same intensity, the power of concentration, the instinctive ability to grasp, to correlate, to analyse. But there the resemblance ended and the differences began. Hidayat Ali Beg had a deep love for history, a profound insight into its relevance. His son, though equally erudite, would never have been able to explain how it helped anyone to know in exhausting detail about events of the past. In their frequent discussions this point was raised persistently. The son openly sceptical, the father passionate.

'Lessons, Parvez,' had said Professor Beg earnestly, 'history teaches lessons. Lessons inherent in mistakes made, in actions and their consequences, in pitfalls of power. In turning men into demigods and gods into mere tools of manipulation. History is like a road map, son, with danger signals posted at every turn for one capable of deciphering them.'

But the son had been as doubtful as ever. And the differences of attitude continued.

Today, sitting behind his immense desk, Parvez Ali Beg was concentrating on the security plan for August 15, 2001. The day India was going to celebrate fifty-one tempestuous years of freedom. Which also happened to be the day when the World Energy Conference would be inaugurated in the presence of about sixty VIPs from around the globe.

The date was what one could call packed, thought Beg wryly, and security systems would be stretched to their limit. Planning was everything. God was in small details, it was said. Well, the security systems had to assume a godlike nature in that case. He grimaced and pored over the plan once again.

'Sir,' the polite voice of his assistant interrupted his reverie.

He looked up, frowning, 'I told you I wasn't to be disturbed, Khanna.'

Atul Khanna's tones became even more polite, yet firm, 'I am sorry, sir, but you had said that you wanted this fax urgently. The police record of Alam Khan. Just received it.'

'Yes, yes, I do. Just leave it there, I'll go through it in a minute. And Khanna, before I forget, there is a

small matter I want you to look into. Nothing urgent
you understand, but I gave my word.'

'Of course, sir,' said Khanna crisply and took out a
small diary and a pen from his pocket. 'Yes?'

'Have you ever heard of a fellow called Abumiya?
Lives in Chandni Chowk, has a reputation as a gun
dealer?'

'Offhand, not that I can remember. But then I
wouldn't. It's not my area of concern, you know that.'

'I know. So can you find out about this man for me?
His dealings, his regular contacts. That sort of thing.'

'Sure, sir. I will immediately detail a man today. Do
you know the address of this Abumiya?'

Parvez told him.

It seemed to be the standard police resumé of a
professional killer encapsulating in two pages a lifetime
misspent in crime.. Alam Khan alias Aliawar Khan, forty
years old, born in Padder, a tiny hamlet near Sheikhupura.

At an early age he took a train to Lahore, his first
crime, for it was a ticketless journey. Duly caught and
briefly charged, Alam Khan learnt a lesson from this
incident, and developed a lifelong allergy, not for crime,
but for getting caught. He started small, with petty
larcenies, but his talent was noticed and he soon found
himself an insignificant part of the Ranbir Singh gang,
the largest in Lahore in terms of turnover and activities.
From then on, his career was assured, and finding himself
skilful with guns, he practised diligently and soon became
a member of the elite core group of hit-men in the
gang.

All in all, he had not done badly for himself, either
professionally or personally. This was evident by the fact

that his two wives were seen crying copiously in the hospital six months ago when he had his first heart attack.

As for the present, enquiries elicited that he was away from home on a business trip. Destination unknown, as usual.

Parvez frowned, and closed the file with a snap. Damn, nothing here, nothing at all. And actually, he didn't really know what he expected to find. With Alam Khan dead, succumbing to a mixture of drugs and a massive heart attack, his existence had become a negligible factor in the scheme of things. So what was he looking for? But there was something wrong, something crooked in the pattern. Why couldn't he grasp exactly what that was?

With a muttered imprecation Parvez put the file aside, and lit up, the kick of the tobacco calming his mind for a while.

So much for cutting down on his smoking as he had promised his wife last night. She would grill him alive if she saw him like this, showering him with dire warnings of impending heart attacks .

He paused, startled. Some thought had clicked in him. Now what could it have been? Smoking, nagging wives, heart attack, that's it. Heart attack! That was what was in his subconscious.

For Alam Khan had died of a massive heart attack, brought on by a normal dosage of chemical drugs. And Parvez had assumed that it had been an undiagnosed heart condition. But that was a fallacy. This had not been his first heart attack but the second. The first was at a hospital in Lahore with two wives crying their hearts out. But what did that prove, thought Parvez with a frown. Why should that fact disturb him?

And then it dawned on him. The whole thing was incongruous because his first attack was on record, not a hushed-up affair! Now, if an organisation like the Quom-e-Majlis wanted to recruit a paid assassin, what would be the first thing they'd do? Get a brief on his record. Which meant that the Majlis knew of Khan's heart condition. And that was a conundrum, the curious factor to be understood, explained satisfactorily.

Why should the Majlis risk giving a crucial contract to a man with a weak heart? Especially when they could have had someone fit and with equal expertise to do the job? As good as Alam Khan was in his profession, there was never any dearth of efficient executors in this expensive segment of the crime pyramid. So why select a man with a limited threshold for stress? Physical health had to be one of the prime considerations while choosing a killer.

Unless . . . .

With a jerk, Parvez got up, knowing he was near to answering his own query, close to solving the puzzle. He trod restlessly, his thoughts rapidly accelerating.

Unless, in some way Alam Khan's weak health was an asset, a definite profile plus? Now that might sound bizarre, but the first principle of detection was to fit conclusions to facts and not vice versa.

Shorn of incidental trivia, the glaring fact was that the Quom-e-Majlis had chosen a man with a known heart condition to assassinate Govind Gunaji.

Conclusion? They wanted a man with just that characteristic.

Why?

The answer was, had to be, that he was never meant to be involved in the assassination.

That he was a smokescreen.

That his arrest was a part of the Majlis plan, with the CBI grilling a natural corollary. Chemical investigation a standard part of the enquiry.

Even a normal dose would lead to another heart attack and death.

Result? Information fed to the CBI by a witness who could not be cross-questioned on details of identity. Or locations.

But the question remained. Why?

Why this elaborate smokescreen? What was it supposed to hide?

The time-span of the assassination? The scene of the crime?

Or, the target itself? Could it be that Gunaji was not the actual target? But Gunaji had seemed to be such an ideal quarry, his killing having a ripple effect on the entire political spectrum.

Or maybe it was too ideal, too obvious? Was the Majlis more subtle in their strategy? Was he making too much of a previous heart attack in the police records? If the answers to the above were yes, yes and no, then he had some serious thinking to do. The whole premise had to be re-examined and conclusions re-analysed. The who, why, how, where and when, would have to be answered again, the most crucial question being, if not Gunaji then who was slotted to be the sacrificial lamb in this game plan?

Sparse grey hair, prim spectacles on a stern nose belied by a kind smile and twinkling eyes, Professor Satyen Sengupta was both genial and friendly. Finding his audience was female and pretty, Sengupta was positively

beaming at her as they sat on chairs on the lawns outside
the library of St Stephens College.

'You are from Rawalpindi, my dear? Nice city, nice
city. And how is Salamat Kidwai?'

'He sends you his regards. He suggested that I should
approach you for information as you have specialised in
the history of India's freedom struggle.'

'Hmmm? Oh. Ask anything. I will help any way I
can.'

'Well, there was a small group of freedom fighters
from Calcutta in the 1940s called Hind Mata Sevak
Sangh. Have you ever heard of them?'

'Hind Mata Sevak Sangh? Give me a minute to think,
there were so many such groups you know. Okay, I know
which one you mean. A close group, shrouding itself
with secrecy, identities concealed. A freemasonry of
unknown rebels with a united federal India as its
covenant. Is that what you are talking about?'

'Yes!'

'Well, what do you want to know?'

'Anything you can tell me.'

'You understand, because of the inherent secrecy of
the organisation, not much was known, and the little
that was, was shrouded in mystery and myth. Basically
they were staunch patriots with the twin ambitions of
rooting out British imperialism and encouraging
secularism at the grassroots. Impressive ideology matched
by creditable performance. An extensive but quiet
presence in a fairly large part of Bengal, ample funding
from unknown sources, a variety of activities, but most
of them of a non-militant nature.'

'But aren't there any identities available at all? Any
rumours, myths, anything?' she asked frustratedly.

Sengupta cocked his head, arching his eyebrows in a quizzical gesture. 'Actually it's curious that you ask me that. Because one of the things which intrigued me about this organisation when I was researching Bengal's freedom movement was a legend emanating from the Sangh.'

'A legend?'

'A legend about a young man, a member of this group. The scion of a rich well-known family of Calcutta. Brave, innovative, wily and resourceful. A powerful young Turk with many brilliant operations to his credit. Nothing on the records, nothing that can be proven. As I said, a legend, a myth if you like.'

'But even legends have a names! What was he known as, do you know?'

'Only the first name, and that too in abbreviated form.'

'And what was that?'

'Manu.'

'Manu,' she said softly, taking a deep breath. 'That's it? No surname, not even a hint of one?'

'No. Nothing else'

'Guesses perhaps. What could Manu be in its stretched-out form? Manav, Manohar, Manikchand, what?'

'I have no idea at all, my dear. I told you, all that is known is the name Manu.'

'And I suppose you have no idea where this Manu could be now?'

'None at all.'

'Damn, damn, damn!'

'But what do you want with Manu? What is so urgent about a comparatively petty freedom fighter?'

'It is something that goes back a long way.' She shook her head in frustration. 'It is certain that Manu met Jawaharlal Nehru early in the morning on June 3, 1947.'

'And why should that be so important? Wait a minute, June 3? The day of Mountbatten's ill-fated conference on India's Partition? But even then, what is so important about an insignificant meeting between a minor revolutionary and Nehru? Unless you know more about this appointment than I do.'

'That's the thing – there was no appointment made, amazing that one was granted. The circumstances under which it was done were incredible to say the least. And followed by one of the most inexplicable reversals of a decision in the history of India.'

'Nehru's rejection of Partition. And you think there is a connection between the two. Not necessary you know. More like a coincidence, don't you think?'

'No, I don't. The context was much too mysterious, the coincidence much too pat.'

'Then you are saying . . . what are you saying? That this man from Calcutta was a courier of information? Information so critical that it made Nehru turn Indian history on its head in a matter of hours? Improbable. Most unlike Nehru.'

'Or maybe a pointer to the magnitude of the disclosures.'

'Do you have any proof for such rash conjectures, young lady?'

'Strong suppositions based on logic. Witnesses with curious accounts of events. Together pointing irrefutably towards a certain conclusion. But as for evidence, I can get that only when I reach the source of this particular puzzle. So I ask you again, do you have any idea who this Manu is or where I can find him?'

'The Indian Moses who delivered his people from the agony of Partition? Interesting. And if you find him, explosive. But unfortunately. I have no further details about him, though if you like I can go through a few books and see if I can find a clue for you. Now, what's your contact number?'

Satyen Sengupta saw her walking away, his face a study in frowning concentration. Then he nodded decisively and walked rapidly towards the librarian's office to make a call. He was soon listening to a distant buzz, impatiently tapping the table while he waited for someone to pick up the phone. Someone did. The right person.

'Hari, Satyen Sengupta here. I want to talk to Govindji.'

'Sorry, sir, he is in a meeting.'

'Then give me an appointment. It's urgent.'

'What is it about?'

'Something I need to discuss with him. At the earliest.'

'Can you come tomorrow? 10 a.m.?'

'Fine. I will be there.' Reflectively he put the receiver down. Govind Gunaji would be interested in the story of Manu.

Sometimes chance plays tricks on the destinies of human beings in its own enigmatic ways. It was chance that made Anees take a nap that afternoon to forget the loneliness and the memories. He slept only fitfully. And woke up shaking with the nameless fear of an unremembered nightmare, which had stalked him through the ravages of his comatose mind. Drenched in sweat, he decided to do something he hadn't done in days. He put on his singlet and shorts

and went jogging. Passing the Police Ground, the
Central Library and Hansraj College, he crossed over,
on his way to the Ridge and Hindurao Hospital.
He ought to have been a mere running blip on the
road which flanked the graceful portals of St Stephens.
But chance played a dirty trick once again. Casually
glancing at the smart young things gathered at the bus
stop, a normal reflex action in any male, Anees
encountered something more critical. He saw the face
which had recently chased him in his nightmares. The
radiance which could bring out all his latent yearnings.
He saw Reshma.

He should have had enough strength to walk away, he
knew. Anything else would be risky, in more than one
way. But he couldn't, not again. He had managed it
once, in Chandni Chowk, but now there was an urgency
in him to be near her, talk to her, touch her. He
succumbed to the temptation.

She was enmeshed in thought when a deep familiar
voice whispered harshly to her. Shock dulled her reaction.
And the fact that it was not a surprise, that her instinct
had told her it would happen. Dazed, in slow motion, as
she turned towards the dark shadows of his face, she felt
a burgeoning fire in her belly.

'Anees!' she whispered. 'What are you doing here?'

'I could ask you the same question, I suppose,' he
said derisively. 'If I bothered enough that is.'

Defenceless she stared at him, at the bitterness, at the
hatred. She couldn't find a vestige of love there in those
eyes which were capable of so much warmth. And she
could not blame him either.

'Anees. How are you?'

'How do you think?'

She kept silent. The ordeal of the guilty. The pain of the accused.

He took her by the arm, pulled her a little away from the crowd, setting her against a narrow wall, shading her white face from the prying eyes of the world with his brooding bulk.

'Can I ask you something?' his sharp voice grated on her conscience. 'I asked it before but I never got an answer. Maybe you can give me one now?'

'What?' she mumbled.

'What right did you have to do what you did? To me? Him? Do you think the reasons were compelling enough for the sin you committed? Do you have the capacity to make me understand?'

'Understand what?' she asked desperately.

'Oh, you know very well, Miss Innocent. Can you offer me any rationale at all to justify your delightful little Judas act?'

She pleaded quietly, 'It was the only pragmatic decision, Anees. Anything else would not have worked. My family would not have allowed it.'

'Ah yes, and that was the only thing that was important to you, wasn't it? Your world, your family, your community. I could only provide you with a few moments of illicit excitement. Never a part of that world. Damned solely by my identity. That didn't trouble you earlier when you professed your undying love so charmingly in pretty quotes?'

'I thought it wouldn't matter. It doesn't – to me. But that's not enough to live, Anees. I understood that but too late in the day. No man is an island, you know. And a woman, an Indian woman, even less so.'

'Brave Reshma,' he mimicked cruelly. 'Smart Reshma too. Playing your own version of Kipling's *Never the twain shall meet*.'

'I haven't made this society, Anees.'

'Oh, you haven't made it, you just condoned its injustice. But don't worry, what you have started, I'll finish. I don't like anything half-baked, you know.'

'What do you mean?'

'Sweetheart, you will see. Soon, very soon. This charade of sham fraternity, of false unity, has to end. And we will end it, I promise you that.'

'We? Who's we, Anees?'

He grinned lopsidedly, bent forward to whisper huskily in her ears, 'You kept your secret, didn't you? So very well too, not letting out a hint till it was all over. Now I'll keep mine. But let me tell you this – liberation is on the cards, my love, our liberation from a lie. Finally, I'll get rid of you, won't I?'

He tweaked her nose, the gesture an achingly familiar one, turned ugly with the cruelty underlying it. Then he turned and jogged away, never once looking back.

Eleven

Zahera was in the living room, working on her next day's lecture when Reshma came in. She looked up, instinctively removing her spectacles as she took in the young tormented face, the deep eyes blinded with pain, body unnaturally stiff.

'Reshma,' she asked sharply, 'what is it? What is the matter?'

'Nothing really, I am just tired. Give me a minute to catch my breath and I will be fine, honestly.'

Zahera understood that she was being shut out, accepted it gently.

'So where did you go today? You were to meet some professor at St Stephens, right? Any luck there?'

She could hide her misery under the guise of her quest. She willed herself to stop feeling. Rewind. Reconnect with the real.

'Actually yes and no. I met him, I did get some information. But once again I seem to be stuck. And I don't know where to go from here.'

'You know, Reshma, I have been thinking. This Manu you have told me about – somehow that name has a familiar ring to it. I have been trying to think for the last few days exactly why should that be.'

'Maybe you are thinking of *Manusmriti*,' said Reshma wryly.

'No, no, but talking of books, I think I saw the name in some book somewhere. An old book, for I seem to associate it with whiffs of dust. And musty damp. Yes, an old book I am sure.' She clucked irritably, 'Just can't remember.'

'Do you know how many Manus there must be in India?' asked Reshma patiently. 'The chances that your Manu has anything to do with mine are nonexistent.'

All professors have this inbuilt ability of taking frivolous suggestions in their stride, and Zahera smiled perfunctorily without the smallest break in her thought process.

'Let's see now, where did I see this book? In the Jamia Millia Library? JNU? Central? Someone's house, perhaps? I really must remember, something very indelible about this Manu there was. With a smile Reshma left her alone with her musings and went up to her room. She had half an hour before dinner in which to nurse her headache and heartache.

* * *

AUGUST 11, 2001

When Satyen Sengupta entered the sanctum sanctorum of the Arya Andolan Sabha, Govind Gunaji stood up in a rare gesture of deference and clasped his hand warmly.

'How are you, Satyenbhai? Seeing you after a long time.'

'I know. There was something I needed to discuss with you. Important I think.'

'Go ahead. What is it? Is there is anything I can do to help?'

'No, no, it's nothing for me. A piece of information you ought to know about.'

'Okay, tell me. What is it?'

Helplessly Sengupta looked around at the motley group of visitors, avidly listening to the exchange. Gunaji understood, imperiously gestured to the crowd to leave his room, waited silently as they made a rapid exit, then turned towards Sengupta.

'Now you can tell me, yes?'

Sengupta nodded. After a while said, 'A girl came to meet me yesterday, a journalist from Rawalpindi's newspaper *Indian Morning*.'

'For an interview?'

'No, for information. Trivia from the past, you would have said. Insignificant chapters of Indian independence.'

'Obviously not so trivial or you wouldn't be here. What was it?'

'She was looking for information about an ancillary rebel group which operated from Bengal, a secret society with the name of Hind Mata Sevak Sangh. Heard of it?'

'No, should I have?'

· 'Not really, most haven't. But anyway I told her what I knew, which was precious little.' He shrugged, 'Her disappointment was highly disproportionate to the subject matter, you understand?'

'So you probed?'

'So I probed. I asked her about the object of this enquiry and she told me. It was fascinating.'

'In what way?'

'Before I tell you, let me just recapitulate it for you. You remember the summer of 1947 when India was on the verge of getting independence, at the cost of Partition?'

Dourly Gunaji said, 'I was fifteen then. I remember very well. The suspicion, the tension, the enmity, the desperation, I have experienced it all. I also remember that half the country was grimly readying itself for the inevitable, while the other half had blind faith in Mahatma Gandhi's magical ability to prevent it. And ultimately it did seem to work, for there was no Partition.'

'Yes, but according to this girl, it was not Gandhi but someone else who worked the magic. An unknown man who with unknown means capped a volcano on the point of erupting. It is this man she is trying to locate.'

For a minute Gunaji was still as he tried to absorb the information. Then he softly said, 'Could she be right? Was there really such a man?'

Sengupta shrugged, 'Certain facts she related to me convinced me of his probable existence, yes.'

'And what was this man's name?'

'As I said, HMSS was a highly secret society, given to code names. The only known name of this man was Manu.'

There was a long pause, with Gunaji immersed in thought. He emerged from it with a glint in his eyes. 'Tell me, Satyenbhai, interesting though the story may be, it is not like you to be swayed by romance. Let's come to the point, shall we? In what way is this incredible bit of history important for me? For us rather?'

Sengupta smiled calmly. Bent forward for added emphasis and whispered. 'Find the man, Govindji, find him and make him a symbol. An epitome of righteous Hindu power. The Hindu who saved India from divisions dictated by Islamic fundamentalism. The Lok Sabha elections are in four months. Make this man a rallying point of the Hindutva consciousness, the one-man army who kept intact the Vedic dream of *akhand Bharat* (undivided India). It can work. With the right publicity, it can work like magic. Do you see what I mean?'

Slowly, very softly Gunaji said, 'Yes, I see. You are right, encase the story in some clever publicity, touch it with fire, and it may flare up beautifully. Sway the masses with its message. But the question is, where do I find this man?'

Crisply the historian said, 'The girl. She is very persistent. Very innovative too. If anyone can find Manu, it is Reshma Kapoor. Keep a tab on her movements and she just may lead you to him. If he is alive, that is.'

'You have her address?'

'I have her phone number.'

Gunaji thought it over, came to a decision, picked up the intercom and tersely gave a few instructions to the man at the receiving end. Then he turned back to Sengupta, pushed a piece of paper in front of him and said, 'My men are coming in. Could you write down the girl's phone number? And details about this Manu.'

Gunaji surveyed the bent figure diligently scrawling on the paper, 'Satyenbhai, I'm very grateful for this, you know that. It could be a brilliant manoeuvre, indeed.'

'You don't have to thank me, Govindji, what are friends for?'

Gunaji smiled, 'Well then, as a friend, what can I do
for you?'

Sengupta looked up. 'My nephew is bidding for the
Haldipur project,' he said simply.

Gunaji's smile widened as he raised his hand in
farewell.

They both understood each other perfectly.

Reshma came down early in the morning in a state of
depression. Four days left for the Energy Conference to
begin. Seven days for her departure from Delhi. And
then? It would be good-bye to her story of the decade.

Morosely she tramped into the living room, only to
encounter a beaming Zahera, and fond as she was of her,
the last thing Reshma needed was blithe spirits. 'Good
morning, *Maasi*,' she said sourly, looking with a jaundiced
eye at the sudden excitement this simple greeting
produced. 'You seem exceptionally cheerful this morning.
How come?'

It ought to have been impossible but Zahera's eyes
shone even brighter, 'I was waiting for you. Look what
I have found!'

'What?'

'Remember the book I was telling you about, the
one which I was sure had Manu written on it? I have
found that book!'

Slowly Reshma came alive, stared at the dusty
greenish tome the older woman was waving at her
triumphantly, and quietly held out her hand, once again
hope coiling up within her, insidiously. Silently she opened
the book to read the words written on the flyleaf. The
prominently printed title of the book. The name of its
author. And below it written in careful longhand, the ink

fading with age, a name, a city, a date. Obviously the
owner of the book putting his stamp on his possession.
The date was January 11, 1945, the city was Calcutta,
and the name written with a flourish – Manu.

Reshma looked up in wonder, shook her head with
awe.

'You see?' smiled Zahera. 'Your Manu seems to match
this one in terms of name, residence and time-span
doesn't he? Now check this.'

She turned to the next page. The yellowing paper
was dominated by a hand-scrawled figure of a Goddess
wearing a crown of thorns, in chains, and carrying a
tricolour flag. Hind Mata!

And below that was a quotation written in a neat
handwriting.

Reshma softly read out the lines squiggled on the
page.

And how can man die better
Than facing fearful odds
For the ashes of his fathers
And the temples of his Gods?

She took a deep breath, 'Macaulay? From Horatius?'

Zahera nodded, 'Yes, Macaulay. The reason why the
name Manu stuck in my mind. It was the quotation you
see, it was my father's favourite, he would have tears in
his eyes while reading it to us.' She shrugged, 'So there
it was, the book was right in my house, in Parvez's
library.'

Reshma narrowed her eyes in concern, 'You said you
borrowed it. But from where? Do you remember? Don't
tell me, please, that it was from a public library?'

Decisively Zahera shook her head, 'No, I am sure it was not a general library. A private one rather, someone's house I think. But for the life of me, I can't recall whose.'

'Oh no, *Maasi*,' groaned Reshma. 'If you can't then I am sunk.'

'No, no, *beti*, I'll get it. Give me some time, I will remember.'

'But time is what we don't have!' she wailed. 'I am in Delhi for just seven more days. And the conference starts after four. Seven days. That's all I have to solve the puzzle of Manu. Not much can happen in such a short time, can it?'

AUGUST 12, 2001

She was wrong. Events have a momentum of their own. And time is relative anyway. A nanosecond can carry the genesis of a cataclysm within its ephemeral span. An instant creak with the weight of posterity. Seven days can generate ripples affecting many generations to come. Already the plan was operational. The sequence set in motion with precision. Today the chain would accelerate. Explode. Insanity would break out. Everywhere. And the anarchy which would follow would threaten to engulf the very fabric of Indian harmony. Once again the concept of the two-nation theory would draw blood from the unity of a country. And the dormant dream of Pakistan prove a nightmare for a subcontinent.

The first spark of the conflagration burst through that day. On time. In rhythm with the predetermined schedule. The first event of a systematic progression, ending in chaos. And death. A ruthless, cold manoeuvre

which could topple India, poised once again on the verge
of another abyss. The prevented past and the ugly present
would merge together to demand answers from a
speechless nation. India would have another appointment
with another crossroad. And Partition would loom darkly
on the not-so-distant horizon.

The first act of this drama of death choreographed by
the Majlis would open in the morning. The actors would
be largely unimportant, their presence on the stage due
to chance and their bad karma. The venue of the drama,
however, was one chosen with great precision and
thought, to cause the maximum damage. The stage
chosen for the event – the Inter State Bus Terminal
(ISBT) of Delhi. Opening time for the show – the early
hours of August 12, 2001

At 7 a.m., the scene at ISBT is always tumultuous. A
frenetic medley of confused movements. Time-bound
hurry. Harassed search. Passengers herded with their
luggage safely inside buses. Any man becomes necessarily
an island in that sea of humanity, intent on his own self,
his purpose paramount. Certainly no one has time to
observe their surroundings in detail, nor the inclination.
Normal humanity produces a reaction of irritation at
ISBT. The abnormal a fleeting second glance.

The man with the briefcase did not qualify for either.
Too effacing to irritate. Too ordinary to appeal. None of
his actions unusual. He went towards the paan shop.
Bought a packet of low-priced cigarettes and a paan.
Walked further ahead to the information booth, asked
details about the bus going to Lahore. Bought a
magazine, settled himself in a corner of the dirty waiting
lounge on a cracked plastic seat, the briefcase below

him. Read the magazine quietly, unconcerned about the
paucity of natural light in that shadowy corner. After
nearly ten minutes, he stretched, took out a cigarette and
lit it. Seemed to realise his mistake after a moment as,
with an apologetic glance at the family of four nearby, he
got up, walked towards the exit door. A conscientious
man, concerned about the effects of nicotine on small
children, you would think. He strolled out. Merged in
the crowd. Unnoticed by anyone. Equally unnoticed was
the fact that the briefcase had been left below the seat,
tucked near the wall, away from prying eyes. The man
did not come back to claim his property. And the clock
ticked steadily away.

The explosion which ripped apart the walls of the lounge,
shattering windows, bursting shrapnel, was heard as far
as the Red Fort. The police would not find any concrete
clues. No letters would be received claiming responsibility.
The debris settled, the damage to property would be
pegged to the tune of Rs two crore. The number of the
injured would slowly totter up to a hundred. And the
final death toll would be a shocking forty-four. The tally
would include six children.

Any kind of news has automatic wings in Delhi, a city
where information is a prime obsession. Calamities speed
up the internal network. Within ten minutes, reporters
and television news units were there. Within an hour, the
whole of Delhi was buzzing about the tragedy at ISBT,
conjectures and theories burgeoning thickly. They would
soon be getting thicker. Before the day was over, Delhi
would be in a shocked spin. And newspaper headlines,
the next day, stun the whole country.

A mere two hours after the ISBT disaster, death would once again hover over the city, and finally, slam the New Delhi Railway Station with its shadow. A bomb would explode in the second-class waiting room. Similar techniques, no careless clues. Death toll ten. Chaos total.

The third tragedy would rupture Palika Bazaar, Delhi's underground beehive of a market. With its stifling tiny shops, twisting, confusing passages, and sweaty multitudes in search of bargains, the market would prove to be a perfect target. The strategy used a variation on the explosion rhapsody. Less dramatic. More terrifying.

Palika Bazaar breathes through its numerous ducts which recycle oxygen continuously. The air-conditioning is barely adequate but manages to keep the temperature levels fairly low, the air reasonably fresh. It was this life-support system which was infiltrated and contaminated. Certain chemicals added in the central channel. The poison flowing through the network of conduits to all corners of Palika Bazaar. The gas which suffocated, paralysed and ultimately killed. The collective crowd in that cloistered space 'soft' targets.

The first intimation came at mid-afternoon, the first signal an unusual stink. Not particularly noticeable to the shoppers used to the constant gamy smell in the air. But the odour intensified, dispersed rapidly. The first victim succumbed within five minutes, a sixty-one-year-old shopkeeper who suddenly clutched at his throat and sank to the ground. An anxious crowd gathered around the man and discovered to their dismay similar symptoms in themselves.

That was when the shouting began, the screaming of mortal terror which makes men into beasts intent on survival. By this time the effect was felt everywhere, and panic struck with a vengeance. Coughing, choking, desperate humanity, striking, pushing, clawing their way out of that underground hell. Some succeeded, many did not. And even those who did get to fresh air, found themselves succumbing to the gas on the lawn outside. By this time telephone calls had been desperately made and police cars and ambulances could be heard. Within no time at all the police cordoned off the area, helping out the victims. Rushing them to nearby hospitals via ambulances, cars, auto-rickshaws, even motorcycles. The air-conditioning was shut off and Palika Bazaar became an airless hole where eleven bodies lay contorted in ugly death. Two more were trampled to death on the spiral well of the main exit. Three died in the Lok Nayak Jai Prakash Narain's hospital's emergency room. Others who eluded death, found that they carried its legacy in the form of side-effects for many years to come. Appalled by the unprecedented savagery of the attack, horrified Connaught Place reacted en masse. Traders shut shops, shoppers went home trembling. That evening the commercial heart of the capital was a deserted place of shadows and fears.

The fourth and the last violent act was one which evoked the least concern in the local populace, but the maximum at the international level. It was once again back to the tried and tested. Enter the ubiquitous bomb, but at an unanticipated site. Its target this time a sudden break in the logical progression of the day's disasters. Logical would have been the international airport, to complete the triumvirate of exit-entry points in the city. Instead the dewy white walls of the powerful American Embassy became the unhappy target.

Situated on Shantipath in Chanakyapuri, the fortress-like embassy is one of the most tightly manned and protected of all foreign missions in the capital. No one would ever know how it was managed and how anyone could infiltrate the security channels. And yet at 6 p.m., a bomb exploded in the bathroom next to the secretarial offices. One clerk and two security officers were killed on the spot. Five others were injured. And for once Chester Forbes, the suave Ambassador with a reputation for keeping his cool, was shaken to the core.

As was the whole embassy, traumatised by the violence, insular fears reactivated forcibly. Wires hummed throughout the night, and by the next morning the international arena was buzzing with the news that New Delhi was under the siege of extremist violence. Red alerts were issued from powerful capitals to their missions. Keep your antenna honed. Take ultra-protective measures. New Delhi was unsafe territory.

* * *

AUGUST 13, 2001

Next day, newspapers screeched out the previous day's bloody tragedies in bold black headlines. The unprecedented violence had sent the capital reeling with shock. Temporary paralysis set in, the domain of babus rattled to the very bottom of their terrycotton trousers. Harried top police brass went into a spin of activity, directing operations, tightening security, digging evidence. In every street, every shop, every restaurant, every house, citizens were seen huddled, in whispered parleys, espousing convoluted theories and relating conjectures. Delhi's ever-active grapevine worked overtime, churning out the most bizarre rumours. Fingers were pointed in diverse directions as people primed themselves for more horrors. And a shrill footnote to the dirge was the bleak thought of the approaching conference. With India the prima donna of the world for the two-day period – would the choreography of death become more bloody?

It was a question which begged answers, and the people gathered in the room were there to try and do just that. Collectively they represented the supreme power in Indian polity. And bore its legacy of chronic unrelenting pressure. It wasn't easy to keep the federal fabric of India in prime condition. Even at normal times, the diversity was extreme, unity a fragile concept needing constant reaffirmation. And abnormal times like these could stretch the nation's faith to its limit. Give sleepless nights even to a Solomon, which these three would be the first to concede they were not.

But they were well-meaning. With a real depth of feeling for their country. A vision of its future. And an India broken and hurting was not a part of that vision.

In the last two years of statesmanship, no one had seen India's premier so obviously worried. Normally he wore an armour of calm which could and had defeated any number of calamities. But the last twenty-four hours had not been exactly easy on Shiv Charan Shukul, and the strain was showing.

Shukul looked around the small round table and at the faces of his three colleagues. The helplessness he felt was mirrored in theirs but he remained hopeful. They were good, these three, his star performers. Brilliant troubleshooters, innovative and resourceful. Hopefully they would prove adequate in the present exigency. He rubbed his old forehead to ease the pressure, suddenly feeling his age.

The emergency meeting of this select committee, hurriedly summoned that morning to attempt crisis control, was proceeding in fits and starts.

'What is the report from the Jai Prakash Narain hospital, Farzana?'

She grimaced, 'Four more people are on the critical list. Prognosis uncertain. Ten others have been shifted to the general ward in a fairly stable condition.'

'What about the railway station blast? Its victims?'

'In a bad state. They have been admitted to Safdarjung and Willingdon hospitals. Five of them critical cases. Others disfigured, handicapped, scarred.'

'And I suppose the ISBT survivors are in a similar condition?'

'Yes. Worse. I have here with me detailed medical statements of the victims and our compiled figures. Maybe you can go through it later.'

'Leave it with me. I am visiting these hospitals in the afternoon. I will need it then.' He turned towards S. Aravindan, India's suave, soft-spoken Foreign Minister, who looked distinctly hot today. 'Have you had a talk with the American Ambassador, Aravindan?'

'The conversation I had with Chester Forbes cannot exactly be termed a 'talk', Shukulji. Calling it a mudslinging match would be more accurate, I think. Anyway they have requested extra security and I have acceded to the request. Just as I have acceded to similar demands from the British High Commission, the Chinese,

French, Israeli embassies, with a few others in the pipeline. Plus there have been umpteen panic calls from desperate sources, worried about the security factor at the approaching conference. I have tried to pacify them but I myself need assurance that adequate steps have been taken in this regard. Foreign offices around the world are questioning our ability to protect their delegations. And with ten heads of states scheduled to arrive for the conference, I cannot blame them.'

'Farzana?' fielded Shukul.

She sighed, 'You also know, Aravindan, that no security is foolproof, but yes, it will be increased, tightened, made more extensive. We are cordoning off all exit and entry points to the city. Road checks are being set up on all nodal routes. The hotels where the VIPs will be staying will be under a literal siege by security personnel. Exact procedures and watertight movements are to be executed. The venue of the conference, Mahatma Gandhi Memorial Bhavan, has been sealed off and will open under unprecedented security. Every head of state will be accompanied by an armed escort and bulletproof vehicles. We will bring in reinforcements to augment our security forces which are stretched to the ultimate point. We shall assign extra Central Reserve Police Force and Border Security Force units to our city force.'

'What a mess!' said Shukul frustratedly. 'And that too now, at this sensitive juncture. Who is responsible for this outrage? And why are they doing it? Farzana, has any group come forward to accept culpability?'

'No.'

'Any leads in the on-going criminal investigation?'

'Not much. Medium-strength bombs were used. In open spaces they may not have created too much damage.

In the carefully chosen closed areas, swarming with people, they were devastating. A common link is obvious in all episodes. Similar modus operandi. A synchronised agenda. Obviously one single group is behind the plan. But as to its identity, or its purpose, we haven't got anything. Not yet.'

Softly Aravindan said, 'But the rumours are there. People are already talking. Which way is this ill-wind blowing, Farzana?'

No one would ever know the exact genesis of the rumour. But suddenly everyone was talking about it in hushed tones. A startling bit of information, ascribed to impeccable sources. The exact identity of the source shrouded in the garb of confusing *avatars*. It was told and retold with great certainty, each new version losing nothing with added masala. And slowly the whole of Delhi seemed to be in the know of this great secret. Believing it implicitly. Resenting the implications, burning with a muted anger. Suspicions flared quietly, evident in imperceptibly changed personal equations. A certain withdrawal, an avoidance of contact, blatant aspersions on a particular community.

The changed atmosphere was, however, a natural result of the virulent bit of gossip. For it was whispered that the police had definite evidence to pin the crime on a particular group. And was hushing it up in a bid to retain communal harmony, on blanket orders from the apex powers.

The group was rumoured to be a right-wing separatist, fanatic, militant organisation.

Its name – the Quom-e-Majlis.

Its agenda – the creation of Pakistan.

The whispers went on, increasing in intensity, in rage. Delhi did not know it but it was sitting on a simmering volcano.

An impatient Anees was stopped at the main gate by the guard who talked briefly with someone inside the house, and after giving him a curious hard stare, went to open the huge gate. The second guard, meanwhile, came forward with the visitors register, thrusting it in front of Anees with a pen, and waited patiently while the name, address, time of entry and the purpose of the visit was noted. Then he handed him the pink entry slip. The ritual had been neatly completed by the time the first guard turned back. Which is why he never realised that his comrade had by mistake defied the boss's orders. The voice on the phone had given strict instructions that the visitor's entry should go unrecorded.

'I had told you not to come here, Anees. Ever. It is imprudent. You should know that,' the voice was cold, controlled.

Anees instinctively folded his arms across his chest as he sank deeper in the plush chair, 'I couldn't get you on the phone. I needed to talk.'

'What about?'

'This thing that is going on. Yesterday. So many deaths, so much blood. I heard people saying that the Majlis is responsible. Is that true?'

'Yes.'

'You didn't tell me about it.'

'It's a 'need to know' principle, Anees. You did not need to know this.'

'But I don't understand. What do you hope to achieve? It will simply generate anger against Muslims. Maybe incite a backlash against them. How will that benefit you?'

'Psychology, Anees, it is a part of mass psychology. Human nature is a funny thing, it depends on how you manipulate it. Presently we are the perpetrators. Guilty without a shred of evidence.'

'But guilty, nevertheless.'

The soft tone became even more sibilant, 'I can't tell you much, my angry friend, but let me just point out a few facts about human nature to you.'

'I'm all ears.'

'Right now Hindus are full of righteous anger. Muslims of humiliating guilt. The burden of collective responsibility can be pretty exhausting you know. It's an emotional tug-of-war, an instinctive communal loyalty versus humane morality. And right now the latter is winning hands down. Because its cause seems to be justified, the other undeserving.'

'So?'

'So your ordinary Muslim is experiencing the barbs, the bitterness, the fulminating anger, occasional assault. He simmers with anger, but it is of the muted variety. Because somewhere in him he believes that the aggression is justified to a degree, the demon of collective responsibility is at work.'

'What's your point?'

'Simple. If it is later proved that the community he belongs to is as innocent as a newborn babe, his status changes to that of a scapegoat! And the anger which has been there within him all the time will erupt into reactive violence. This will instigate a greater backlash from the

Hindus, which will fuel his fears further. It will become
a vicious cycle. That is where we come in.'

'How?'

'At the lowest point of Muslim alienation, the Majlis
will step forward. Drum up propaganda. We will become
the innocent martyrs persecuted by the Hindu majority.
The ordinary Muslim will empathise with the alienation,
the persecution. He is experiencing it himself you see.

Suddenly his future, his identity, will seem to be on
the block. The pressure will build up, the fear consumes
him. To him the Majlis will appear as a savant, someone
offering a sane, safe haven. Pakistan will not seem as
unpatriotic propaganda but the just revolt of the
oppressed. The two-nation idea which would have taken
years to gain momentum, will ferment in a matter of
months. The schedule for the birth of Pakistan will be
dramatically shortened, fast-forwarded. The beginning of
the end.'

Anees narrowed his eyes, 'All very interesting in theory
but could prove weak in practice. How will you convince
anyone that yesterday's black deeds do not belong to the
Majlis? The problem with rumours is that if they are
easy to spread, they are much more difficult to scotch.
To counteract them you need overwhelming proof. How
do you get that? How do you hammer home your
innocence, beyond all doubt?'

The smile was sly, secretive, 'The proof will be
overwhelming. Innocence will be proved without a doubt.
You will see.'

'So yesterday's violence was necessary?'

'Essential. The whole of Delhi is in chaos presently,
disorder is rampant. It is this situation which we'll turn
to our benefit. For in the heart of chaos are the seeds

of future order. Our order. Pakistan will happen, and we will see it happening in our lifetime.'

If Parvez Ali Beg was worn out and tired, which he was, he managed to hide it beautifully. Keeping your cool was an art you compulsively learned in this job and a crisis-ridden day was all a part of the game. The only difference anyone saw in Beg at such times was an increased consumption of cigarettes and tea, which rose in direct proportion to the intensity of the crisis.

'Sukhram, what's happened to my tea?' snapped Beg without looking up from the file he was studying.

'Sorry, saab, I have brought it. Shall I keep it here?'

'Uh, huh and send Khanna inside.'

Beg was deep in the file when a cheery voice intruded on his concentration, 'You called, sir?'

'Oh, yes, Khanna. Just checking on arrangements for tomorrow. That's when most of the conference delegates are coming?'

'Yes, sir, we have received a hundred and fifty intimations for the 14th. Around seventy will come on the 15th morning.'

'I want you to personally ensure that the police make stringent, watertight arrangements for their safe transport. Liaise with the foreign office, position some of our best men at the airport. I don't want any hitches at all, you understand?'

'Don't worry, sir, I have met Vinod Rastogi, the Chief Protocol Officer, and the Deputy Commissioner, Ranjit Chaddha. We went through the minutest details before we set the schedule. The number of cars, luxury buses, security guards, the duty timings, everything has been worked out.'

'All quiet on the Western front today?'

Khanna grimaced, 'Till now, yes. But by the time this conference is over I'll have turned into a wreck.'

'Join the gang, buddy.'

'One more thing. You remember a few days earlier you had asked me to check on Abumiya, a Chandni Chowk resident?'

It took a second for Beg to react. 'Yes, what about him?' he said without much interest.

'The report has just come in, you may want to go through it.'

Impatiently, 'Not now, Khanna. Later perhaps. It is not that important.'

'It may be,' said Khanna quietly.

'What do you mean?'

'An unusual connection.'

Parvez frowned, 'Exactly what are you talking about, Khanna? What have you found about Abumiya?'

'Two facts. He has been an illegal gun-trader for the past ten years. Something of an expert in explosives too.'

'And the second fact?'

'From some of the papers we found at his house it's evident that for the last one year, Abumiya has forsaken his other clients, servicing just one major one. Would you like to guess who this one major client is?'

'Not the Quom-e-Majlis?'

'Got it in one shot.'

'My God, what are you waiting for? Bring in Abumiya immediately! Take him apart, put the fear of God into him, make him sing.'

'Can't. He vanished. The minute he realised someone was sniffing around, he simply folded up his operation. Crawled back into the woodwork.'

'Damn!'

'I want to know something, sir.'

'What?'

'Why did you ask for this enquiry on Abumiya? Did you know something I don't?'

'No, my house guest had requested more information about the man. I decided to oblige.'

'Your house guest?'

'A young girl, a Rawalpindi journalist. Come here to attend this conference.'

'But why this curiosity about a shady character? Was he a part of some story she was following?'

'No, I asked her. It seems she had gone visiting in Chandni Chowk where her servant is staying with her sister. That's where she heard rumours about Abumiya. And asked me to enquire about him.'

'Seems like an incredible story. A young girl goes to meet her servant, hears that the servant's neighbour is a notorious character and gets all panicky. To the extent of asking her host to investigate the man? Sounds fishy to me.'

Beg nodded crisply, 'Yes, I agree. I will ask her tonight. Any other developments?'

'You mean in our wonderland? Well, mostly peaceful. News of small skirmishes is coming in. Nothing major however. Not yet. But rumour has it that Govind Gunaji has given a clarion call to all Hindus to unite and carry on the good fight.'

Beg groaned, 'That's all we need.'

'Yeah, don't we just? You seen that movie, sir, *One Flew Over The Cuckoo's Nest?*' Before the night is over I'll fit the part beautifully. For now I'll take your leave, got to practise the call of the cuckoo, you see.'

*   *   *

It was after dinner that Parvez decided to gently explore his young guest's mind. Zahera was edged close to the TV, chin in hand, intent on every word of her favourite talk show.

He took his coffee cup, and quietly placed a chair next to the settee where Reshma was sitting with her legs folded under her, looking like an unhappy little girl. His voice was gentle as he said, 'Reshma?'

She looked up, tried to smile, failed, 'Yes?'

'You remember you asked me to find out about a Chandni Chowk resident, Abumiya?'

Abrupt interest, slightly wary, 'Oh, of course. Did you investigate? Did you find anything?'

'Well, yes, more than we bargained for.'

'What do you mean?'

'Your information was right. He is an illegal gun-trader. But we have also discovered something more significant about him, especially in the present context. He could be a major supplier of weapons and explosives to the Quom-e-Majlis.'

'Quom-e-Majlis. You mean the organisation rumoured to be responsible for yesterday's violence?'

'Yes.'

A long worried silence.

After a while, Parvez asked patiently, 'Reshma, may I ask you a question?'

She nodded.

'Why did you ask me to check on this man?'

'I told you. I had gone to meet *Amma* who lives in the same building.'

Gently he cut her short, 'You told me that earlier but I think there is some other factor too. Or you wouldn't get all worked up about rumours which don't touch your life in any way.'

She did not respond, seething with inner disquiet.

'Reshma, I must insist on an answer. National security may be involved.'

A deep breath and she confided, 'I met someone there. And I came to know that this friend had come to visit Abumiya. I was curious.'

'A friend. Male? Female?'

'Male.'

'His name?'

'Anees Bakhtiar.'

'An old friend?'

'Yes. His family is close to mine in Rawalpindi. I have known him since childhood.'

'What does he do? I mean, what's his profession?'

'He is an army officer. Presently stationed in Amritsar.'

Persistently he probed, 'And he is in Delhi on holiday? Personal matters?'

'I don't know.'

'Didn't you ask him?'

'No.'

He inspected her pained face quietly for a moment, 'Reshma, did you know he was in Delhi?'

'No.'

'His family did not mention it when you were planning to come here?'

'No, his mother did not know it either.'

Sharply, 'What do you mean? She did not know that her son had gone to Delhi? Where did she think her son was − in Amritsar?'

She quietly responded, 'Well, yes, but then she was informed that he had taken casual leave.'

'Which she didn't know about?'

'No.'

'Casual leave to come to Delhi?'

She grimaced, 'No, casual leave to go to Karachi. But he never went there. That is what worried her.'

'And then you meet him in Aasmaan Mahal. He told you that he had come to see Abumiya?'

'No.'

'Didn't you ask him what he was doing there?'

'We didn't talk.'

Parvez narrowed his eyes, 'He saw you?'

'Yes.'

'But he didn't talk. Nor did you?'

'No.'

'Why? You said he is your childhood friend?'

'He was my friend, I mean. We kind of broke up.'

The young face was weary with a dark burden. Deep waters, he gauged. To be charted later perhaps. Peripheral at present. Cautiously he groped, 'Let me put things in perspective over here. This Anees Bakhtiar. An army officer. Takes leave from his station, gives his destination as Karachi. But that seems to be a camouflage. Instead he comes to Delhi on a visit shrouded with secrecy. And meets a nefarious character with definite links to the Majlis. Does he owe allegiance to the Quom-e-Majlis, do you know?'

'I don't know. I wouldn't have thought so. He was never a fanatic. I do know that for a fact.'

'In the past maybe. But people change. Can you be sure now?'

'No. Not any more.'

'And you have no idea where he is staying in Delhi? Or who his friends are?'

'No, but I ran into him again two days later,' she blurted.

'Where?' he said curtly.

'In Delhi University, near the bus stop of St Stephens College. I had gone to meet a history professor.'

'What was he doing there?'

'He was jogging.'

'Jogging? Did he see you?'

'Yes, he is the one who approached me.'

'Talked to you?'

'Yes.'

'About what?'

'That is personal, Uncle. Not germane to the issue.'

Eyes narrowed, he reflected. Tacitly accepted her point. He drew a diary from his pocket, took a pencil from the table and looked up, 'I will need details about this Bakhtiar, Reshma. His Pindi address, his family details, physical description, whatever you know.'

She tugged at her lower lip anxiously, 'Now?'

'Right now.'

The interruption came when the inquisition was nearing its end. Or rather it was less an interruption and more a mini-storm. A quiet Zahera was overpowering enough. Zahera with her soul on wings was devastating to say the least. She stood up and turned to Reshma happily. 'I've got it,' she yodelled. 'I told you I would get it, didn't I? I've got it.'

A rueful smile flitting on Parvez's face fractured the tension in the air, 'Zahera, exactly what is it that you have got? Can you please clarify?'

'Something which Reshma wanted me to remember!' she said triumphantly.

Reshma's maudlin mood evaporated. 'You remembered where you got the book from?' she screeched in excitement.

'Yes, didn't I tell you about the marvels of subconscious? I was listening to the talk show and . . .'

'*Maasi*,' she interrupted, 'tell me where you got the book from, please.

'No, listen to this. A participant was making a point about powerful women, and in that context he mentioned a name. And voila! I got it, I tell you.'

'My *jaan*, will you please tell us immediately what exactly it is that you have got?' asked Parvez.

'I got the book from her library. We had gone there for dinner once, you remember, Parvez, and I saw the book. I asked her if I could borrow it and I forgot to give it back.'

Mustering great patience Reshma spaced out her words, 'Just who are you talking about?'

Zahera beamed at her anxious face, paused for added drama and then said simply, 'Farzana Hussain.'

It was the night of the knives. Shadows came out from dark corners to add another ugly chapter to the story of inhumanity. Pockets of Delhi became fortresses of fear, as from unknown crevices anonymous faces crept out with weapons to trap the hapless. Govind Gunaji's call for redemption and retribution found an echo in many a burning mind. By the dawn of the next day, the night would claim ten more lives. And Hindu-Muslim amity, already stretched thin, would be tested to its limit.

Parvez Ali Beg wanted very badly to sleep. In his tension-ridden job sleep was a necessary panacea, to relax his tired brain. It refused to come. What was irking him most was his own instinct, screaming out, jolting his weary mind to attention. It was the Anees Bakhtiar factor which was troubling him. And the Alam Khan enigma. Two odd and unusual events, separate, yet could there be a connection between them? Alam Khan was a plant, he was sure, brought in to confuse, to distract attention. And now this Anees Bakhtiar. He needed to get it into perspective. Investigate it in depth. He had told Khanna to immediately fax the Amritsar Cantonment for precise, detailed information on Bakhtiar, including the exact times of his absences in the last one year. By tomorrow he would get it. The explanation for his visit could be innocent and Bakhtiar's presence in Delhi legitimate. But he wouldn't bet a crooked coin on that supposition. His seasoned nose had smelt something fishy. Tomorrow would decide whether he had caught only a minnow or netted a big catch.

Twelve

Beg's instinct would not be the only thing that would be put to the test today. The day would initiate other progressions too. Tumultuous movements, merging into others, gathering force, cascading ruthlessly towards a savage culmination.

It hadn't been easy even for Zahera to secure an appointment with Farzana, despite the fact that she was not just Parvez's wife, but also one for whom Farzana had an immense though rueful respect. When the beleaguered Home Minister answered the late night call and heard that the reason for the appointment sought was of a personal nature, she had become impatient, and tried to postpone it to a later date. Zahera had insisted, cajoled, and finally, Farzana had agreed. Seven in the morning. And that too only for fifteen minutes. Could Zahera make it? She could and here she was, tagging Reshma along.

By this time Reshma was panicky, 'We are going to the house of the Home Minister of India, when Delhi is in turmoil, to ask her about the ownership of a book! Zahera *Maasi*, she will slaughter us!'

'Nothing of the sort, not when we explain its significance. Now you keep your cool and let me do the talking. You have never seen her before have you? She can be pretty formidable.'

But from a distance Farzana did not really match that description, bunched up in the garden chair in a simple cotton *salwar-kameez*, hair falling all over her shoulders. She looked more like a college girl suffering from examination stress, than the most powerful woman in the subcontinent.

But the minute she became aware of their presence, the vulnerable look vanished. Her aquiline features were shrouded in a familiar mask. She rose quietly, as did a mild-faced, bespectacled man siting next to her.

'Her husband, Shaukat!' whispered Zahera abruptly. 'A nice guy who lets Madam trample all over him.'

The barest of greetings and the briefest of introductions. A cool, firm handshake from Farzana, a warm engulfing one from Shaukat, cordially beaming at them. 'It is nice to see you again, Zahera,' he said genially. 'And Reshma, you are from Rawalpindi, I believe.'

Farzana cut through the small talk firmly, 'You had some work with me, Zahera? I am sorry to hurry you this way, but I do have to leave for the office.'

'I understand perfectly. And if it was not urgent we would have never imposed.'

She nodded gracefully and waited.

Zahera removed the book from her purse and handed it over to her. Farzana scowled, rapidly leafed through the pages. Waited for an explanation.

'This is a book I borrowed from you a few months back. I forgot to return it earlier.'

For once Farzana was speechless, 'You wanted to meet me just to return a book?'

Hastily Zahera interrupted, 'No, no, actually I need to ask you something regarding the book.'

'Really, what?'

'Open the flyleaf. You see an inscription written on it? By a Manu from Calcutta in the year 1945. And on the next page there is a figure of Hind Mata and a quotation by Macaulay.'

A brief flicker in Farzana's eyes? Or was it mere imagination on her part?

Reshma couldn't be sure and certainly when Farzana looked up her voice was as cool as ever, 'What about it?'

'Well, do you know who this Manu could be? Reshma is trying to trace him.'

Farzana interrupted, 'I don't think I can help you in any way. If I remember I bought this book at a sale. Secondhand you understand.'

Shaukat who had bent forward to pick up the book, interrupted softly, 'No, Farzana, don't you remember? You picked up this book at your grandfather's house, if I am not mistaken.'

A definite trace of annoyance flitted over her face.

'I don't think so, Shaukat. But really is it that

important? Even if it had been given to me by Nanu, well, the chances are he bought it secondhand himself, so it's the same thing, really.'

'But still, can we meet him? What's your grandfather's name?'

'Altaf Naqvi.'

'Well, we would like to ask Mr Naqvi, on the off-chance that he may know who and where this Manu is,' beamed Zahera.

Curiously Shaukat asked, 'Just who is this Manu? Why is your friend trying to trace him?'

'Yes,' reiterated Farzana, 'I would like to know that myself.'

Zahera looked at Reshma, said softly, 'You explain.'

Shaukat broke the deep silence which wrapped them after her narration petered to a close.

'Amazing,' he breathed. 'Absolutely amazing. If true. Is it?'

'I have told you all that I have found out. Now you judge. You understand, only Manu can give concrete proof in this case. I can only conjecture,' shrugged Reshma.

'Fascinating but far-fetched,' murmured Farzana. 'And anyhow it has nothing to do with my grandfather.'

Shaukat stared, 'But didn't you tell me that your grandfather was a freedom fighter. In Calcutta.'

She nodded impatiently, 'So? There were any number of them.'

'But, my dear, don't you realise? As one of his tribe, he may have known this Manu! Perhaps the book was given to him by Manu!'

'I don't think so. I have never heard him mention that name.'

Zahera broke in, 'Farzana, where does your grandfather live? In Delhi?'

'In Mehrauli, in a farmhouse,' she replied shortly.

'May I have his address, please? I would like to meet him. Perhaps I could call him.'

With extreme reluctance, Farzana nodded, rapped out the address, 'He is an old man. I don't want him disturbed, you understand.'

Wryly Shaukat interrupted, 'He is not exactly helpless, Farzana, God bless him. Tough he is and capable of taking more than this in his stride. As for being lonely, doesn't he live with that Bengali friend of his, Manmohan Ghosh? In fact, come to think of it, this book may belong to Ghosh. He is a voracious reader if I remember, and has quite a collection.'

He paused, then sat up, 'Wait a minute. Manmohan. Manmohan?'

'Manu?' said Reshma softly with suppressed excitement. 'Mrs Hussain, is it possible?'

'No, highly far-fetched.'

'But was he a freedom fighter?'

Reluctantly she admitted, 'I believe he was.'

'Well, where is he from? Can you tell me something about him?'

'What little I know, yes. He is an old friend of Nanu. From Calcutta, I believe.'

'Calcutta? The headquarters of the Hind Mata Sevak Sangh! He could have been a member of that organisation!'

'I don't think so.'

'Wait a minute,' said Shaukat thoughtfully. 'Didn't you say, Reshma, that every member had a tattoo of Hind Mata engraved on their chest?'

'Yes. Why?'

'Now I don't know how conclusive this is, but Manmohan Ghosh does have a similar kind of a tattoo.'

'How would you know that Shaukat?' snapped Farzana.

'I came on him at the Mehrauli farm while he was gardening. Bare-chested. It seemed odd, incongruous with his persona. Possibly that's why it remained stuck in my memory.'

Reshma was resonant with excitement, 'Really? Is it possible? Could he really be Manu? Oh my God!'

Zahera gestured her to silence, 'Farzana, what about his family? How does he happen to stay here with your grandfather?'

'His wife died and he is alienated from his only son. A decade ago, Nanu went to Calcutta and met Manmohan *Kaka* again. He found a lonely man, and as Nanu was lonely too, he invited *Kaka* to come and stay with him in Mehrauli. He does some gardening, some odd jobs. But mostly his status is that of friend and companion.'

Reshma said softly, intensely, 'I would like to visit Mr Naqvi today. If he is not too busy?'

'I suppose you can. But go after 4 o'clock in the afternoon. He is more hospitable then.'

'And Mr Ghosh will be there?'

'Yes, he always is.'

Anger seared. Clogged the rational. Erupted violently. Simmered in frustrated rage. It was unbelievable, unacceptable. He really did exist! The killer of a dream. The destroyer of destiny. He really was. Not just a part of imagination, an aberration of the mind, an ugly rumour born out of frustration. But the reality of a nightmare. For so long the rumour had hummed in the air, whispered in pain, in fear, with hatred, like a black dirge in the background. An implausible rumble that fifty-four years ago the seed of Pakistan had not died an unfortunate death, but had been murdered. The infant entity executed in the womb. Killed on the verge of birth. The myth of a man who had, in mysterious ways, blocked the birth of a young nation. Unacceptable. Unbelievable.

But today the myth had proved to be tangible. The unbelievable had been shown to be true. And the anger had seared. Painful. Uncontrollable. The man who had killed a birthright was real. And living. Everything pointed towards it. All indications were clear. The chain of evidence was too cogent, too precise.

Manmohan Ghosh had to be the man who had manipulated destruction. If it had not been for him the unthinkable would never have been thought of. By everything fair and just in the world, Pakistan would have been a fifty-four-year-old country today. With a blessed separate entity of its own on Allah's good earth. Not just a tortured fantasy of a few visionaries.

The fire in the mind intensified. Helpless hatred deepened. The creator of this chaos had no right to live.

But before that the guilt had to be proved. Innocence could not be punished. That must be ensured.

And if it was proved beyond doubt that Manmohan Ghosh was culpable, he would have to die. Without option. And not just because of the immense satisfaction inherent in the idea. The act was one of practical necessity.

For even now Manmohan Ghosh could become an

effective weapon in the hands of zealots. And consequently a threat. To THE plan. THEIR plan. If Manu's role was discovered, and proved, and splashed in the media, he could overnight become a strong symbol of nationalistic fervour. An icon of unity. And that could not be allowed. Not at this juncture when every tiny development was crucial. Action had to be immediate. Reaction total. Jury, judge and executioner all rolled into one.

The fevered hand reached for a phone. Urgent whispers were understood. They would be obeyed implicitly. Fanatically. The order was clear. Quick trial. Instant judgment. In case of negative decision, the penalty was pre-decided. Terminate.

The man who had been called Manu was relaxing in the garden. With a smile he looked around the place that had given meaning to the twilight of his life. After his wife's death he really had thought there was no point living. And then he had found some solace. Nothing earth-shaking or significant. Just the gift of a friend, a modest farm, a garden. For a younger Manu, caught in the vortex of movement and passion, like a kaleidoscope of vivid graphics, these would have seemed a yawningly dull sepia print. In the flush of heady youth, Manu would never have predicted such a passive staid existence for himself. But then life taught its lessons. And one accepted. As he had.

Just for a moment he wondered at the curious turns in his life. The crossroads in his life. And the choices he had made. Once again, doubts gnawed. With a wry shake of his grizzled head, he bent down to energetically pull out the persistent weeds cleaving at the roots of the bougainvillea. Weeds were a life-sapping monstrosity, sucking at existence, insidiously killing the plant. Just like doubts. He should know. He had lived with his own for years now.

He sighed. Time for a cigarette. The one luxury he had refused to give up, and roundly cursed the gaggle of doctors who advised him otherwise. He fished out a cigarette from a crumpled packet in his khaki shirt and lit up. With eyes closed he leaned back, and let his vibrant imagination go beck to the past.

He smiled, this man who had been called Manu in that misty-magnificent decade of white-hot passion, a part of him remaining in the convoluted, glorious span when every breath had vibrant life and life held so much meaning.

And then had come the culmination of that meaning. Once again he remembered his paroxysm of rage at the thought of Partition. The desperate strategy. The audacious planning. The flawless execution. Surging hopes drenched in pessimism. And then the triumph. Emphatic, glorious success. India would remain whole. Unbroken. He remembered the thrill of that moment when he knew that he had achieved a feat comparable to that of David. He had defeated the communal Goliath.

But unlike David he had not gone on to become king. Or the trappings that came with it. That power could have been his for the taking. It had been offered by a grateful premier as a gesture of appreciation.

The fact that he had rejected it would be labelled by many as impractical idealism. Certainly his son had thought so, the swelling bitterness of what might have been consuming the affection between them. But idealism had been the natural morality of his times, and he had not regretted the rejection of parasitic power.

The regrets would come later. When the leaders betrayed the dream. When politics became an arena for self-serving manipulators. And ethics became a joke. Then came the sick realisation that the vision of their India had been brokered away by khadi-clad vultures. That the concept of secularism had deteriorated pathetically into a vote-catching trick. That India was slowly, inexorably breaking into hurting segments, helpless under the pitiless weapons of religion, community, sect.

That was when he had realised that by trustingly gifting away power he too had betrayed his country. By abdicating his inheritance he had allowed the political jackals to stake a claim.

His were the sins of omission but nevertheless they were sins. His and of countless others of his ilk. Freedom fighters who had untiringly fought for years the enemy without. But were myopic about the enemy within. They had been the tigers of their turf. If hyenas now ruled, they were equally culpable.

Manu came back to reality. Shrugged away the past with a pang. The anger had come too late. The years had whisked away the leaders who had known him. And the rebel in him had been lulled by the tedium of the mundane. It had been easy to sway with the tide, let it all go.

And later it had become too dangerous.

The right-wing elements had always been there, espousing rabid, narrow theories of dissension and hatred. But in the last few years a disturbing trend had emerged. Slowly groups were slinking in from the fringe, infiltrating the mainstream, gaining increasing acceptance, progressive power. And that was the menace. His act in 1947 was like the fable of the blind men and the elephant.

Perception depended on perspective. And all of them dangerous to the unity of the nation.

For the insidious two-nation theory was not defunct, merely somnolent. The communal genie was bottled but not dead. And so Manu had to remain in the shadows, his identity and his work hidden from most except a trusted few. It was essential for the subcontinent that the genie stayed supine.

India could not afford to uncork this particular genie.

It was nearly two hours later that two men came on a motorcycle. Thin, ordinary, nondescript. Common men with common faces. And their job, common enough not to arouse suspicion.

Politely they told the servant who opened the door, 'We are from the Election Commission conducting a survey for the coming elections. May we talk to the owner, please?'

The servant frowned, 'Well, sahab has gone out.'

Their faces duly registered disappointment. They had let Altaf Naqvi safely pass them by on the road before entering the farm.

'Oh! Well, is there anyone else we can talk to? We just need some information.'

'Yes. There is Ghosh sahab. Shall I get him?'

'He lives here? Then please do.'

The door was opened again after a few minutes. This time it was an old man. White hair. Strong face with translucent skin. Sharp intelligent eyes behind gold-rimmed spectacles. Wiry, thin frame with traces of latent strength. And when he spoke it was with a clear diction and flawless English.

'Yes? What do you want?'

'We have come for a voter list survey. We wanted to talk to the owner of the house but he has gone out, it seems?'

'Yes, Mr Naqvi won't be back for some time. Can you come later?'

'Well, it is rather a long way. Couldn't you help us? We just need some information which I am sure you can give.'

'I suppose I can. Come in. But may I see your identity card?'

It was swished out instantly.

Manmohan Ghosh carefully surveyed the legend on the little bit of plastic with its official seal. Satisfied, he gave it back and opened the door wider.

'Come into the study.'

The windows were shut, the curtains drawn. Manmohan Ghosh was going to sit down on the settee when there was a rush of movement behind him. Hands covered his mouth. Something sharp touched the back of his neck. A shiver ran through the old spine. But the spirit, as fighting fit as ever, refused to show fear.

'What is the meaning of this?' asked the old man derisively.

'We just need to talk, Mr Ghosh. Just a few answers from you.'

'What do you want to know?'

'Ever heard of an outfit called Hind Mata Sevak Sangh?'

If he was shocked he managed not to show it. His tone was deliberately casual, 'No, I do not. What is it, a new political party?'

'No, a dissident group based in Calcutta during the Independence movement.'

'Oh. Well, ancient history. Sorry I know nothing
about it.'

The move was sudden, sharp. A hand whipped
forward, clutched the front of his cotton shirt, ripped it
downwards. On the bony chest, amongst the meagre
white hair was a delicate splash of colour. A Goddess,
tattooed in delicate colours, colours, girdled in a black
chain.

'Hind Mata,' said the visitor softly. 'The sign which
marked the members of the organisation. That is what
we were told to look for. Now, Mr Ghosh I ask again,
are you a member of the Hind Mata Sevak Sangh?'

The old man stared. Harshly he asked, 'What if I am?
Why do you want to know? Who are you anyway?'

'Never mind that. Answer a few questions please. And
this time you'd better not lie to us.'

'What do you want to know?'

'There was a member of HMSS who went under the
name of Manu.'

Ghosh blinked rapidly, staring in dawning fear at the
harsh face above.

The voice of his interrogator was silky smooth.

'Are you Manu?'

The old eyes were wary.

'Well?' said the man harshly.

There was a pause of deep thought. Eyes narrowed,
the wrinkled face hardened with decision.

'Yes,' confessed Manmohan Ghosh.

The sanctum sanctorum of the CBI Directorate was fast
reshaping itself into a crisis control centre. Constant
phone calls, a relay of messages, hurried consultations.
Arrival of the delegates from the USA? Confirmed. Safe

escort to the hotel? Positive. Delays, fumbles, last minute hitches? Alternatives pre-decided, enforced immediately. The chain of command was clear, responsibilities in proportion to the level of decision-making. Before the day was over, the Indira Gandhi International Airport would be reeling under a continuous wave of unprecedented security.

But that was not the only focus of danger, though it was the major one. Smouldering with yesterday's violence, the city was dangerously susceptible. One spark, and the area could flare up like a box of firecrackers. The police *chowkis* dotting the sensitive zone were on their toes, on red alert for any sign of violence. Their forces strengthened in numbers. Emergency squads on instant call.

The entire CBI office, including the telephone operators and the peons, were feeling the pressure. The air humming with breathless tension. The constant stress, the feeling of being perched right on the edge, with a grandstand view of the apocalypse.

Emergencies sift out the leader from the led, and Parvez Ali Beg was always in his element when he was proving his awesome mettle. In a turbulent world, his was the stable voice of sanity, of control, of authority. In the medley of movement, with the storm raging around him, he was as calm as a saint.

But the teacups and cigarettes had doubled since yesterday.

'Khanna,' he rapped out softly at his junior. 'Have you checked with the Sarai Rohilla police *chowki*? Have they managed to suppress the demonstration?'

'Yes, sir, but they had to put three of the chief demonstrators in jail.'

'Tell them to keep them there. They can be released later. What about Turkman Gate? You told me there could be some incident there?'

'Yes, it seems an old Hindu woman was beaten in the early morning. Tension prevails, reaction could brew. The *chowki* may have to use tear gas in case of violence.'

'Tell them to go ahead. Control at any cost is the mantra today. And Khanna, has that file come from Amritsar Cantonment? About Anees Bakhtiar? If it hasn't, shake them awake. Tell them it's a National Emergency. Tell them anything but see to it that I get that file today.'

'Will do, sir, I will go and put the fear of God in them.'

It was nearly four in the afternoon when Reshma's car turned into the curving path leading to the farmhouse.

She saw a wiry old man walking stick in hand, slowly climbing the three shallow porch steps.

'Excuse me,' she called out, hurriedly stepping out of the car. The old man turned, stared hard at her face.

'Excuse me, I have come to meet Mr Manmohan Ghosh. Are you he?'

'No, I am not. But who are you?'

'I am Reshma Kapoor, sir, I am a journalist.'

'Well?'

'If you are not Mr Ghosh, you must be Mr Altaf Naqvi, Farzana Hussain's grandfather?'

'You know her?'

'Yes, she gave me your address.'

'Oh, I see. Come in then, Manmohan must be inside. You want to meet him? Come in.'

Atul Khanna came in with a thin bunch of papers in his hand.

'This has just been faxed to us. The service record of Anees Bakhtiar. Had to give the Amritsar Cantonment a bit of a shake up to get them cracking.'

'Thanks. Any new development?'

'So far so good. New Delhi's been amazingly peaceful. Don't uncross your fingers though.'

Beg smiled, 'I won't.'

His smile petered out as he read the closely typed papers.

The first few pages were a chronicle of the career of an exceptional officer. The brilliant young scholar who joined the army as a lieutenant and became a captain within a year. An excellent officer with a reputation for being a troubleshooter par excellence. And an ace marksman to boot, having won innumerable trophies in rifle shooting.

With a track record of this sort and glowing commendations from all his seniors, Anees Bakhtiar had been clearly slated for bigger things.

And then an ugly anomaly had insidiously crept in. A year ago, Bakhtiar's boss, Major Sukhbir Bindra, noticed a deviation of behaviour in the star performer of his unit. Prolonged depression. Frequent insubordination. Increased skirmishes with his colleagues. And a violent episode where Bakhtiar had registered an informal protest that he was being subjected to discrimination because he was a Muslim. Unwillingly Major Bindra had put a painful question mark on the record of his favourite junior.

In the last six months Bakhtiar's aberrant behaviour had assumed disquieting undertones. Increasingly he seemed to lose interest in all military activity, except rifle shooting, which he still practised diligently. Irreverent, bitter exchanges with seniors were reported with greater frequency.

As for his leave pattern, the graph was one of acute ascendance. The angry major in fact had thought it fit to note one particular incident when Captain Anees Bakhtiar had taken an unexpected holiday on June 15, the day when he was supposed to attend an important training programme. The reason given was flimsy and unconvincing. His present leave was equally baffling, his excuse doubtful. The Major would have, in fact, turned it down if it had not been for Bakhtiar's insistence, and the plea that it was absolutely urgent. He planned to recommend a reassessment of Anees Bakhtiar when he came back from his unexpected leave.

There was an unusual urgency in Beg's voice when he summoned Atul Khanna to his office. Quiet for once, Khanna responded immediately.

'Yes, sir?'

'You have the phone number of the Amritsar Cantonment?'

'Yes, sir, shall I connect you? To the army PRO?'

'No. To Bakhtiar's immediate boss. Major Sukhbir Bindra, isn't it? Contact him right now.'

The call had to go through two secretaries, the caller's identity and the urgency emphasised before the gruff voice of Major Sukhbir Bindra came through.

'Hullo, Major Bindra here. What can I do for you?'

Atul Khanna matched the curtness, 'The CBI Director, Mr Parvez Ali Beg wants to talk to you. Hold on, please.'

'Major Bindra, I need some information on a priority

basis,' Beg's quiet tones had the kind of authority instinctively understood by the Major.

'What about, sir?'

'About Captain Anees Bakhtiar of your platoon.'

A brief pause. Then, 'What is the nature of the information, sir?'

'I want an exhaustive record of the Captain's absences in the last one year from the Cantonment with the exact dates.'

'Well, we can manage that, though it will take some time to compile it. When do you want it, sir?'

'How about yesterday? This is urgent, Major.'

'Okay then, give me two hours, I will fax it to you.'

'Thank you. And one more favour.'

'Which is?'

'I want you to personally examine every bit of the Captain's belongings, his room, his locker, letters, everything, every tiny scrap.'

The gruff voice rasped with disbelief, 'What! Why, for God's sake?'

'I have my reasons, Major.'

'But what do you expect to find in this search? If I agree to it, that is?'

'Your job is to find anything suspicious, anything out of the way. A diary, some vague jottings, any papers with incongruous information. Anything which smells.'

The voice had hardened with dislike, 'I'm sorry, but I cannot accede to your request. For this I need a definite order from an authorised superior as laid down by the chain of command.'

Beg cut him short with silken sarcasm, 'Would you consider the Home Minister of India a clear enough superior in your decorous chain of command?'

'Yes.'

'Then expect a call from Mrs Farzana Hussain within ten minutes.'

'Just a minute, sir,' said the Major in a shaken voice. I have to follow certain rules, you understand. But if it is that important I will conduct the search personally.'

'And immediately if you don't mind.'

'Yes, sir. Could you please tell me what is so urgent about it? I mean, what should I write in the record as the justification?'

'Put it down as internal security,' said Beg harshly. 'Call it National Emergency.'

With old-world courtesy, Altaf Naqvi escorted Reshma inside, calling for his servant, Leelavati.

She came wiping her hands on her grimy sari, 'Yes, saab?'

'Two cups of tea, please.'

'I will just get it. And saab, Farzana memsaab rang up in the afternoon. It sounded very urgent.'

'What did she say?'

'I don't know, saab, Dada took the call.'

'Well, where is he?'

'In the study. Some guests had come to meet him.'

'Are they still inside?'

'No, they went two hours ago. But he is still in there. I didn't wait to disturb him.'

Naqvi nodded, turned around to smile at Reshma, 'He is in the study. Come.'

Manmohan Ghosh wasn't there. Instead there was only death. Sprawled on the sofa, splashed on the walls, stained on the carpet. The body a cold contorted spasm of violence. The fearful pallor in the rigid, wrinkled face testimony of a vicious painful death. Manmohan Ghosh had been tortured before being slaughtered like a goat – a deep slash on his neck cutting right though to the spinal cord, nearly decapitating him.

Reshma gasped in terror, and stumbled back, bumping into the old man who was as white as the corpse on the sofa, breathing suspended, body rigid with shock. She gulped, clapped her shaking hand to her mouth to stop the uncontrollable scream rising inside her. Touched his arm with cold trembling fingers, 'Mr Naqvi, oh God, Mr Naqvi!'

He shivered to life under her clutching hand. Took a deep breath, pushed her gently away, stumbled towards the sofa where the cold shell of his friend lay. Touching the chalky forehead, he fell to his knees in a helpless gesture, hands in the air, '*La Illaha Ilalha . . .*'

Reshma inched softly ahead, touched the shaking shoulders, 'Who could have done this, Mr Naqvi?'

He did not reply, staring dumbly at the dead man, muttering his prayer like a man possessed.

Painfully Reshma said, 'I'll have to phone the police.'

He raised his head at that, and looked at her, tears streaming down his parched skin. Nodded mutely, took hold of himself. He jerked up, faltered away from the sofa towards a small table near it.

That was when he saw the thin paper, next to the flower vase, fluttering under a paperweight. With narrowed eyes he picked it up and slowly read it. The exclamation which was choked out of him stopped her in the process of dialling, and she looked back with concern.

'What is it, Mr Naqvi? What is written in that paper?'

The look he gave was uncomprehending, ravaged, like a lamb who does not understand its own slaughter.

'Mr Naqvi, what is it?' she asked sharply again, putting the phone down and moving towards him. Stretched out her hand and after a moment's hesitation he handed it over.

In a wobbly whisper she read out the bold words written in black. 'Death to the betrayer of Pakistan. Death to the killer who shattered its dream fifty-four years ago. But we will never give up. Pakistan is ours and we will get it. All traitors will be killed by the sword.' She looked up in shocked comprehension, 'Below it someone has signed Quom-e-Majlis.'

'Quom-e-Majlis,' he took a deep breath, his inherent strength slowly returning. He repeated slowly, 'But why? Why should they kill him?'

'Because they came to know his real identity, perhaps. Act of retribution.'

'His real identity? What do you mean by that?'

'Mr Naqvi, I know something about Manmohan Ghosh. He was Manu, wasn't he? From Hind Mata Sevak Sangh?'

He stared, 'What! Who told you that?'

Her face softened and she touched his arm gently, 'I know a few other things which he kept a secret from the world. The fact that fifty-four years ago he wrought a miracle. I don't know how he managed it, but he did. He stopped Partition.'

Slowly he said, 'You know Manu was instrumental in that? How do you know? Not many people do.'

'It's a story I have been following for some days now. Today I got some information which pointed very clearly to the fact that Manmohan Ghosh was Manu. This murder affirms my suspicion. But it is too late for me, for him, for the nation. Damn, how could they kill an old man like this so savagely!' she said disjointedly. 'We must phone the police.'

'Not from here, I think. If I know anything about police investigation, we are supposed to leave things untouched,' he said.

'Okay. Then where?'

'Come to the library.'

The library was a beautiful symmetrical room, deeply etched with the personality of its owner – calm, serene, yet bright. 'Shall I call?' she asked jerkily.

'No, sit down. I will. It's my duty.'

She did not argue the point, tried to sit but found herself unable to remain stationary. She got up restlessly, and went towards the shelf of books automatically, took out a tome and flipped it open. A blue inland letter caught her attention, and quietly she read the contents.

The ambulance wailed along the dirt tracks followed by two police jeeps, the speeding procession garnering curious attention on its way. Certainly it more than caught the eye of the man perched atop a motorbike a little way from Naqvi's farm. He waited only to make sure that the black convoy turned into Naqvi's farmhouse before taking out a mobile phone from his pocket and punching a few buttons.

'Hullo,' he said gruffly. 'Vishwas here. I want to speak to Govindji.'

'What about?' snapped the voice from the other end.

'About kicking your ass. This is damn urgent you idiot! Now do you want to call him?'

'Okay, okay.' A few seconds later Gunaji came

through. A slightly irritated Gunaji, 'What is it, Vishwas? I'm in a meeting here.'

'Sorry, sir, this is important.'

'Well, what is it?'

'I followed Reshma Kapoor to a farm in Mehrauli. She went inside half an hour ago and hasn't emerged yet. But two minutes ago, an ambulance and two police jeeps went inside the farm.'

Gunaji's voice sharpened with interest, 'Have they indeed? Why?'

'Can't find that out, sir. I thought maybe you could.'

'How would I be able to do that?'

'Well, the assistant police commissioner is your friend.'

Gunaji cut him short, 'I will call him, and call you back. And give me the exact address of this farmhouse. The assistant commissioner will require that.'

'Here it is – Altaf Naqvi, 2210 . . . .'

After exactly nine minutes, the mobile phone came alive. Eagerly Vishwas took the call, hoping it was Gunaji with some information. It was. And a very excited Gunaji at that. 'A murder, Vishwas,' he said rapidly, words rolling over one another energetically. 'The daylight murder of a man called Manmohan Ghosh. Did you get the name? Did you understand?'

'Manmohan. You mean Manu? He was Manu? You mean Manu was killed?'

'Looks like it, doesn't it?'

'If it's true, it's terrible news, Govindji. Your plan of using him in the revival of Hinduism crumbles.'

'Not so. In fact this could benefit us more. Do you know who are his killers?'

'Who?'

'A paper was found which clearly says that the Quom-e-Majlis accepts responsibility. Now if this is true, I can exploit it to the hilt. Used strategically, the information is pure dynamite which will kick-start Hindu sentiments in the right gear.' He ruminated thoughtfully, 'Okay, Vishwas, you keep a check over there. I'm coming along immediately. Sit tight.'

The phone call from Beg came when Farzana was in the midst of a cabinet meeting and it took some amount of insistence on his part to get through to her. In the background he could hear voices, and identified one of them faintly as that of the Prime Minister. From the raucous sounds, the meeting was vituperative to say the least.

'Parvez, can this wait for fifteen minutes?' snapped Farzana impatiently.

'No, it can't. It's about Manmohan Ghosh. Your grandfather's friend.'

She said caustically, 'And this is more important than an impending national crisis? What about him?'

'He is dead. Killed. At your grandfather's farm in Mehrauli. By the Quom-e-Majlis. Important enough?'

For a long tortuous moment there was silence while the background cacophony continued. Then Farzana said in a strangled tone, 'My God! But why?'

'Because they discovered that he was Manu. Avenging history. You know the story. Reshma told you this morning.'

This time the silence seemed to stretch for an everlasting span. Thinly she whispered, an unusual fear lacing her words, 'They killed him because he was Manu? Oh my God! What about my Nanu! Is he okay?'

'Yes, physically speaking, yes.'

'Mentally too. Nanu is tough as nails. He is there at the farm?'

'Along with Reshma. And by now the police.'

'Look Parvez, I can't leave this meeting and go there immediately. Do you think you can?'

'I'll send my best troubleshooter immediately,' he promised. 'Another murder by the Majlis is bad enough. If the newspapers get to know the Manu angle as well, it will be a disaster.'

'Yes, I know. God! That cannot be permitted. I never knew. I never understood. Nanu, dear God! I will talk to the police commissioner right now. This has to be hushed up. At all costs. You understand Parvez? At any price.'

Thirteen

Atul Khanna reached the Mehrauli farmhouse at about the same time as Govind Gunaji sailed in though the door, doing nothing to improve Khanna's temper.

'Oh, hell!' snarled the troubleshooter supreme of the CBI.

Welcome to one big royal mess, thought Khanna viciously as he strode up the porch, impatiently showing his ID card to the cop stationed there. 'How did you allow Govind Gunaji to go inside? Weren't you given instructions that no one should be allowed to enter?' he asked the young man coldly.

'Yes, sir, but how could I stop him?'

'Why, is he your *chacha*?'

'No, sir, but he is an important man and important men have great reach,' said the cop simply.

'God bless you, son, you will go far,' said Khanna

wryly, and walked, in uncertain of what he was walking
in on.

Within ten minutes he knew that if the whole thing had
not been so dreadfully tragic he would have been
pardoned for assuming that he had strayed into a
melodramatic Parsi play. In one corner a dead body lay
sprawled on the sofa, surrounded by a group of police
officers busy with the mechanics of a murder
investigation. The effect of melodrama was heightened
by the fact that Govind Gunaji, flanked by two suitably
feral acolytes, had chosen the centre of the room to
have a vociferous argument with the inspector. He wants
the spotlight, thought Khanna derisively as Gunaji
informed the inspector in no uncertain terms his opinion
of uncooperative officials, and hinted at dire retribution.
The inspector, riled by these bullying tactics, and buoyed
up by strict instructions from the police commissioner,
had managed to hold his ground till then.

'We cannot allow your photographer to take pictures
of the victim, sir,' he said sharply. 'This is a murder
investigation, not a political circus.'

'Political circus, huh? You don't know what a political
circus I can make this into. Let me just call a few
newspaper and television offices.'

Oh-oh, grimaced Khanna, this is where I come in.

'Just a minute, Mr Gunaji,' he said quietly, stepping
forward for the first time.

Rankled by the interruption, Gunaji looked around,
stared at Khanna from head to foot. 'What is it?' he snapped.

'I want to know what is your interest in this
unfortunate murder. Why should a politician of your
stature interfere in police matters?'

'You want to know, do you? Well, I want to know who the hell you are,' snarled Gunaji.

Khanna once again whipped out his ID card and waited patiently as Gunaji keenly scanned it, 'Okay, so you are the blue-eyed CBI man. So what?'

'So my question holds. I will not ask you how you knew about the murder, though it is curious to say the least. But I would like to know the reason for your interest in a shocking but apolitical tragedy.'

'This murder is very much connected with politics, and I think you know it. If this was really an ordinary murder I wouldn't have seen a CBI wonder boy descending on the scene, now would I?'

Khanna chose to ignore the question, 'Mr Gunaji, why don't you tell me your exact interest in this affair? I may be able to help, you know.'

Gunaji glared for a fulminating second, then suddenly nodded.

'All right. I will. I have information that this man has been killed by the Quom-e-Majlis.'

'That is yet to be verified. Moreover, the murder could be for entirely personal reasons. Do you know how many people are daily murdered in the city just for greed? These could have been thieves trying to hide under nebulous political creeds. Why should the Majlis murder a harmless old man?' Khanna was provoking, probing, trying to get under his skin. Just how much did the wily fox really know?

Gunaji said pedantically, 'He was not just a harmless old man. Fifty-four years ago he did something which makes him a hero in my eyes. But I am sure the Majlis does not share my views. For them he was the man who killed their dream. It's not amazing that they exterminated him.'

'Excuse me, Mr Gunaji,' said Khanna with polite scepticism. 'This is reality, not some thriller. Exactly what are you talking about?'

Gunaji's eyes narrowed in anger, 'I am talking about the fact that Manmohan Ghosh was Manu of the Hind Mata Sevak Sangh. Do I need to say any more?'

'Manu? I don't understand.'

'Mr Khanna, please don't consider me a simpleton. Anyway, whether you really do not know or are simply lying does not concern me. The story of Manu's life and Manu's death belongs to the nation and that's where it will reach.'

Khanna swore impiously. 'All right, I grant you we know something about the man's role in 1947. But there is no evidence to prove that Manmohan Ghosh was that man,' he pointed out.

'That is the reason I have come here,' said Gunaji softly. 'To get that evidence.'

'And how do you propose to do that?'

'From Manmohan Ghosh's friend, Mr Altaf Naqvi. I want to talk to him. He will confirm the truth.'

'He is in shock right now. Maybe after a day or two?'

'Which will give you a chance to tell him your brand of truth? Either you let me talk to him now or I go to the press. You decide.'

It took Khanna about a blink of a second to do that, 'I will have to ask my boss about this. Excuse me for just a minute.' Imperceptibly he signalled to the inspector, and the message was received and understood. While Khanna was on his mobile phone, Gunaji would not be allowed to go out of the room.

The news of Gunaji's entry into the macabre mix of politics and murder managed to jangle even the cold nerves of Beg. He heard Khanna quietly, then rasped, 'Give me some time here to find a solution. Can you hold the war horse for a while?'

'Not long, sir, he is raring to go.'

'Okay, twenty minutes? You can manage that?'

'Yeah, that I can. I hope.'

'Good.'

Beg put down the receiver, and without bothering to ask his secretary to dial, punched a few numbers.

'Mrs Hussain, please. This is Parvez Ali Beg.'

'The cabinet meeting is . . . .'

Beg cut him short, 'This is an emergency. Immediately, if you don't mind.'

When Farzana came on the phone, you could have touched the tension in her voice, coming through metres of wire.

'Yes, Parvez? What is it?'

'The Manmohan Ghosh murder. A serious development.'

'What?' she asked sharply. 'My grandfather?'

'No, he is okay. But Govind Gunaji is on the scene.'

'You mean in person? But how? Why?'

'He knows about Manu. And he wants to use Manu for his rightist propaganda. Publicise Manu's contribution in 1947 to the whole nation.'

The silence stretched, became unbearable.

'Oh God. Let me think.'

It was a while before she spoke again. And it was the crisp, decisive voice of a mind made up.

'Okay Parvez, leave this to me. I can see only one way out of the mess.'

'After fifteen minutes we will have to let Gunaji talk to your grandfather. To get evidence about Manu being an alter ego of Manmohan Ghosh.'

'That's okay, let him go ahead and talk to Nanu. God willing, five minutes is all I need.'

She disconnected the call and quickly made another call. For a few minutes she whispered urgently into the receiver and then a grateful look came into her face. When she came back to the committee meeting, she looked tense, her eyes filled with disquiet.

'What is it, Farzana?' anxiously asked Prime Minister Shiv Charan Shukul, expecting another disaster, dreading it. 'What is the matter?'

'Well, there was a bit of a complication, I'm afraid. Under control now, I believe. But you need to know about this immediately. The cabinet needs to know.'

'Go ahead,' he said.

With a deep breath she started, 'The genesis of this problem lies not in the present but in the past. Fifty-four years back to be precise.'

Altaf Naqvi was no longer in shock. He had been, an hour earlier, but that is time enough to recover for those made of sterner stuff. If there was a white line around his lips, and a slight quiver in his fingers, one could overlook that in a seventy-five-year-old man who had recently witnessed the brutal murder of his dearest friend. But the fighting light was back in his eyes and his backbone was once again stiff.

It took an apologetic Khanna ten minutes to make his request.

It took Naqvi half a minute to assent. No, he had no objection to seeing the supremo of the Arya Andolan Sabha.

When Govind Gunaji came in, he saw a seventy-odd-year-old man with a patrician face and a firm chin.

Easy target, he exulted silently. 'Mr Naqvi, I am Govind Gunaji. Maybe you know about me?'

If Gunaji was expecting any gratified enthusiasm at the announcement, he was going to be disappointed.

Casually, almost contemptuously, the old man said, 'I have heard about you.'

'Well, anyway, can I talk to you? It's something important.'

'Yes, you can.'

Gunaji looked at the slim girl siting quietly in a corner. This had to be Reshma Kapoor, 'Maybe we can be alone .'

'The girl stays. She is someone I think I can trust,' Naqvi pointed out with meaning.

Gunaji narrowed his eyes, then looked at Khanna. Before he could say a word, Khanna preempted him crisply, 'Forget it, Mr Gunaji, I am staying too.'

With a glare, Gunaji accepted the inevitable, shrugged, and sat down on the sofa opposite Naqvi.

'First of all, let me offer my condolences.'

'Please,' the formal platitudes were quietly rejected.

'All right then. I wanted to talk to you about a slice of history. Pertinent history.'

One thing Farzana Hussain could not have complained about was getting the attention of the colleagues. They listened avidly to the saga of Manu, their expressions ranging from the unbelieving to shocked.

'I don't believe this! This Manu, he stopped Partition? Arrant nonsense,' said Mushtaq Peerzada, the Minister of Agriculture.

Softly countered S. Aravindan, 'It may not be nonsense, but I don't think we need to get all worked

up about it. You say there is no concrete evidence to
support the story. And the only person who could have
provided the proof, the person who is thought to be
Manu, has been killed. That means that the story cannot
be substantiated.'

Farzana shrugged, 'Histories like these are awkward.
The truth can be kept hidden for a long time but once
a single link is discovered, it's not too difficult to go
right back to the source. If the story is made public,
naturally there will be pressure to discover the core.
Witnesses may come forward. Secret papers may come
out of the shadows. And can you imagine what kind of
holy mess that may create?'

If Shiv Charan Shukul had not been the
Prime Minister of India, you would have said he
shuddered.

He said, dully, 'Yes, I can. With Muslims claiming
rank betrayal. And Hindus crowing with satisfaction. The
divide would widen, the country would become a
tinderbox ready to be ignited by communal passions, and
Pakistan would once again beckon from the edge. God,
I can well imagine what would happen! What do we do,
what is the solution? You said that it is under control. In
what way?'

Farzana leaned back calmly, 'We tell the true story.'

Altaf Naqvi was angry, 'You want to talk history? At this
moment?'

'It also happens to be the cause of your friend's
murder. So I did think you might be interested.'

Naqvi's voice became ice-cold as once again heat
surged through him. And with it hatred, revulsion and
venom.

'I would like to know about your interest in all this first.'

'It's very simple. Appalling injustice has been done to your friend. He belongs to history for the one single extraordinary act he performed. And yet he was relegated to the shadows of political power. It's ironic that Indian history does not mention the name of that supreme sculptor who kept the country's face intact, flawless. Now this is inequitable. Reparation should be made. Will be made. By me. I will bring to his name its much deserved glory. And his killers will be caught and punished. My word to you.'

'I see. And as you are not exactly a social worker, what do you ask in return for this munificence?'

'Nothing, absolutely nothing. A great Hindu, a great Indian should be honoured, even if it is posthumously. I will talk and India will listen. He will take his place belatedly amongst the great men of India. And to accomplish this I need details of the life of Manmohan Ghosh and how he achieved the impossible.'

'I suppose I should act ignorant at this point, but I won't. We are discussing 1947 now?'

'Yes. And the fact that he prevented an ugly event from happening. I am curious – how did he manage it?'

'Well, I would be curious to know about it too. When you find out, tell me,'

'Mr Naqvi, this is not a joke. He must have told you! You were his closest friend! Don't try to convince me otherwise. I won't believe you.'

'This is democracy, not a theocracy, not yet. Believe what you want.'

'Manmohan Ghosh is a man who should have the

gratitude and homage of the whole nation. I request you – help me in achieving that.'

Altaf Naqvi straightened up in slow motion, like an old imperial lion, seething in outrage, 'So that you can squeeze out extra weightage for yourself in the coming elections? Divide the nation further on communal lines? We have already wasted over fifty years of independence in hackneyed political philosophies and unworkable theories. So much blood has been lost, so much time. And it is always the politicians who manipulate events. Play mindless games. Ruthlessly converting frustrations into a vote bank. It's pathetic.'

'It's politics,' shrugged Gunaji.

'At the time of Independence, politics meant leadership. Sacrifice. Not a sick excuse to exploit. Divide and rule, that shameful legacy of the British is still alive and kicking, courtesy the sharks in power.'

Gunaji was on a slow fuse to fury, 'I have not come here to discuss politics with you, Mr Naqvi. If you want to give me information about Manmohan Ghosh, good. If not, well, I will get it by other means. It's not difficult to get facts once one knows where to tap.'

'How can you get at facts which do not exist? You could fabricate truth but I would not let you do that either. You try selling lies to the country and I will prove them to be lies.'

'I will go deep into this. Get evidence confirming that Manu was Manmohan Ghosh. As for the fact that he was the man who kept the country from breaking into two, well, I suppose it is difficult to get such proof. But I know enough of the story to convince the public.'

Naqvi smiled thinly, 'My dear sir, you are off tangent

on your basic assumption. Forget anything which happened later, you will not be able to prove that Manmohan Ghosh was Manu.'

'And why is that, may I know?'

'Because he wasn't Manu.'

Shiv Charan Shukul was bewildered, 'What do you mean, true story?'

'The real identity of Manu.'

'You mean it is not Manmohan Ghosh?'

'No.'

'How can you be so sure about that?'

'I am.'

Aravindan frowned, 'Well, Farzana, let's assume it is not Manmohan Ghosh, but someone else. How will that help us? Gunaji will be able to use him just as well, better in fact if this one is alive.'

'He is alive.'

Shukul shrugged helplessly, 'I see Aravindan's point, Farzana, and it's a valid one. What difference will the real identity of Manu make as far as the political situation is concerned?'

Farzana smiled, 'Oh, revealing the identity of Manu will completely shatter Gunaji's dream. Gunaji automatically assumed that Manu was a Hindu. Anything else is impossible in his limited view. But suppose he finds out that Manu is actually a Muslim? That would turn the whole thing on its head, wouldn't it?'

'Again I ask, how do you know all this?'

'Because I know who the real Manu is.'

'And who is he?'

Calmly she said, 'Altaf Manawwar Naqvi. My grandfather.'

Gunaji missed his beat for just a moment before gathering fire. He quipped, cynically, 'Manmohan Ghosh is not Manu? You honestly expect me to believe that?'

'If you find truth unpalatable, that's your prerogative. But he wasn't Manu and I am telling you this in a charitable spirit. So that you don't waste your time skirmishing with ghosts which never existed.'

'I suppose you will claim that he wasn't a member of the Hind Mata Sevak Sangh, that there was no Manu anyway, and so the question of his role in Partition does not arise?'

'No, I would not say that. Yes, he was a member of the HMSS and a very ardent one at that. Yes, there was a Manu in the HMSS, and he played his role on the stage of 1947. Where you have gone wrong is in blindly assuming that Manmohan Ghosh was Manu.'

'Really?' Gunaji was openly sceptical. 'Then maybe you will tell us who was?'

Altaf Naqvi settled back comfortably in his chair, a look of victory spreading over his lined face. He said, softly, 'I am.'

The shock was like a wet blanket. Gunaji gasped, Reshma stared, Khanna almost choked. And it was only after a few breathless seconds that Gunaji snapped, 'I don't believe you.'

'I told you – that is your problem, not mine. However, I am prepared to substantiate my claim in public, with any number of proofs confirming without a shadow of doubt that I, Altaf Manawwar Naqvi, was known as Manu in my position as a member of the Hind Mata Sevak Sangh.'

The old man bent forward, softly tapping Gunaji on

the knee, 'And now, Gunaji, take me around the country. Let everyone know that one Muslim kept the nation together. That patriotism is not the prerogative of any particular sect, caste, or religion. That India belongs to all Indians who love their country. Go ahead, Gunaji, you wanted to honour Manu, didn't you? Can you do that now? Proclaim that a non-Hindu secured the Aryan dream of a united India?'

Gunaji was never at a loss for words. Today he was.

Naqvi shrugged, 'I pity you, you know, I really do. Manu could have been a brilliant strategy on your part, to build up support in the coming elections. You never expected that he could be a Muslim. Now you have the difficult task of fitting this strange fact within your parochial parameters. The game is lost, Gunaji, don't you think? For once, it's advantage India.'

The long plush car was speeding down the road when the buzzing of a mobile phone broke its owner's reverie. The call was received. No identification was asked, for none was needed. The conversation was brief and crisp. Why this intolerable delay in reporting?

The caller apologised and said they were covering their flanks. They thought it prudent to remove themselves to Agra for a while. Yes, the mission had been accomplished. Identity had been confirmed, with a confession. The execution carried out as planned. No, there was no room for doubt.

The mobile phone was switched off and a look of satisfaction swamped the taut face for a moment. Honour had been restored, anger satiated. The destroyer of Pakistan was dead, and with that thought the burning fire of hatred within subsided.

Now his thoughts could once again turn towards the conspiracy reaching its crest. To the unfolding of the last urgent move of the manoeuvre.

A slow, judicious tempo of violence had to be built up, to end in its logical conclusion. The crescendo had to be sharp, horrific. The act so unthinkable, of such extreme ugliness that immediate revulsion would swamp the nation, grip it with paranoia, and make it shudder.

And this fear would then become the key to their entry into the folds of the Quom-e-Majlis. The mild elements would be kicked to a corner and he, as the master-planner, would be awarded the mantle of Muslim leadership. When parochial obsession rages, patriotism takes a back seat. The idea of Pakistan would be embraced. And thousands would willingly join the Majlis.

The symphony was one of synergy. The composition was perfect. Now the aria had to be flawless. So much depended on Anees Bakhtiar. On his hatred, his passion, and his marksmanship. The final denouement was about to begin. It was a story of hatred, so much of it. For her and for the system which made her do it. That thought would make him press the trigger tomorrow without the slightest hesitation.

He kept the gun down on the table beside him, took another deep swig of cola and then pushed the glass away. He lay down quietly on the narrow bed, hands cushioning his head, eyes closed in quest of sleep. He would not think of Reshma lying in the hospital, huddled, white, shivering and penitent. He had not forgiven her then and he could not forgive her now. Instead he would go over the details of his plan once again. Plan his movements minutely. The finale of his vengeance would

start tomorrow. He glanced at the calendar on the wall
on which he had marked the following day in black. A
significant date for all Indians – August 15, 2001. India's
fifty-first Independence Day!

That simple fact was giving sleepless nights and
nightmarish mornings to everyone whose job it was to
ensure internal security in the country. Even Parvez Ali
Beg seemed affected as he snapped at his secretary, 'Any
call from Khanna yet?

'No?'

'Well, contact him then, can you, please?' He turned
to the man sitting opposite him, a senior officer of the
Bureau, 'Sharma, life is hell. If tomorrow goes without
incident I swear I am going off for Haj. In deep
reverence to Allah for having just about saved my sanity.'

Beni Prasad Sharma, affectionately called Big Ben, was
known for his natural gloom as no one had ever seen
him smile. Belonging to Uttar Pradesh, twenty-five years
of service in the CBI had not made him stop oiling his
hair or chewing tobacco, and given him a jaundiced view
of life in general and crime in particular. He suspected
everything under the sun as a matter of habit and that,
combined with a bewilderingly logical mind, had made
him the best analyst of the Bureau.

Wallowing as he did in pessimism, he was evidently in
his element.

'The PM's speech in the morning,' he said with
extreme despondency, and you could see from his face
that he would be surprised if it was not marked by
'incidence'.

'And if that goes off in reasonable calm, there is the
opening of the Conference scheduled in the afternoon.'

So there wasn't much chance that Delhi would escape unscathed, said his lugubrious expression.

The phone rang and Beg picked it up with alacrity. It was Atul Khanna.

'Khanna, thank God, what's happened?'

'Plenty. All of it surprising.'

'Has Gunaji had his talk with Naqvi?'

'Oh yes, still talking, as a matter of fact.'

'Well, then what's the bottom line? Are we still in control or not?'

'If you call just about managing to prop up a teetering edifice control, then yes, we are.'

'Why, what's happened?'

'Oh nothing much, sir. Except that Govind Gunaji has been delivered a whammy and has yet to recover from it.'

'What do you mean?'

'Altaf Naqvi claims that Manmohan Ghosh was not Manu.'

'Really?'

'Yes. And then comes the punch line. He claims he is.'

'What! Are you telling me that Altaf Naqvi is this Manu whom Reshma was trying to unearth? The one who stopped Partition?'

'I'm not, he is. I am just relating what he stated.'

'Could he be lying?'

'Why should he? Moreover, he is prepared to prove it with evidence, in the right quarters.'

Beg gave a thoughtful whistle, 'But this changes things doesn't it? At least as far as Gunaji is concerned.'

'Yes, sir, it does. The last I saw him, which was five minutes ago, he was still blustering about proving Naqvi's lies, but you could see that the fight had gone out of him. The last thing he needs is a Muslim whose profoundly patriotic act would disprove all Gunaji's pet theories.'

'Hmm. Okay. Khanna, I don't want Naqvi to stay there under the circumstances. Mrs Hussain's house would be the safest place for him right now.'

'I already suggested that. He doesn't want to budge from here. Says he can take care of himself.'

'Well, he will simply have to change his mind then. Insist, and if necessary, force him. I don't want any more incidences.'

'Right on, sir, thy will be done.'

'And Khanna, is Reshma Kapoor still there?'

'Yeah, she's here. You want to talk to her? Just a minute.'

A few seconds of static and then came on a familiar voice.

'Yes, Uncle?'

'You know the whole – about Naqvi's identity?'

Her voice was quiet, 'Yes, I was present when he said that.'

'Okay, I want to know one thing. You will admit it is curious that the Quom-e-Majlis latched on to the Manu story almost at the same time as Gunaji. Frankly, the coincidence is too much for me to digest.'

'For me too.'

'So if we discard chance, then the only possibility is that they got the information from a source. You?'

'I don't think so. I never told anyone the detailed story of my research except you, Zahera *Maasi* and . . .' her voice petered out with uncertainty.

'Yes? You told someone else too, didn't you?'

'Well, yes, Professor Satyen Sengupta.'

'Ah! One mystery solved then. Gunaji got his facts from the good professor. But how did the Majlis get to know about it?'

'I really don't know, Uncle. I didn't tell anyone else, I promise. Maybe *Maasi* might have.'

'I have already asked her and the answer is a definite no. Think hard Reshma, this could be important. Who else did you tell?'

'Well . . .' hesitantly she said.

'Yes?' he responded sharply. 'You did tell someone else, didn't you?'

'I did, but really that's hardly relevant in this context.'

He interrupted quietly, 'Let me be the judge of that. Whom did you tell?'

'Why, Farzana Hussain, of course!'

Through the swirling smoke Beg's face was a study in concentrated thought, busy as he was in mental callisthenics. Slowly the puzzle was falling in place. Piece by piece a pattern was forming. In frustration Beg stubbed his cigarette. The net was closing in silently. Its silken threads hiding an ugly truth he instinctively knew, but could not spell out. Not right now. But he was near, he knew that. He was very near the truth! One bit of inspiration and he could unravel it. He stared at the silent phone, willing it to ring, impatiently waiting for Major Sukhbir Bindra's call. How long did it take to search a Captain's quarters? The Major should have reported by now.

In the meanwhile, he had another puzzle to solve. Was it remotely possible that Farzana Hussain was the information conduit about Manu? Perhaps inadvertently telling the story to a covert Majlis member?

But Farzana was an incisive, clever woman, not an impulsive babble mouth. Where were his thoughts leading him?

The phone rang. It was Major Bindra, crisper than ever, 'Sir, I personally went through Captain Anees Bakhtiar's belongings.'

'And?'

'Well, the only thing I found that could fall under the sphere of 'interesting' is a folder with some personal photographs and newspaper cuttings. Perhaps there may be something significant in them for you. Should I send them with a courier tomorrow?'

'No! That would be too late! I need it sooner than that!'

'Just a minute,' Beg could hear a whispered conference before Bindra came back on the line. 'This is a National Emergency you said?'

'Yes.'

'Right. My courier will leave by a special car immediately. What is the time now? 7.15 p.m.? You will get the folder by 2.30 in the morning.'

'Thanks. In my office please. I will be waiting. And what about Bakhtiar's absence schedule of the last one year? Is that ready?'

'Yes, my assistant is faxing that to you right now.'

For once Beni Prasad Sharma 'Big Ben' had shed his sad face. The big boss had summoned him double quick, and from his voice it was vitally important. He literally ran into the office in his urgency.

'Yes, sir,' he asked anxiously.

'Sharma you have one crucial job to do. Amritsar Cantonment is sending a fax which details certain timespans. I want you to match these with the violent incidences of the previous year. See if they match. Compare them carefully and report to me.'

'What are these concerned with?'

'Leave of absence of a Captain Anees Bakthiar.'

'Tell me no more, sir, I understand I think. I will get on with it immediately.'

He reported within fifteen minutes. In six instances the time-period corresponded.

What was the possibility of this being a coincidence?

One in a million.

And when was the last matching time-span?

The FINCOM bomb blast in Karachi.

Prognosis?

Guilty, unless proven innocent.

It was time to take preventive, precautionary action, decided Beg. He picked up his hotline to the Police Commissioner, P.V. Krishnan, normally the most genial of policemen, today on edge, 'Yes, Beg, what is it?'

'A request. An urgent one.'

'All your requests are urgent. What is it this time?'

'I need information about a Captain Anees Bakhtiar. Priority status.'

'On what grounds?'

'Suspicion of dangerous dissidence. Could be an assassin by ideology.'

'They are the most unpredictable of all.' A deep sigh and then, 'Do you have any possible location in mind?'

'Yes, Delhi University and the surrounding area.'

'On what basis?'

'He was seen jogging in that area.'

'And a man, even an impassioned extremist, does not stray miles from his residence for a jog,' accepted Krishnan. 'Right. Photograph? Description?'

'My man will come to you immediately with mug-shots and a detailed profile.'

'Okay, I will do what I can. Spread the word to my informers in the area. And send a few men to scout around. Would this man be armed?'

'Not only armed, but he is an expert marksman.'

'Wonderful. What's life without excitement? Keep you posted on developments.'

There was no sleep that night for the Director of the CBI or his assistants. Beg was frantic with a nameless fear gnawing at him. A sixth sense warning him of a colossal tragedy about to take place the next day. Time, as fickle as ever, was running out, and disaster was grinning from the shadows. One lead, one miracle, one inspiration – that's all he needed to stave off the danger. God, if only he could get it, and that too in time. Tomorrow might be too late. For him, for India.

If excitement is contagious, fear is even more so. Beni Prasad Sharma, more gloomy than ever, decided to camp out at the office for the night. And Atul Khanna refused to budge too, pointing out validly that with Big Ben around, the boss would need his sunny personality to counteract the gloom. The two of them literally forced Beg to take a catnap on the comfortable office sofa while they kept vigil.

It was 2.15 in the morning when Khanna tiptoed in. He found his boss in slumberland, snoring softly. He shook him awake, 'Sir, the folder has arrived. You want to take a look?'

Ten minutes later, Beg, Khanna and Big Ben were
carefully going through the mixed bag Bindra had sent.
It seemed like a composite of a man's whole life. The
entire existence of Captain Anees Bakhtiar was there,
fragmented in myriad manifestations. Photographs, letters,
newspaper cuttings.

Khanna said wryly, 'For all that he is a renegade, the
guy seems to be a regular romantic. Look at this dried
rose, these Valentine cards!'

Big Ben looked up with disapproval, 'We are
interested in finding evidence of conspiracy. Not pry into
the man's private affairs, if you please.'

Calmly Beg interrupted, 'I don't think so, Sharma,
not in this case. From what I suspect, his ill-fated love
affair could be the causative factor of his defection.'

'Oh,' immediately piped up a curious Khanna, 'you
know the heroine in this case, perhaps.'

'Yes, so do you. You met her today – Reshma Kapoor.'

Even if Beg had not disclosed this fact, the
photographs would have. Reshma Kapoor was everywhere,
smiling, frowning, tempestuous. A slim young girl, with
all the mischief of a coquette, and the yearning of a
Juliet there on her face for all to see. Gloriously,
unashamedly basking in her lover's adoration. A seductive
temptress and a shy Madonna in turn. A woman's
incandescent pride in every movement, every expression.
Revelling in the lambent sun of love, yet loving to play
hide-and-seek with it.

The photographs were all of her only, obsessed with
capturing her image in myriad ways.

With one exception.

The picture had been taken in front of a huge tree.
In the coloured snapshot there was Reshma as usual,

laughing, delight in her eyes, a bursting rhythm in her body lines. But it was the man beside her who caught Khanna's attention. A younger, softer face than that in the stiff army mug shot. A slight smile as he looked down on the girl's head. A very ordinary picture. The kind taken by lovers everywhere. What made it startling were the eyes. Molten lava of emotion, helpless worship, intense happiness, single-minded adoration – the camera had managed to capture that fleeting unguarded moment of painful passion. Cruelly slicing through the facade to bare a man's soul to its very depth. Even Khanna, who generally took matters of the heart with a pinch of salt, was startled for a moment. For in those eyes was a world of hunger, an intensity bordering on obsession, a heat which burned through the photo image and could be felt across the divide of years. Anees Bakthiar had not merely loved Reshma. He had been crazily, dizzily, madly in love, the kind of love that may grab one only once in a lifetime, having the capacity to leave one hollow and bereft. Khanna whistled but for once kept quiet. Which was good because even if he had, he wouldn't have got an answer.

A curious expression on his face, Beg was staring at the newspaper cuttings. Sharma too seemed to have noticed it. 'What is it, sir?' quietly he asked. 'Got something?'

Beg looked up with a deliberately blank expression. Without a word he handed over the clipped sheaf of papers to Big Ben. Instinctively Khanna bent over, and both of them peered at it.

If the photographs had all been Reshma's, the newspaper clippings seemed to be dominated by another woman.

The clippings contained a plethora of news, mostly about the Quom-e-Majlis. But three or four concerned the official visits of a powerful woman. A seminar in Karachi. A conference in Rawalpindi. The inauguration of a dam near Jullunder. Press photographs. Crisp journalese. And the quiet effacing presence of her husband by her side. But clearly it was the woman of feline grace who was the epicentre of attention. Her face instantly recognisable everywhere in the country. The Home Minister of India, Farzana Hussain. Sharma looked up, to catch the curious look still on Beg's face.

'What do you make of this, sir?'

'What do you?'

'Well, he does seem to be unusually interested in Farzana Hussain.'

Beg said disjointedly, 'Yes.' Then got up restlessly, went towards the window to look out at the outside gloom, thoughts churning in his mind.

What he was thinking was bizarre! Inconceivable! And yet, was it impossible? Suddenly he turned around.

'Sharma, get that list of Anees Bakhtiar's absences from his Cantonment.'

'I have it here with me, sir.'

'Right. I want you to check the dates of these newspaper cuttings and match it with the list. I want to know whether Bakhtiar could have physically been in those cities on those dates.'

While Sharma pored over the list, Beg remained near the window, his tense fingers clutching at the window frame. And Khanna quietly smoked, not quite getting his boss's drift but definitely preferring to keep quiet.

Sharma quietly spoke up, 'Sir.'

Beg turned with an anxious enquiring look.

'The four dates were in the early part of the year. He was absent from Amritsar Cantonment on all of them.'

'F . . k,' Beg said crudely, startling his juniors, who were not accustomed to hearing him use bad language. Finally, Khanna's curiosity brimmed over, 'I don't get it. Why is the fact so significant?'

'Taken singly – no. Together with a few other facts – maybe.'

'What facts.'

Narrow-eyed, Beg stared at them silently and then snapped, 'Okay, what we discuss now stays strictly within these four walls, understood? This is just a supposition, without any factual base.'

They nodded.

'How did the Quom-e-Majlis come to know about Manu? Apart from me and my wife, the only other Muslim to whom Reshma told the story was Farzana Hussain.'

'So?'

Beg leaned back in his chair worriedly. Then said softly, 'You remember that report on the Quom-e-Majlis? That its visible leaders were mere puppets, manipulated by a master puppeteer. His persona in shadow, his identity secret, revealed only to a few trusted lieutenants. The brain who planned, organised and dominated the whole show?'

'Yes, I remember. But what you are saying? It is unthinkable, sir!'

'In our profession, Sharma, sometimes it is precisely the unthinkable that must be thought of. Why should Bakhtiar keep these cuttings? Why was he absent from his Cantonment on the days when Farzana Hussain was officially visiting nearby cities? It could be dismissed as chance. Or it could have an uglier explanation.'

He was quiet for a moment, then continued, 'Now consider this. A brilliant man has been newly recruited. His talents are awesome, his potential immense. But before trusting him with crucial assignments, it's necessary to gauge the extent of his commitment to the cause. And that can be done only by the shadowy leader. For that, meetings are necessary but that is not easy, especially if the leader is in a vulnerable position. Such men and women are constantly surrounded with security and scrutiny. And if Bakhtiar has been marked for future critical work, he cannot be seen frequently with the numero uno of the Majlis. Someone might remember, someone might put two and two together and make the right connection. For this reason it is better to arrange such parleys during official tours. They have a transient quality about them, and any meeting can be explained.'

Khanna contained this chain of logic, 'So he is invited to certain cities on certain dates. He goes there, these meetings take place, and he comes back more dedicated than before?'

'Yes. And in the new flush of his devotion, keeps cuttings as mementos of meetings which are of immense significance to him. Is there anything illogical about this scenario so far?'

'Frighteningly, no.'

'And yet, how can I believe my own logic? I have known her for three decades! Logic be damned – it just cannot be. There must be some other explanation. I am missing something, some factor, some perception. Or maybe I am becoming senile or paranoid, or both.'

The ring of the phone saved the two from answering

this awkward question, as with alacrity a relieved Atul Khanna jumped to pick it up.

'Sir, for you. The Police Commissioner, Mr Krishnan.'

Beg hurriedly took the receiver from him, 'Yes, Krishnan?'

'We traced your man in a small shanty apartment in Kingsway Camp.'

'Thank God!'

'No, don't be so hasty in thanking anyone yet. He escaped.'

'What! How the hell could that happen?'

'My men tapped quite a few of their sources while enquiring about him. Obviously one of them tipped him off. When they closed in on him, he had flown the nest. One of those things.'

Beg thought fast, the professional accepting the inevitable. These things did happen – it was a part of the game. The only thing left was to salvage all one could.

'Did you search the place? Did you find anything?' he asked tersely.

'Well, yes, a curious piece of paper.'

'What is it?'

'It's an entry pass, Beg, given by government security personnel manning organisations and residences.'

'I see. Which organisation?'

'No, a residence. The time of the visit is 2 p.m. on August 13, 2000.'

'And the address?'

'48, Willingdon Crescent. You know who stays there, don't you?'

After a long pause Beg responded, 'Could you send me this paper right now, Krishnan?'

'Right. My man will come there within ten minutes.'

Beg kept the phone down quietly and turned to Khanna in a daze.

'What is it, sir?' he asked sharply.

'An entry pass has been found in Bakhtiar's room. For 48, Willingdon Crescent.'

Khanna swore, 'The residence of Farzana Hussain.'

Beg nodded abruptly, 'It seems Anees Bakhtiar went to meet her at her residence on August 13, at 2 p.m.'

'Which gives substance to your suspicions.'

'Yes. Earlier it was just a conjecture that Farzana Hussain had a connection with Anees Bakhtiar. This is proof.'

'What are you going to do about it?'

'I don't know. Wait a minute, wait a minute. What was that date and time?'

'August 13, 2 p.m.'

Quietly Beg sat down on the chair, 'But do you know what that means? There is no way that Bakhtiar could have gone to meet Farzana.'

'Why?'

'Because she was in a meeting.'

'Are you sure?'

Beg said wryly, 'I ought to be. I was there too. You see it was a meeting with the police and paramilitary about the security logistics in the face of the bomb blasts.'

It took a moment for Khanna to absorb the fact and rearrange his perception, 'So this means . . . what does it mean?'

From being worried, Beg was suddenly transformed into a tense whirlwind of energy.

'It means we can't lose any more time than we already have. I was blind, stupid! I need to check some facts immediately. Where is that folder of Anees Bakhtiar?'

As Beg pored over the cuttings, Sharma raised his eyebrows at his colleague in tacit enquiry, but Khanna grimaced and shrugged and remained silent. It was only after Beg put the cuttings down, a set look on his face, that Sharma ventured to ask. 'What is it, sir?'

'Sharma, get me Farzana Hussain's personal file, will you?' Beg barked.

'The one in which we keep a detailed record of her private life?'

'Yes.'

Without a word, Sharma got up, and when he came back it was with a brown box file in his hand. Beg snatched it from him with a muttered thanks and once again immersed himself in reading sections from it. After a long period he closed it with a snap, and looked up at the patiently waiting duo. He shook his head in disbelief and said dazedly, 'I have been nine kinds of a fool. Those newspaper cuttings. I ignored the fact that on each of those visits she was accompanied by someone. Get me her residence member, will you? I want to talk to her.'

'It's 4 o'clock in the morning.'

'I know that. Get her, please.'

* * *

Farzana's sleepy slurred voice came instantly awake the minute she realised that it was Beg on the line.

'Parvez? What is the problem?' she queried sharply.

'I need to talk to you urgently.'

'Don't break it gently, give me the bad news right away, please. What's wrong? Another bomb blast?'

Beg said soothingly, 'No, Delhi is calm at present. But we need to talk.'

A hint of impatience was evident in her voice, 'If there is no emergency couldn't this have waited for a couple of hours?'

'No.'

'Okay, so talk,' she snapped.

'Farzana, you remember our findings that there was an unidentified brain behind the Quom-e-Majlis? The director and planner of operations.'

'Yes, I remember. What about him?'

'I think I know who that person is. And it is regarding him that I need to talk. Could I meet you right now?'

'At this ungodly hour? Why? What is this all about? Surely you can tell me on the phone – considering that this line is squeaky clean. Your men 'sweep' it daily.'

'There is such a thing called internal security, Farzana. Who is there in the house with you?'

'Well, Shaukat went to Meerut last night. And Nanu is sleeping in the guest room.'

'I see.'

'So are you going to tell me about this mystery man?'

'I would rather explain the reasons for my belief first. There are complications and it's going to be a shock for you.'

Farzana said patiently, 'Parvez, I trust your judgment. Can you just tell me the name and let me handle the shock?'

'Okay,' Beg was abrupt, 'Your husband, Shaukat Hussain.'

There was a stupefied silence on the other end, deepening with disbelief.

'My husband?' she croaked. 'Are you serious? Is this a joke?'

'No.'

'Then you are out of your mind! Shaukat, mastermind of an outfit like the Quom-e-Majlis? On what basis, Parvez, on what grounds can you possibly make this kind of allegation against my husband?'

'Farzana just listen to me. Let me explain.'

'No!' she cut him short abruptly. 'You were right. I need to hear this in person. With every scrap of evidence on which you are basing such vicious charges. Meet me here in fifteen minutes.'

She banged the phone down.

A small click downstairs signified another ear on the line. The receiver was kept down more gently. And for a long moment the wrinkled face of Altaf Naqvi remained white-faced in shock. Innocence had made him pick up the phone from his bedroom, curiosity made him listen. Now he had to cope with the bizarre.

Parvez Ali Beg was supposed to reach there within fifteen minutes. He made it in thirteen, but spent a few moments interrogating security personnel at the gate. When he finally presented himself at the residence, the door was opened by Farzana herself. She wished him perfunctorily, indicated a seat, and sat down on the opposite chair.

'And now, Parvez, let's have the explanation.'

'Farzana, you must understand one thing. I am going to talk logic, not emotion. You must gauge the evidence the same way.'

She nodded curtly and waited silently.

'When we first came to know of the existence of a secret leader, we drew some conclusions about the man, based on the style and scope of his activities. A rabid right-winger. He also had to be a prodigy of sorts, with connections in high places. A secure financial background was an assumption, as well as a nexus with other moneyed sources because of his talent for keeping the Majlis flush with funds. But what baffled us most was his access to extremely sensitive secrets of the government. It indicated a dangerous proximity to a major power centre.'

'And that power centre has to be me? Why?'

Patiently Beg said, 'Because of other events, other evidence.'

'I am waiting to hear it.'

She listened to the saga of Anees Bakhtiar. And its derivative deductions.

Furiously she snapped, 'Let me get this straight. Just because some fanatic army officer keeps newspaper cuttings of a few of my official visits where my husband accompanied me, that is evidence of his complicity?'

'No, that is an indication of it. And there is more.'

'Like?'

Silently he removed the pink slip from his folder and handed it over to her. 'We found this in Anees Bakhtiar's room.'

She read it carefully and slowly her face whitened.

Beg handed over a register, 'On my way inside I stopped and interrogated the security personnel at your gate. Anees Bakhtiar's visit is listed in the register with his signature. The person he came to meet was Shaukat Hussain. The purpose of the visit – personal.'

Farzana opened the register and read the concerned entry.

'Well, so, okay, he had a visitor called Anees Bakhtiar, who is a suspect. That doesn't make my husband one too.'

'And the suspicious circumstances don't trouble you?'

'There could be an innocent explanation – a businessman has to deal with myriad complications.'

'I told you Farzana – these are just indications. Pointers which made me probe further. I went through the information file we have on you – which naturally includes your husband.'

'I know. You maintain dossiers of this sort on all key people in the government. So? What have you got against Shaukat?'

'History, Farzana,' Beg said quietly. 'Something which you understand well. As *Abba* used to say, history makes its presence felt in some way in the present. Specifically speaking, I found two important factors in Shaukat's past.'

'Which are?'

'His grandfather, the Nawab of Rajapura – do you know he was a staunch blood and gore kind of believer in the Muslim League? His entire faith was wrapped up in the concept of Pakistan?'

'Well, actually I didn't. There was no reason why he should have told me – probably he found it irrelevant. And that should tell you just how apolitical he is.'

'Okay,' Beg nodded, 'but has he told you about his father?'

'What about him?'

'His father, also a fervent acolyte of the Muslim League, died tragically, killed by his Hindu neighbours in the 1947 riots, which followed Nehru's rejection of Partition.'

'I didn't know that. Actually Shaukat told me his father had died in an accident. But, well, perhaps he did not know himself. He must have been a child. He was possibly shielded from the truth and told a fictitious story.'

Beg interrupted quietly, 'He couldn't have been shielded from this truth, Farzana. His father was burned to death in his own house by a group of violent Hindus. And the five-year-old was a witness to the horror.'

Her face blanched, she sat there shell-shocked. With disbelief. With dread. It took her a moment to gather up her faltering faith. 'I will ask him. He will explain why he kept the tragedy a secret from us – from me and Asma. But that still does not constitute irrefutable proof to substantiate your allegations.'

'That is because you are, for once, letting sentiment obscure logic. And that is always dangerous. You should know that, Fazi.' She turned around to look at the only person in the world who called her by that name. Altaf Naqvi was standing in the doorway, a tall man in every way. The wizened face was marked with deep worry. She got up instinctively, went towards him. 'Nanu, you should be sleeping.'

He gently pushed her away and stepped into the room, 'No, I am not going anywhere. Because this concerns you. Because it concerns my country.'

'You don't know anything about this, Nanu!'

'I know enough to know one thing – you may trust Shaukat, I don't. I never did. You know that.'

'That's just because you have an inbuilt prejudice

against any man who doesn't need to work for a living.'

'No, it was more than that. Anyway the discussion has become academic in the face of the evidence put forward by Mr Beg. Don't reject it because of some misguided sense of loyalty.' He turned towards Beg, 'These facts you have come out with, are you reasonably certain they indict Shaukat?'

'Yes.'

'Then, Fazi, you must act accordingly. You are not just Shaukat's wife, you are the Home Minister of India.'

She was still for a moment, then squared her shoulders and nodded starkly. 'All right, I accept you have grounds to suspect my husband, Parvez. Valid grounds, perhaps. You can conduct an enquiry when he comes back. I will accede to that.'

'And when is he coming back?'

'Tomorrow.'

'No!' Beg reacted sharply. 'It will be too late. Because today is to be the culmination of the conspiracy.'

'What makes you think that?' asked Altaf Naqvi.

Beg studied him thoughtfully, 'You are Manu I am told. That in itself gives you the right to ask. Sit down, Mr Naqvi, it's a long story.'

Naqvi had a frown on his face at the end of it, 'You mean you found a calendar in the room in Kingsway Camp in which Bakhtiar had underlined today's date?'

'Yes. Bakhtiar has been appointed as an assassin by the Quom-e-Majlis. But who is the target? I wish to God I knew.'

Farzana asked sharply, 'Why Parvez, didn't you tell me it was Govind Gunaji?'

'No, Farzana, I don't think so. I have my reasons to discount that as a red herring.'

Altaf Naqvi sharply asked, 'But you are, of course, taking due security precautions?'

'Mr Naqvi, you have been a freedom fighter. You ought to know there is no such thing as foolproof protection. A determined killer can always find loopholes to get through to his victim. He has the advantage even when one knows his identity and modus operandi. Can you imagine how helpless security can be when it has to work in the dark? Offhand, I can think of a dozen possible targets of the Majlis. And my force is already stretched to its limit. It's essential that I have some idea about who the supposed victim is – or it's all over and the Majlis has won the game.'

'Another 1947 you mean?' Asked Naqvi softly. 'No! India is on its way to soar in the world arena. We can't let divisive forces eat into our roots!'

'So suggest something.'

Naqvi got up agitatedly, 'It's essential for you to put yourself into the mind of your enemy. Feel his thoughts, tap his ideas. Get a grip on your opponent's reason, then preempt his moves. Lay your traps.'

'Nanu, that was then. Things are more complicated, now, it's not that easy any more,' said Farzana softly.

'That's where you are wrong. Eras change, human nature remains constant. The facade mutates, the inner core doesn't.'

'The Quom-e-Majlis is a ruthless sect of rabid insurgent elements,' pointed out Beg wryly, 'not exactly the type of rebels your generation specialised in.'

'Rebellion is always of the mind, son, you rebel not with swords, or guns, or bombs – but with the anger of your thoughts, with the frenzy of your passion. They are the real incendiaries in any form of insurgency. The rest is merely the means, ineffective without its fountainhead. It is that seed which you have to probe and assess, only then can you offer resistance.'

'Okay, I grant you that. How do I go about it?'

'Understand the blueprint of their strategy. What has the Majlis tried till now? What have they achieved?'

'Obvious, Nanu. Fear, retaliation, communal tension.'

Naqvi shook his head impatiently, 'No, that is the symptom of the disease. The real sickness goes deeper. Polarisation, Fazi, they have managed to polarise two coexisting communities. You must have read, communal riots are breaking out already in different parts of the country, anger is deepening, as is suspicion. It's an untenable situation for both. An ambiguous status quo.'

'All right, so where do they go from there?' asked Beg

'If I was a Majlis man, at this point I would be planning a trigger. A trigger which could take the status quo to the point of no return.'

'Exactly, and the perfect trigger would be provided by the assassination of Govind Gunaji or some other eminent Hindu leader,' said Farzana. 'Which is why I do not see why you are negating Gunaji as the possible victim, Parvez.'

'No, Fazi, it's you who don't understand. Just think for a moment. What will happen if they assassinate Govind Gunaji today?

'The whole thing will reach its logical climax. Resulting in uncontrollable Hindu reprisals. Extreme escalating violence.'

'And how will that help in achieving their aim, considering their objective is not mere senseless death but division of a country?'

'Why, the reprisals will isolate the Muslims further. Make them feel insecure in this country. The need for a land of their own will be increasingly felt.'

'No, your analysis is fractured and faulty! Because you are forgetting the guilt which presently consumes the community at present. The assassination of Govind Gunaji at this point would merely increase it. The reprisals would make the radical cabal squeal for Partition, yes, but not the ordinary peace-loving Muslim, and contrary to their image, the majority falls in that category! In fact, it would make them turn against the Majlis and reject them.'

He got up, restless with foreboding regarding the future, and continued. 'The game plan of the Majlis is not to make believers of the right-wing hotheads – you don't need to convert converts. No, they are targetting the nonviolent moderates. Radicals spearhead rebellions, but moderates provide the strength and substance. Without their support any revolt ultimately fails.'

'And how do they get this support?'

'By changing the present perception of the moderates that the Majlis is uncontrollable, has gone berserk. And that can be done only if Hindus act in an equally ugly, vindictive way. If that happens, the guilt will be neutralised, reaction will set in, and all the suppressed anger will erupt. And from that anger, that alienation, will come real grass-root support for the idea of Partition.'

'How can the Majlis accomplish that?'

'Simple. By killing, not a Hindu, but a Muslim leader! And manufacturing evidence to blame it on a right-wing Hindu group.'

It took them a little while to trace the tactical maze laid down so precisely by a seasoned terrorist. And some more to digest it.

With a deep sigh Beg said, 'It sounds logical to me, Farzana?'

She nodded crisply, 'Probable.'

'So, Mr Naqvi, to take your argument further, which Muslim leader would be the target?'

'To make a guess I have to once again think like the man whose mind has conceived the plot. And you say that mind belongs to Shaukat.'

'Yes.'

'I dispute it,' retaliated Farzana.

'That may be. But giving Mr Beg's instincts and experience a certain weightage, let's consider the situation from that perspective.'

'And what is your perception from that angle, Mr Naqvi?'

'Well, it calls for the assassination of a Muslim leader who commands immense respect, cutting across community lines. Someone who is at the apex of power, with acknowledged contribution to the nation. And who is known to be a staunch nationalist. The killing of such a person would be considered unjustified in every way. And there is one Muslim leader I know who fits the bill perfectly.'

'Who is that?'

'The Muslim woman who has reached unprecedented heights of political power. Who has become an international symbol of the subcontinent's emerging woman power. India's Home Minister, Farzana Hussain.'

She sat up, stunned, 'That's preposterous! Nanu, that's utter rubbish. Me? You think my own husband is going to target me? You are talking nonsense now!'

'Why?' he asked simply.

'Why? How can you even ask that? Because I am his wife! The mother of his daughter!'

'Fanatics know no family.'

'He would have to be evil to plan this sort of thing!'

'Fanatics find it difficult to distinguish between good and evil. Their mania becomes everything.'

A brief knock on the door, and a tumultuous young figure in a neat school uniform unceremoniously barged in. Two ponytails blazing with two bright red ribbons, impatience marking the wilful young face, 'Mamma,' wailed Asma, 'you have to give me a hundred rupees for the school donation! My bus will come any moment now!'

Just for a moment, the country had to take a back seat as a young girl and her small needs took precedence. Farzana sped inside.

Altaf Naqvi turned around to look at Parvez calmly. 'Well?' he enquired.

It was with a deep sigh and deeper reluctance that Beg acquiesced, 'I have to agree with you. It is logical. Farzana is the perfect target for the Quom-e-Majlis at this point.'

'So what are you going to do about it?'

'Throw a protective net around her. Double the security force. But there is a problem.'

'What is it?'

'Farzana is infamous for her intrinsic hatred of excessive security. In her present frame of mind, she may not cooperate.'

'Then find other ways of ensuring her protection, Mr Beg. Her life is invaluable and not just because she is my granddaughter. Her assassination will cause incalculable damage to the harmony of the nation. It has the capacity of creating a groundswell of support for a separate land. And once that happens, once the movement reaches the grass roots, it is the beginning of the end. No amount of military force will mend matters. And this time there may not be another Manu to stop the catastrophe.'

'I know, which is why the security has to be perfect.'

'But didn't you say that no defensive strategy is foolproof?'

'Yes, but in this case I have an ace. And I plan to use it.'

'And what is this ace?'

'A girl who was the beloved of Anees Bakhtiar. A girl who can identify him even in a crowd. I must talk to Reshma Kapoor.'

Her mind swirled. The unbelievable was being told, had to be heard, had to be accepted as the truth. Tears welled up and the faces of Zahera and Parvez were blurred. Her ears buzzed with the resonance of words that hurt, that killed, that skewered. And yet they went on, sentence by sentence, piling up evidence, culminating in a damnation which was as complete as it was terrible. And the pain was like a whirlpool, dragging her ruthlessly down in its swirling terror. A pain so intense that it numbed all feeling. The words finally stopped, helplessly she looked up, tears pouring down her face.

'I don't believe it,' she whispered. 'I don't believe it,' she repeated piteously. And then it became a litany of pleading, of anger. 'I don't believe it, I don't believe it, I don't BELIEVE IT.'

Empathy encircled her in the form of Zahera's plump arm.

'Hush, sweetheart, hush, don't, baby, quiet now, quiet.'

And she did quieten. Her senses dulled. Lassitude swept through, sensitivity subsided. And then she began to think, to analyse, and ultimately to digest. You couldn't argue against logic. You couldn't fight against the probable. You couldn't debate the small inner voice which whispered that it all jelled.

After a while she detached herself from Zahera's arms, sat up and said, 'You are sure about your facts, Uncle? You are sure about Anees?'

'Yes.' There was a world of sympathy and understanding in his eyes. But that was not going to help her. The only thing that could help her today was her own inner force.

'So, what do you want me to do?'

'I want your help.'

'Parvez! How can the poor girl help you, for heaven's sake?'

'The Special Protection Group guarding Farzana will have a copy of Anees's photograph. But that may not be enough. For we do not know his plan. Or the diversion used. Or the pre-decided direction. In that pressing mass of bodies, amongst the sweltering multitude, perception is befuddled, individuality is lost, and one face is like any other. My people are trained to identify people even in those circumstances, but it is not easy. They may make a mistake. Miss out a sighting.'

'So?' snapped Zahera.

'Reshma wouldn't make that mistake. Because she is familiar with not just the eyes, nose, hair, chin. For all these can be camouflaged, you see. But there are some things which are difficult to disguise. A turn of the chin, a gesture, a nuance of expression, an angle of the face. That is what she can see with the vision of her mind, her memories. If anyone has a chance of locating Anees before the act, it is Reshma. Will you do it?'

'You are asking me to play Judas,' she asked softly.

'I realise that. It's your country too, you know.'

'I loved him very much. I still love him.'

'Some things are greater than the greatest love.'

'Why does this country need a Manu at every turn? Why does someone have to sacrifice his or her all to keep its harmony alive? Why does it demand blood at every stage?'

Parvez did not answer. There was no answer.

She got up from the sofa, adjusted her *dupatta*, squared her shoulders, 'Give me five minutes and I'll come along with you.'

Zahera's anxious eyes followed her as she left the room and then turned their fire on Parvez.

'Okay, let's have the real story now, Parvez,' she said acidly.

'What do you mean?'

'You told her you need her to identify Anees. Now that would have been perfectly understandable if you feared an assassination via a human bomb. But you do not. The fact that Anees is an excellent marksman means that the assassination attempt will be made from some distance, am I right?'

'You might be. So?'

'So you don't need her as a lookout. You are using her as a decoy. As a protective shield. Hoping that she will manage to either draw him out or deflect the bullet. I think its despicable.'

He said softly, 'Extreme situations demand extreme sacrifices. The operation has to be aborted. Or it will be another turning point in the history of this nation with repercussions reaching down to future generations. If by adding Reshma in the picture I reduce the odds, I will do it without a single moment of hesitation. I said it before – it is not just my country.'

Fourteen

The Press Trust of India's news report: Prime Minister Shiv Charan Shukul addressed the nation on the occasion of the fifty-first year of India's independence from the ramparts of the Red Fort amidst unprecedented security. Stop. In spite of the tight police *bandobast*, a massive crowd had collected to listen to the PM. Stop. In his speech Shukul assailed the reactionary forces for instigating violence in the capital. Stop. He assured the citizens of Delhi that the situation was under control. Stop. He promised strong action against the offenders. Stop.

The teleprinters at the PTI offices were beating a merry tattoo, feeding the story to the hungry news networks, the language staccato, with clients including small and large newspapers all over the subcontinent. Desk editors everywhere tore off the report and anxiously scanned it. And then threw the report into the tray labelled OUT, with a sudden relaxing of tensed muscles. Routine stuff. No bomb, no explosion, not a whisper of violence. In fact, the usual political verbiage. Nothing untoward at all. It could be dealt by the sub-editor later on. And thank God for that.

* * *

10 A.M., NORTH BLOCK

Parvez Ali Beg looked a little like a spider sitting with a Buddhaesque calm in the midst of the crisscross lines of the information network. Phones jangled constantly, as did hot lines, feeding him information, enabling him to keep his finger on the city's pulse. The phone rang again. 'Khanna? Where are you speaking from?'

'I am following Farzana Hussain's car, sir. We are now leaving the Red Fort grounds.'

'Heading for?'

'Her office.'

'Peaceful so far?'

'Very peaceful, sir.'

'And Reshma is with Mrs Hussain?'

'In Madam's car, yes. But it beats me how you managed to make Madam comply. Most unlike her.'

'I threatened her with my resignation,' Beg wryly said.

'Well, sir, your tactics may be questionable but your choice is flawless. Reshma is learning the drill like a professional. A sharp girl, if I may say so.'

'And also pretty,' added Beg acidly.

Khanna chuckled, 'I didn't notice. By the way, any news of Shaukat Hussain?'

'No, I have spread a quiet word around for information. I will let you know if anything comes in.'

'Yes, boss.'

'What is your next destination?'

'Right now Madam's residence. At 11 a.m. we go to the Doordarshan studio. Madam is participating in a panel discussion on television.'

'Okay. Keep me posted.'

*   *   *

12.45 P.M.

Atul Khanna's car was just behind the official white Ambassador of the Home Minister as it neatly passed through the gates of Doordarshan. Time for a report, he thought and removed his mobile from the pocket.

'Yes, Khanna.'

'Leaving Doordarshan premises, sir.'

'All clear so far?'

'All clear.'

'What's your destination now?'

'Madam's office.'

'Okay. Remain alert.'

*   *   *

1.15 P.M.

A tight mesh of security had been thrown over the entire area surrounding the Mahatma Gandhi Memorial Bhavan, the venue for the World Energy Conference.

Built in 1952, it had been planned as a massive modern conference hall in memory of that apostle of peace who had believed that the meeting of minds was the grand road to world peace. With Prime Minister Jawaharlal Nehru taking a keen personal interest in the building, it had become Delhi's premier auditorium from the first day of its inception. Lavish care by succeeding governments had ensured that it retained its magnificence. Now the hall had been geared up for its role as the host to one of the biggest conferences of the decade. And in view of the eminence of the delegates and the inflammable condition of the city, the security systems were chokingly tight.

All the interconnecting roads were closed to traffic, leaving only one main arterial avenue which had a series of checkpoints. Suspicious men in khaki stopped every vehicle, subjected the passengers and interiors to careful scrutiny, and then, with utmost reluctance, allowed it to pass. This procedure, conducted not once but three times had the effect of deflating even the most pompous, and this was just a preamble. At the gates of the Bhavan, metal detectors had been put up as a security measure, and this was followed by a quick but thorough frisking. By the time the delegate was allowed into the graceful portals, you couldn't blame him for being limp with relief.

The unpretentious van drove slowly along the route and whirred to a stop in front of a checkpoint.

The driver put his face out of the window, waiting for the questions.

They came, sharp and hissing, ready to sting. The sting missed its mark by a mile as the man foolproof answers.

'This is the Doordarshan mobile van, sir, we have got permission.'

'But some Doordarshan representatives have already passed! They have been here since the morning, setting up their equipment!' There was a worm of suspicion wiggling in the statement.

'I don't know any of that,' said the man with supreme unconcern. 'You want to talk to the producer sitting behind?'

The policeman nodded sharply, and the driver, with a shrug, tapped the sliding partition. The panel slid open, and large unfocused eyes behind ugly tortoise-rimmed spectacles peered fuzzily at the policeman. It was a middle-aged face, the wrinkles in tune with the tired mop, the limp moustache. But it was the voice which was unusually arresting. A deep cultured baritone with a precise accent.

A voice is as exclusive as the ears, and just as difficult to disguise. Anees Bakhtiar's face had been changed by a make-up expert. No amount of camouflage could, however, could hide the strength of his diction.

'What is the problem officer?' he asked officiously, letting a tinge of impatience seep through.

'Your driver says this van is from Doordarshan. But I clearly remember letting a Doordarshan van through.'

Patiently, he said, 'Yes, yes, that was our advance team in charge of installing infrastructure. This is the primary DTV van.'

'What is that supposed to mean?'

'Direct telecast, of course.'

'Can I see your identity please?'

With a sigh Anees removed a card from his pocket and handed it over. The identity card was a work of art

executed by a master. The photograph matched the face,
and the script bequeathed a name and history to it. The
face, according to the legend belonged to one Ramesh
Katiyar, aged 45, resident of 34, Rajouri Gardens, New
Delhi. Presently gainfully employed by Doordarshan in
the capacity of Senior Producer.

The ID card was handed back.

'Mr Katiyar, you have permission from the
Information and Broadcasting ministry for this direct
telecast?'

Silently another official-looking paper exchanged hands.
A ruffle of pages. A keen inspection.

'Well,' said the cop doubtfully, 'it seems to be all
right.'

'Then can we go? We are getting late.'

'It's just that your name is not included in the media
list I have with me.'

Anees said impatiently, 'I was assigned on this job just
two days ago. They must have left out my name by
oversight.'

The policeman was truculent, 'That may be, but I will
have to phone the Media Centre and ask them before I
allow you to pass. Wait a minute please.' He went back
to the makeshift tent with its compact communication
box, keeping a wary eye on the van while he dialled a
number.

'Hullo, Media Centre?'

'Yes?'

'Sub Inspector Duleep Singh of Control Post One.
Who's speaking?'

'PR Officer S. Sharma. What can I do for you?'

'I need a verification, please. How many Doordarshan
vans have been allowed entry to the premises?'

'Two.'

'But in my sheet there is mention of only one.'

The voice drawled wearily with boredom, 'Someone goofed up. In my list here it is very clear that two vans are to be allowed entry – one in the morning and one an hour before the inauguration. What is the matter?'

'Nothing. Who's in charge of today's telecast, do you know?'

'Senior Producer Ramesh Katiyar. Why? Any problem?'

'No, sir, none at all. Just checking up. Thank you.'

The self-styled PR Officer smiled thinly as he kept the receiver down. For the last fifteen minutes he had been waiting for this call, and now that his job was over he could rest easy till the real PRO came back. Which would not be very soon as the gentleman was presently in a Karol Bagh flat where his married girlfriend lived. Wrapped in sexual bliss, if S. Sharma had any thought to spare, it would be of gratitude to his friend, Armaan Shakeel. Shakeel, who knew Sharma's proclivities, had nobly offered to act as a stand-in for an hour or so at the Media Centre. Enough time for a quick and deliciously illicit bedroom romp. And with his good friend Armaan manning his post, he had nothing to worry about.

The van passed through the rest of the roadblocks smoothly and soon entered the parking lot. Exactly a hundred metres away from the entrance of Mahatma Gandhi Memorial Bhavan.

The time was thirty minutes past one. Farzana Hussain was scheduled to arrive at 2.10 p.m., with the opening ceremony slated for 2.30 p.m. Quietly, the phony television producer set about his activities, all of which would have baffled a genuine producer in the extreme.

He removed a panel from the ceiling and took out some metal pieces concealed there. Metal clinked as the pieces were arranged on the seat. Carefully, Anees Bakhtiar began to fit them together, imposing order in confusion, fusing together a cohesive metallic pattern. The pieces fit each other admirably – Abumiya, the gun dealer, would have deserved a pat on his back if he had been around. The completed product was a lethal 5.56 mm rifle with a silencer and telescopic sight. A deadly instrument by any measure, and in the hands of a marksman like Anees Bakhtiar it was as good as issuing a death warrant to someone.

He kept the rifle in the false ceiling and signalled to the driver of the van.

'It's time for you to go, Suleiman. But let's recheck the drill. The Maruti is in this parking lot some hundred metres away?'

'Yes, it's already there. I just checked.'

'A Maruti with a souped-up power engine, I believe.'

'With a bulletproof body. Yes.'

'Okay. You go to the car and wait. The minute you hear the shots, bring the car ten metres to the left of the van.'

'Right.'

'That's where I will meet you. Clear?'

'Yes, very clear.'

'Then go.'

'God be with you. See you later.'

Anees nodded and waited till Suleiman had left the van. Now to add the last minute touches and he would be ready. He removed a letter typewritten on an Arya Andolan Sabha letterhead and pinned it prominently on the van door. A perusal of the black-lettered missive would have made it evident that it claimed responsibility for the Farzana Hussain killing and pithily promised more of the same if Muslims continued to threaten Hindus.

Then he threw a paper carelessly inside the false ceiling, smug in the certainty that the CBI would soon tear the van to pieces. The paper would provide vital proof that a zealot belonging to the Arya Andolan Sabha was the assassin.

Anees sat back with satisfaction – the scene was set. From a small aperture he had a clear view of the entrance, and the sweeping passage which led to it. He placed a small, powerful telescope on the aperture and adjusted it. Now to wait for Farzana Hussain.

*   *   *

2 P.M.

'Sir? Atul Khanna.'

'Yes, Khanna, what is it?'

'We are about to leave Madam's office.'

'Reshma is still with her?'

'Sitting right next to her.'

'And nothing suspect so far?'

'Not a whiff. You think we got the wrong end of the stick?'

'I don't know. Anyhow I have Govind Gunaji covered securely.'

'No news from that front either?'

'No.'

'Well, maybe Anees Bakhtiar has choked to death on his conscience.'

'Very funny. Your next destination?'

'Mahatma Gandhi Memorial Bhavan. The inauguration of the World Energy Conference.'

Minutes passed and the pressure built up. It always did. A familiar pain he had still not learnt to deal with. Starting in a small way as a niggling anxiety and then skulking its way to greater strength. Soon he would be playing God. He briefly felt the power of the act, and the terror of that power. For it is unnatural that one man should turn God. It is aberrant that one man's evil decides the death of another. Just for a minute Anees let himself imagine the nanosecond of destruction when his bullet would penetrate the flesh of a human being. Tear through the tissue. Cut up muscle. Rape internal organs. Slam against bones. And then with clinical efficiency snuff out the last spark of life, contemptuously slashing out an exit from the falling body. He could see it in his mind's eye, he had seen it before. The stricken disbelief in the victim's eyes, the pain which convolutes the body to a screaming rigidity, the blood spurting, flowing. Taking away with it the life force. He had done it before in the name of duty, played God for his uniform. How could he justify it now?

Suddenly there was no time for the fancies of his conscience. No time to think. For a car came sweeping into his vision, the dust it generated unable to hide the numberplate, or the vague outlines of the passengers. Farzana Hussain had precipitated on the scene a few silent moments away from her planned death. And her executioner was ready for the kill. With quiet efficiency Anees removed the rifle from its hideout and took his pre-decided position near the window, opened enough to provide the conduit to the bullet.

Passion chills when your finger is on the trigger. Then it becomes only a matter of coordination between the eye, muscle, nerve, and brain. Erupting finally in a spectacular dance of death. His finger tightened momentarily on the trigger in anticipation of that final moment. He concentrated. With a curious detached efficiency. The door of the Ambassador was being opened by an SPG commando. A white *salwar*-clad leg slithered out in a gentle flow of motion, the foot encased in a brown moccasin. The body uncoiled gracefully. Its slim lines stretching out to its full height. A long slender neck, topped by a shapely head.

Anees caught his breath. Hard. It was a terribly familiar head! Achingly so. His focus sharpened critically and his pulse went into a panic. For he was seeing the unbelievable, the impossible. The face was one which for so long had been his personal hell and torment. There could be no mistake – the young girl who was continuing her 180 degree appraisal was none other than Reshma!

Sweat broke out on his temples as he desperately tried to regain control. What was Reshma doing here? In Farzana Hussain's car? And where was Farzana for that matter?

That was the moment Farzana chose to make her appearance, slipping out of the car smoothly, adjusting the folds of her sari and saying a few words to the girl standing beside her. Immediately they were surrounded by a gaggle of SPG men, gimlet-eyed with restless vision.

He had expected that, planned for it. For good as her security mesh was, there was one loophole and he had closed in on that.

Flanking the gravel corridor where the car had stopped was an expansive courtyard beyond which was the hall entrance. At the centre of this courtyard there stood a mammoth granite bust of Mahatma Gandhi. All savvy politicians stopped there for a moment to pay homage to the father of the nation before entering the hall. The gesture was first initiated by Jawaharlal Nehru and over the years had become a sort of tradition. Farzana Hussain too would follow the rites of passage. A natural deference would make the SPG fall back a step. The pause would be of less than a minute. But it would be enough.

He looked through his telescope at his target who was rapidly walking towards the statue with the gait of a much younger woman. Surrounded by the SPG. And flanked by Reshma. Once again he felt unnerved and dazed by her presence there.

Who? How? For what reason?

He took a deep breath, primed himself once again, pulling together his shaky concentration. Farzana had reached the Gandhi bust and was standing still with her hands folded, head bent in front of it. Reshma was right next to her, and just for a heartbeat his hunger controlled him. But he was a professional. He had to ignore the peripheral, the time-span was shortening dangerously. The schedule going awry with each passing moment. Farzana would be moving any second now. Don't react, act. Immediacy taking precedence. Purpose paramount.

He bent his eye to the telescopic sight, positioned it carefully and clutched the trigger with a slightly trembling finger. The aim was everything. Anything else could wait. His gunsight was directed straight at a vulnerable point. The angle set precisely to enable the bullet to hit Farzana Hussain's slim back. The framework was perfect, action had to be initiated, every minuscule delay carrying with it the penalty of failure. Voluntarily his finger tightened on the trigger. And for the last time he checked his target through the lens. The trajectory of the bullet would have a clear, unimpeded corridor in which to move, to reach, to slam. He pressed the trigger, setting off an irrevocable sequence.

What made her do it? An accidental overture, a wild insight, an eerie premonition. Or simply mischievous fate which takes unholy pleasure in scrambling up human destinies. Reshma, who was standing quietly a respectful foot behind Farzana, choose that very moment to step forward, her body shielding half of Farzana's. The bullet hit her arm instead of its target.

She felt an unexpected thump and then an intolerable pain exploded through her body as the little lump of metal smashed through the muscles and tissue of her right arm. Hit the bone, the forcible impact changing the direction of its trajectory. Surged out of the arm, soared upwards, crashed into Farzana's shoulder, the resistance of bony tissue slowing down its already debilitated force, and finally losing heart, embedded itself in the muscle. Farzana Hussain was hit, but on the shoulder, not even close to fatal.

Blood. Too much blood. Spurting over her chest, running rivulets of life, now ebbing away in glorious technicolour. Even from the distance he could see the incomprehension of the sacrificial lamb on Reshma's face. Feel the scream retching through her, its echo carving a valley of pain in his mind. He saw her falling to the ground in a heap, her white *dupatta* draped over her like a shroud.

Everything around him turned grey, everything else was out from his consciousness. His capacity for thinking, for feeling, for wanting, was all wrapped up in that white sad broken bundle lying a hundred metres away from him. The past was forgotten, the present nonexistent, the future not there. Only two thoughts hammered in his scorched brain. His love was dying, perhaps dead, and he had killed her. Sanity could have yet saved him. Sanity and the sense that though the mission was terminated in failure, his escape route was still alive, throbbing with a running engine some ten metres away. All he had to was to use logic, hold on to reason. But logic and reason could not penetrate that dark hell of pain. The searing heat of bloody death had melted his hatred, leaving just passion, madness, and love.

Blindly, frenetically, he threw open the van door and rushed out in a manic frenzy to reach her, touch her, hold her, his woman whom he had loved more than himself.

He broke into a run, closing the distance between them, oblivious to the surroundings, his mind concentrating on the image of that supine white shroud with a yearning which can break a man apart. Somewhere a scream rang out, someone was shouting Reshma's name. With fleeting surprise he realised that it was emerging from his own tortured throat and dismissed the fact as incidental. And then he saw it happening. His screaming agony seemed to have the power to raise the dead, for a movement was visible in the huddled inanimate body of his Reshma. The *kafan*-like *dupatta*

seemed to raise its head, a parchment face shimmered in
the sun's light, and Reshma was staring straight at him.
Into his very being. Just for that one infinitesimal second
it was like the beginning of the world. The beginning of
their world. The shared passion, the oneness, the
incandescent madness, all merged in that one glorious
perfect moment of pure, joyous love. Hatred could not
be sustained in this deluge of powerful passion and just
for that moment they surrendered to its force, drowned
in its vortex. And then the guns thundered from all sides.
The SPG commandos, stunned for a moment by the
unexpected, came alive. A barrage of bullets exploded in
rapid succession and ended the life of Anees Bakhtiar. He
did not feel the pain, he was not conscious of the
engulfing darkness, he had no thought for his impending
death. His last vision on earth was Reshma's tormented
face contorted in a rictus of anguished love. That
perception calmed his inner devils, laid to rest the ghosts
which had devoured him. He had discovered his love
once again and in that discovery Anees Bakhtiar died an
intensely happy man.

*   *   *

When it comes to a catastrophe, the government
machinery can turn from excruciatingly slow to rapid
efficiency with bewildering speed. The aftermath of Anees
Bakhtiar's death saw some lightning measures of damage
control as Atul Khanna's genius came into play. With
one dead body, two injured women and a snowballing
crisis on his hands, it would have been easy to go
haywire, or to go off at a tangent. He did neither.
Instead he swiftly took charge, homing in to the essential,

rapidly formulating a defence plan, improvising as he went along.

One thing was clear. The human factor was secondary, to be considered later on. Right now it was imperative that the proceedings of the World Energy Conference should be unimpaired by these episodes. Within minutes a cordon was thrown over the whole scene and Anees Bakhtiar's body was summarily bundled away, the blood on the floor cleaned up. A security officer was deputed to take Reshma in a car to Safdarjung Hospital for emergency treatment. The assassin's van was impounded and removed for an extensive search, and a party of officers assigned to track Anees Bakhtiar's escape route. A few journalists immediately swooped on the scene, avid for details, but were frustrated by the cartel of hard-faced officials with clamped mouths. Their names and the name of the publication they worked for noted imperceptibly. Later in the day the editors of each of the publications would receive a personal call from the Prime Minister's Office, requesting them to 'kill' the story. National pride was at stake. And anyway the story was no big deal as the attempt had failed abjectly. Would they cooperate? They did – by publishing a watered-down version. It made the headlines without creating ripples and acted as good PR for the security arrangements. The readers were merely informed that an unidentified hothead belonging to an extremist organisation had attempted to infiltrate the Mahatma Gandhi Memorial Hall. When apprehended, the man had tried to shoot his way to his freedom and had been killed in retaliatory gunfire. End of chapter. No mention was made that Farzana Hussain had been the target.

But the most vital action was effected by Farzana

Hussain. Hastily escorted to a safe annexe off the hall, she summoned her own personal doctor on her mobile telephone. When he came rushing, in some haste, he received precise instructions – stop the blood, kill the pain, keep me on my feet. His argument that the bullet needed to be removed was despotically dismissed and he was requested to do as he was told. Knowing just how stubborn his patient could be once she made up her mind, he accepted the inevitable, shrugged and got down to his job. The wound was disinfected and wrapped tight in bandages. A local anesthesia to deaden the spot, her body pumped with painkillers, and Farzana was ready to participate in the inauguration ceremony. If anyone took note of her stiff walk and white face, it was shrugged off as incidental. Certainly no one would have believed it possible that she had faced death a few moments ago, and carried its legacy within her in the form of a bullet. Fortified with courage and an indomitable will, the operation on her shoulder was delayed by nearly four hours while she bravely played her role. By that time a vague rumour of an attempt on the life of the Indian Home Minister had died a natural death.

This, however, was merely a cosmetic operation. The real surgery was undertaken by Parvez Ali Beg and stretched into the early hours of the next morning. Farzana Hussain's permission was requested to search her house and her husband's office. For what? Evidence proving Shaukat's involvement with the Quom-e-Majlis, his complicity in the treacherous attempt. After some hesitation permission was granted with the proviso that she was to be informed before any action was undertaken.

A secret can remain hidden when its circuits are masked in enigma, hidden in shadow. But if a single conduit is exposed, reaching the genesis becomes a simple matter of logical progression. The search at Shaukat Hussain's bungalow and office was dictated by this elementary precept and was fruitful. Within half an hour, enough evidence was gathered to indict Shaukat with half a dozen transgressions. The foremost charge being instigation to subversion, conspiracy to kill, traitor to the nation. The proof conclusive enough to hang Shaukat Hussain from his neck till he was dead.

Farzana Hussain was resting fitfully when the phone rang.

'Farzana? Parvez here. How are you feeling now?'

'I'll survive. Well, do you have something to tell me?'

'He is guilty, Farzana. Guilty as hell. I have unearthed plenty of evidence to prove that he was the mastermind behind the recent conspiracy. If you want to see the proof . . .'

Abruptly she said, 'No, I believe you.'

'There is something else I need to tell you.'

'Well?'

'We evaluated the material my men brought from your husband's office. Based on those findings, we pulled in some Majlis members, gave them the third degree.'

'Did you manage to break them? What did they testify?'

'Plenty, all of it worse than we thought. The conspiracy did not end with today's attempt. That was to be just the flag-off. Tomorrow the programme escalates, widens its base.'

'What do you mean?'

'More assassinations, in strategic parts of the country. The would-be assassins primed and ready in place.'

'Who are their targets? Do you know?'

'Yes, once again the pattern of deception. The Majlis is not aiming at Hindus. Instead prominent Muslims are to be its victims. The list includes politicians, academicians, businessmen.'

'And I suppose the killers are to leave the calling card of the Arya Andolan Sabha,' she said in clipped tones.

'In every instance.'

'God! It's diabolical! If this programme succeeds, do you know what it can do to India?'

Wearily Beg acquiesced, 'I know. I don't want to think about the consequences, but I know.'

'So what are we doing about it, Parvez?'

Quietly he said, 'I think we have in hand an almost complete list of the targets. We are informing the local police in every instance. They have been ordered to provide tight security to each suspected victim. In addition, our officers have already left for these cities and will ensure that the safety net is foolproof. In many cases, I am personally talking to the alleged victims and asking them to give full cooperation to the police. The city's security systems have been placed on red alert.'

'And you think this will be effective?'

'Inshaallah.'

'Yes, I know. What about my husband? What steps do you propose to take about Shaukat? I don't need to tell you the necessity of discretion in this case.'

'We are tracking his moves, following leads. A quiet dragnet has been spread through Delhi, right up to Meerut. I am expecting a break soon.'

'And then.'

'We capture him, bring him back to Delhi, charge him. You know the drill.'

Harshly she said, 'No! You won't do it that way!'

'I don't understand.'

'You will be showcasing my husband as a traitor, a renegade, a major conspirator of right-wing insurgency. That is intolerable, unacceptable.'

'Well, Farzana, I can understand your feelings, but . . . .'

'Screw my feelings,' she said crudely. 'I'm talking about my political career here. It can never recover from this sort of stigma. There will be disbelief. And there will be whispers. My credentials will be forever doubted. Perhaps I too was an accomplice in the subversive agenda? Why not? Elliptical references, unconfirmed allusions – without substance, without form. Their very elusiveness making them difficult to deny. I can't afford that, Parvez, not at this juncture.'

'It's a problem, yes. But what can you do about it?'

'I can't. But you can.'

'What do you mean?'

She said, softly, 'No trial, no publicity. Hush it up.'

'Can't be done, Farzana. Not a scandal of this magnitude.'

'It's got to be done. Both our careers are on the line here. Just think. The manner in which I'm building up a mass base, how long do you suppose it will take me to become the prime minister of India? A few years at the most in the ordinary scheme of things? I am on my way to becoming the most powerful woman in the world, Parvez! Help me in this and you will be there at the top right along with me.'

A drawn out pause and reluctantly Beg reiterated, 'No, I can't do it.'

She snapped, glacially, 'You owe me one, you know. There were many other contenders for the post of the Director of the CBI. I had to pull quite a few strings to get you where you are now. I thought I could count on you.'

He said, quietly, 'You can, but not when it comes to betraying my country. And reprieving a traitor definitely comes under that category.'

'Who is asking you to let him go free?'

'But you said that I should hush it up.'

'Yes, by ensuring that there is no enquiry.'

'That is not possible. We will have to conduct an inquisition.'

'Dead men can't be questioned.'

'What? What the hell are you saying?'

She hissed, softly, 'Arrange an encounter. Make it look like an accident.'

The director of the CBI is necessarily quite blasé, always ready to cope with the unusual. But Parvez Ali Beg was distinctly shaken and asked incredulously, 'You don't mean that?'

'I do. Kill the bastard.'

Fifteen

Holed up in a safe house in Meerut, Shaukat Hussain was distraught. And the stress was increasing with every hour spent without any news of the assassination. At around 3 p.m. he switched on the television. It would be in the headlines, her killing announced in a soupy sepulchral voice by the newsreader with a hangdog look. And with her death he would come alive, his dream would take on vivid hues, his horizon inch nearer.

Not many people who had known him as an insipid, hesitant man would have believed his savage elation. Or understood it. But then there had always been layers to Shaukat Hussain which no one had ever been able to gauge. Beneath that placid and dull veneer was a frothing, shrieking reservoir of dank ooze. The stored lava of all his hatred, his hurt, his pain. Its embryo buried in that inferno of his childhood, which had devoured his gentle spirit, his naive trust. The scene gouged him within with dark indelible strokes of incandescent, grisly orange heat. His *Abba's* shrieks jarring his soul in stereophonic sounds. And the shrunk, charred, unrecognisable body – a symbol of his destroyed innocence. For years he had carried that sperm of venomous madness within him, hiding it and carefully camouflaging it in excessive normality. Taking refuge in obscure shades. Desperately trying to keep afloat in the mindless whirlpool. Avoiding humanity, accepting loneliness, for that way lay the semblance of sanity.

And then suddenly salvation had come in the shape of a woman. A girl of almost abounding passions, infectious zeal, bubbling life. Gratefully he had clutched on to her – she would provide him with that slice of sanity he so badly needed. He had been immensely grateful, touchingly amazed when she had accepted his proposal so promptly. That this vibrant young spirit should agree to be a part of his middle-aged monotonous life was for him like a blessing from Allah. It was with buoyant, boyish hopes that he had celebrated his *nikah* with Farzana.

Perhaps that was the reason that disillusion, when it came, was in inverse intensity to the hope which had preceded it. For all his mildness, he had never lacked perception and it did not take him long to realise that it was not him she had married. To put it crudely, the *nikah* had been between a girl with ambition and a man with the means by which she could fulfil them. It was his money, the security he offered, the magical password he possessed which could open enclaves of power for her. He had been merely a stepping stone in her ongoing surge to the top. The betrayal had eaten

into him. The bitterness making him retreat further into
his shadows.

But this time it would be shadows of a different kind.
For the lessons had been learnt. From a master in the
art of survival like Farzana. The first axiom was that no
one gave away strength as a gift – it had to be acquired,
created, snatched if necessary. And the second that
dreams were the fuel of greatness, the propellant to
power.

He thought deeply. And rekindled the vision he had
inherited through the faith of his fathers. He would give
shape to the fantasy which had inflamed his *Abba*. He
would become the Moses who would guide his people
to the promised land. He would create Pakistan. He had
chosen to join the Quom-e-Majlis for the precise reason
that at that point it was a headless outfit drifting in the
morass of polity. The vague outpourings of its puerile
leaders making it a wasteland of frittered energy. He had
given them a purpose, a direction. Shaped them into a
combative force. And in the process he had fuelled his
own ambitions, his own dreams.

Today he would come that much nearer to achieving
his vision. His exhilaration was at its crest.

And the plan was a masterly one, indeed! For a nation
jolted by the assassination of their Home Minister by a
Hindu zealot, there would be other shocks in store. A
spate of killings spread over the country's sensitive,
trouble spots. Targetting prominent Muslims, evidence
pointing conclusively to the Arya Andolan Sabha. The
whole country would be revulsed, horrified. An
international furore would confront the tottering Indian
government for their failure to protect minorities. Fear of
a Nazi-like holocaust would be regenerated with a

vengeance. Vocal disclaimers by Govind Gunaji would be dismissed, disbelieved. The chaos would be total. Rampant chaos would rule and Muslims would press the panic button.

For Shaukat Hussain, it was poetic justice that Farzana's assassination was to prove a trigger. The signal for submerging India in waves of violence which would end up destabilising it. His cup of anticipation was running over, his elation increasing by the minute.

The bubble burst when the 3 o'clock news did not have any news of Farzana's tragic death.

It did have a report on the inauguration of the World Energy Conference though!

With Farzana queening it on the stage, the cynosure of flashlights! He reeled with disappointment. Anees Bakhtiar's first attempt at the point of entry had obviously failed. A black rage shook him. Nothing should go wrong now! His plan had succeeded perfectly! Nothing should scuttle it! Damn her, damn her, damn her.

But soon hope was resurrected. Anees may have had to abandon the first plan for logistical reasons, but a backup strategy was in place. If the first attempt failed, he was to try killing her at night on her way to the official banquet. Anees Bakhtiar could not possibly fail a second time! Could he?

By 7 p.m. Shaukat was biting his nails, by 9 p.m. he was frantic with anxiety. He tried calling some of his trusted henchmen, without any result. No, Anees Bakhtiar had not contacted them. No, they had not heard anything.

Finally by midnight, he gave in to his inner turmoil. He called up his residence.

The phone was picked up by the servant on the seventh ring. Shaukat was alert for accents of misery and panic which should have been there. All he heard was polite, sleepy lethargy.

'Give it to memsaab,' he snapped.

'Saab, can I take a message instead?'

Hope surged within him, 'Why? Can't she come to the phone?'

'She is sleeping. She is not to be disturbed.'

'Well, it's urgent. Wake her up, please.'

With trembling hands he waited. Thoughts suspended in his misery. What had happened? Why was she still alive? Where was Anees Bakhtiar?'

A soft voice said 'Hullo.' Farzana, in person. Shaking, he kept the phone down. It was unbelievable, but true. The assassination attempt had failed. She was alive, and he felt like death himself.

His anxiety made him forget a few ground rules. He remained on the phone long enough for the 'tap' on her phone to work. The Meerut telephone exchange managed to locate the source of the call and informed Atul Khanna accordingly. The quarry had been unearthed. Now for the trap.

It took the small handpicked group of men approximately two hours to reach Meerut and the mediocre yellow-coloured bungalow from where the phone call had been made. The instructions were explicit. Watch carefully. Wait for an opportunity. Relay moves. It would be a long night's wait.

At daybreak Shaukat Hussain drove out of the house in his black Ford. At a careful distance, Atul Khanna followed him till he got on the Delhi highway. Then it was time for someone else to take over. Accordingly a mobile phone rang in a truck a few miles away on the highway, waiting for this call. A few crisp words were spoken, the driver nodded and started his vehicle. He had a date with Shaukat Hussain though the latter did not know it.

The news broke fairly early, in the breakfast show news bulletin. Though the body had been horribly mangled amongst the debris of the car, the police had managed to identify it because of the papers in the briefcase. It was unfortunate, but the Home Minister of India had suffered a painful personal loss. Her husband, Shaukat Hussain, the Nawab of Rajapura, had died in a terrible accident on the Meerut-Delhi highway when his car smashed into a truck. The truck driver was absconding. An inconsolable Farzana Hussain, hugging her 12-year-old weeping daughter, Asma, had declined to comment and requested privacy. Prime Minister Shiv Charan Shukul, cabinet ministers, and sundry VIPs were arriving at her residence to offer their condolences.

But the killing of Shaukat Hussain was just a preamble to Operation Fightback. The violence planned next day was an abject failure, partly due to the efficient security measures taken, and to the depressed morale of the perpetrators. Two men did get killed, but as one of them was a businessman and the other a politician, the police was able to hush the murders up, implying that the motive in both cases was personal.

Under the command of a CBI Director on overdrive, there was a concentrated blitzkrieg on the

Quom-e-Majlis. Its offices in all major Indian cities were raided, plenty of evidence collected, its leaders taken into custody. The charge was a universal one – conspiracy and sedition. If proved in the courts, the penalty would be imprisonment ranging from one year to a life term.

Within two days, most of the Majlis leaders were in jail, their offence non-bailable. A few lucky ones who managed to escape the police dragnet went underground in panic, suspending operations indefinitely. Unnerved, the financial sponsors of the party obliterated any traces of their association, freezing funds, promises forgotten. It was business first after all and no one wanted to be a part of a ship which had sunk so ignominiously. In one fell swoop the organisation's back was broken. It would be a long time before it recovered enough to raise its head. Parvez Ali Beg managed to do exactly what he had started out to do. As far as the Quom-e-Majlis was concerned, Pakistan had faded from its horizons and sunk to the depths in a murky haze. The rout was complete.

* * *

AUGUST 20, 2001

Another cabinet meeting of the Indian Government. But unlike those in the past, this one was not marked with dour and dismal faces. There was celebration in the air, relief on the faces, and the ministers were actually smiling. For India had once again faced a tough squall and sailed to safe shores. The successful conclusion of the World Energy Conference had put a bright feather in India's diplomatic cap and pats on the back were the order of the day. Triumph, after the recent vagaries of fate, was sweet indeed.

Nowhere was this more evident than in the calm visage of Shiv Charan Shukul, who was positively beaming as he surveyed his flock, 'The Conference was successful, and even more important, it passed peacefully. The security aspect, as you know, was an extremely worrying factor but nothing untoward happened and I thank the Lord for that.'

'I think you should also thank Farzana Hussain for that,' put in Soren Banerjee, the Defence Minister wryly.

'She did a remarkable job, yes. But then she is a remarkable woman, indeed.'

'To show such courage in the face of a personal tragedy of this dimension is not easy,' reflected Nandan Naik, Minister of Information and Broadcasting. 'I was told that she has gone to Rajapura for a few days?'

'Yes, to conduct her husband's last rites and to be with his family.'

S. Aravindan, Minister of External Affairs, intervened, 'As she is not here, I would like to give some information to the cabinet.

In December, the United Nations is planning to hold a symposium comprising the most powerful women in the world. The topic of the conference is to be: Emerging Woman Power in the 21st Century.'

'And?'

Softly he said, 'They want the Indian Home Minister, Farzana Hussain, to be the chairman.'

Jagdish Chowdhury, the Finance Minister, bent forward avidly, 'Indeed? That is quite a positive commendation!'

Aravindan quietly said, 'It is a signal honour for Farzana Hussain as well as for India.'

Mushtaq Peerzada interrupted sharply, 'Excuse me, instead of discussing international honours, I would like some clarification on the internal situation from the Home Ministry.'

Shukul bend forward, 'Well, as Madam Home Minister is not present, maybe I can answer your queries. What do you need to know?'

'It has come to my notice that the CBI is conducting raids on the offices of the Quom-e-Majlis all over the country. I would like to know whether this has been authorised by the Home Ministry.'

'To the best of my knowledge, it has.'

'On what grounds?'

'The CBI has recovered comprehensive proof regarding their complicity in the recent wave of extremist violence. There is also some evidence that the conspiracy was on an all-India level.'

'What sort of proof?'

'The Home Ministry is preparing a report in that regard. You will receive your copy soon. Right now all I can tell you is that ·the situation is completely under control. The divisive forces have been defeated. There is no threat to India's internal unity.'

'And the Manu factor?' asked Peerzada. 'Has that been negated? Govind Gunaji is nothing if not stubborn.'

'This time he had to back out. Making a hero out of Altaf Naqvi has no part in his narrow schematics. The story of Manu will forever remain where it has been till now – in the realm of rumour. It will never be substantiated.'

Soren Banerjee puffed on his pipe and said, 'I would like to know about the extremist who was apprehended and shot by the security personnel at the Mahatma Gandhi Memorial Bhavan.'

Shukul shrugged, 'It happened. One of those things. What do you want to know?'

'For a start, which group was the assassin affiliated to?'

'In strict confidence, he was a member of the Quome-Majlis.'

'But that news has not been made public.'

'It will not be made public. The CBI spokesman has already made it clear that the man who was caught was insane, with a history of schizophrenia. There was no connection between him and the Majlis.'

'But that is falsifying the facts! People deserve to know the truth.'

With rare acerbity Shukul bit out, 'The elections are going to be held after three months. This government is already being criticised for increased terrorist activities under its rule. You want to incite more trouble? We are not teaching a kindergarten, Banerjee, we are running a government. As far as I am concerned, I accept this version implicitly and I would advise all of you to do the same. We don't need a deepening rift in the fabric of the nation. The country cannot afford more controversy and bitterness, not at this point.'

The Minister of Industry, Farhad Hashmi, enquired curiously, 'What do you mean, at this point?'

A smile slowly splintered the old face as he looked at S. Aravindan and angled his head, 'Aravindan, I think you should tell them the news.'

Aravindan twinkled and sat up, cleared his throat and looked round the table, each expression, each movement emphasising the importance of the moment. 'Today I had an official visit from Mr Chester Forbes, the American Ambassador.'

'Regarding?'

'To enquire about the steps taken regarding the bomb blast at the American Embassy.' He shrugged, 'I told him that the Quom-e-Majlis was clearly responsible for the act. And I gave him some details about the raids and arrests we have carried out. On the whole, he was pretty satisfied.'

'Is that the news you were talking about?' asked Banerjee sceptically.

Aravindan smiled, 'No, while he was there he dropped a very strong hint.'

'Regarding?'

'You know that for the past many years we have demanded permanent membership of the United Nations Security Council.'

'Which the United States has always opposed.'

'Yes, but indications are that US perceptions are changing on the issue.'

He bent forward and confided softly, 'The United States of America is now ready to support India as the sixth permanent member of the UN Security Council.'

There were muted gasps of surprise, of wonder, of doubt.

Aravindan continued smoothly, 'And with the US supporting India, our membership to the Security Council is assured. The odds are that we are about to join the most exclusive and powerful club in the world.'

A spirited hum broke out, and excitement spiralled.

With a deep sigh Shukul leaned back, 'In the fifty-first year of independence, our subcontinent has come of age. The moral voice of the world has become a superpower.' He shook his head in growing wonder and smiled at his inner vision of the future.

'Gentlemen, the twenty-first century belongs to an united and resurgent India,' said the Prime Minister of the subcontinent.

* * *

AUGUST 22, 2001

A stark Delhi morning shrouded the city with grey. The sombre cast of the day seemed to creep into Reshma's bedroom as she lay passively under the coverlet. She had been released from hospital nearly three days earlier, where she had undergone a relatively minor operation on her upper arm. Though the physical wound had been taken care of, the mind had yet to heal. Wrapped in the silence of misery, buffeted by inner storms, Reshma huddled within herself, desperately putting a distance between the world of the living and herself. The anaesthesia had worn off, but not the shock. And depression seemed to have trapped her in the deepest craters of black torment. She had slipped away to some remote corner of mental existence where nothing living could touch her.

The pain was too recent, remorse too intense. Reshma remained a mere shadow of her vibrant self. And the ghost of Anees Bakhtiar hovered around her.

Ruthlessly Rukshana Bi pulled the curtains, opening the window to let in the cool spray. She went towards her lethargic charge and gently shook her awake.

'Come on, Nyani, this won't do,' she said urgently. 'Get hold of yourself, *beti*, how long will you continue this way?'

'*Amma*, please, just let me be, will you?'

'Beg saheb wants to come up and meet you. Why don't you get dressed so that I can call him?'

She was bairly presentable by the time Parvez Ali Beg and Zahera, tiptoed in. Supported by fluffed-up pillows, hair combed, *dupatta* in place, Reshma was wan and white, but at least she was back in the world of the living. It was with a relieved smile that they enquired about her health, and she lied with serenity. It was her guilt. Her cross. She would not let anyone else in that penance.

'Reshma, I need to tell you this. Yesterday, Anees Bakhtiar was buried with complete military honours.'

Pain flooded her. Swamped her senses. Anees Bakhtiar's passion, his hunger for life. Now cold. Rejected. Relegated to the ground.

She took a deep breath, and stumbled on, 'Military honours? How is that possible?'

Beg explained quietly, 'On no account can there be any connection between a military officer and an assassin of the Quom-e-Majlis. You understand – that is not good for army morale.'

'And so?'

'Major Sukhbir Bindra has informed his platoon that Captain Anees Bakhtiar had been sent to a troubled area on special duty to control insurgency.'

After a pause he continued, 'He died four days ago in a bomb blast. His mother was informed accordingly and his closed coffin was send to Rawalpindi.'

Not just cold but shrouded in deceit. Oh my love . . .

'I must request you to maintain this story when you go back, Reshma.'

She mutely nodded and then whispered, softly, 'So it's all over.'

'Yes, but there is one thing I don't understand,' Parvez stated quietly. 'I thought maybe you could explain.'

'What is it?'

'He had a backup car ready and waiting quite close to the van. After the assassination attempt failed, he could have easily made his escape. Instead he came out in the open, towards certain death. Why?'

'Because of me,' she said bitterly. 'He thought I was dead, killed with his bullet. So he came running towards me. And was hit. Perforated. Everywhere.'

'He must have loved you very much indeed,' said Parvez with compassion.

Reshma nodded silently.

Zahera bent forward, and patted her cheek gently, 'May I ask you something? It is obvious that you were both deeply in love. What went wrong?'

'It wouldn't have worked,' she said starkly. 'I was scared.'

'Scared of what for God's sake?'

'Social stigma. Family ties. He was a Muslim, you see, and I was a coward. I could not risk breaking up my world for the sake of love.'

'So you broke up the relationship?'

'It was inevitable.'

'Why?'

'I haven't made this society. Or its rules. I just live in it. To break traditions, to go against the tide needs courage. I didn't have it. Not enough.'

'And so you decided to dump him?'

'It was not as cold-blooded as it sounds, Zahera
Maasi. Nor so simple. It broke me apart. It hurt, but I
had to do it.'

She shrugged and smiled bitterly.

'I thought I could condition myself to love someone
more acceptable,' she said harshly. 'Like Pavlov's dog.'

'And then?'

'I told him. He went berserk. He just couldn't,
wouldn't, accept the fact that I was rejecting him on
grounds of religion.'

'That's when he turned dissident?'

'That must have been the beginning, yes.'

'What was the end?'

'You think there was one?'

Parvez quietly said, 'I think there must have been.
The change in him was too drastic.'

Zahera softly warned, 'Give her time, Parvez, she
doesn't need any pressure right now.'

'No, I want to. For too long I've kept it inside me.'
She took a deep breath and said in a voice shivering with
memory. 'This happened one month after our break-up. I
discovered I was pregnant. With a three-month old foetus.'

'Oh God! What did he say?'

'Nothing. I didn't tell him about the pregnancy.'

'He didn't know about it?'

'He did later on. When it was much too late.'

'You mean . . .'

'I aborted the foetus. I killed my baby. Our baby.'

The only sound in that room was the soft sobbing of
Rukshana Bi with her hand clamped on her mouth.

Reshma shuddered, 'I was very sick after the abortion.
Amma was with me – she was the only one whom I had

told. She was scared and phoned Anees. That was when he came to know about the baby and the abortion.'

'What did he say?'

'Nothing. He just stared. So much hatred, so much bitterness! He could have killed me at that moment.' Reshma shrugged, 'Anyway, it does not matter any more, does it? Anees is dead. As for me, I'm living. Not alive. But living.'

Zahera said sharply, 'Don't be maudlin, Reshma!'

She smiled bitterly, 'Oh, don't worry, Zahera *Maasi*. I can't be like the Reshma of folklore, who died for love. A modern girl like me has to be sensible. You can't call it betrayal, you give it the fancy name of pragmatism.'

'What will you do?' Zahera probed gently.

'Go back to Rawalpindi. Get married to a man my family approves of. Don't create waves, don't upset the status quo. The good daughter. The acceptable wife. And my children will thank me for not plunging them into an identity crisis because of my youthful blunder.'

'But will you forget?'

'That I killed the man I loved? And the baby who should have been born? No, but I can always push it to some safe corner of my mind where its existence will be known only to me. I can act out a charade. For I am an Indian girl. And we are happy cowards, ace survivors. I too will survive.'

* * *

AUGUST 25, 2001

Altaf Naqvi was weeding an unruly patch near the entrance of his Mehrauli farmhouse when the noise of a car, stopping at his doorstep, attracted his attention.